THE KEY TO CIRCUS-MOM HIGHWAY

ALLYSON RICE

THE TOTAL HUMAN PUBLICATIONS

The Key to Circus-Mom Highway is work of fiction. Names, characters, businesses, and incidents either are the product of the author's imagination or are used fictitiously. Any resemblance to actual persons, living or dead, is entirely coincidental.

Copyright © 2023 by Allyson Rice

All rights reserved. No part of this book may be reproduced or used in any manner without the written permission of the copyright owner except for the use of quotations in a book review.

Noël Coward quote, from *Blithe Spirit,* ©1941, used by permission of Alan Brodie Representation Ltd.

Three's Company theme lyrics, written by Joe Raposo and Donald Nicholl, used by permission of The Joe Raposo Music Group, Inc.

Dorothy Parker quote, from the story "But the One on the Right" appearing in *The New Yorker* magazine, ©1929, used by permission of Condé Nast.

Lyrics from Human Sexual Response's song "Jackie Onassis," by Larry Bangor, Rich Gilbert, Rolfe Anderson, Dini Lamot, ©1980 Future Fish, used by permission of the writers/band members.

Kai Skye (Brian Andreas) StoryPeople quote used by permission of StoryPeople.

THE KEY TO CIRCUS-MOM HIGHWAY

"Key to the Highway" Words and Music by William Lee Conley Broonzy and Chas. Segar, Copyright ©1941, 1944 SONGS OF UNIVERSAL, INC., Copyright renewed, All Rights Reserved, Used by Permission. *Reprinted by permission of Hal Leonard, LLC*

Excerpt from *The Open Door* by Helen Keller, © 1957 by Helen Keller. Used by permission of Doubleday, an imprint of the Knopf Doubleday Publishing Group, a division of Penguin Random House LLC. All rights reserved.

The Lewis Carroll quotes from *Alice's Adventures in Wonderland* and *Jabberwocky*, the Tom Lehrer lyrics from *Be Prepared,* the Jacques-Charles and Albert Willemetz lyrics from "My Man" (translated to English by Channing Pollock), the Charles Dickens quote from *Martin Chuzzlewit,* the Ralph Waldo Emerson quote, the Amelia Earhart quote, and the William Blake quote are all in the public domain.

Every effort was made to trace and contact all copyright holders. Any oversight will be immediately corrected.

Library of Congress Control Number: 2022910346

ISBN 978-0-9821855-4-4 (paperback)

ISBN 978-0-9821855-5-1 (ebook)

ISBN 978-0-9821855-6-8 (audiobook)

First paperback edition January 2023

The Total Human Publications, Los Angeles, California

ALLYSON RICE

Book Cover Design by Allyson Rice

Cover Layout by Robert Zoltan

Book Cover Background Photo by Luckypic, licensed through Shutterstock

www.AllysonRice.com

ACKNOWLEDGMENTS

*"After the verb 'to love',
'to help' is the most beautiful verb in the world."*
-Bertha von Suttner

I would like to thank my father, Paul R. Rice, who urged me to write solo rather than always in collaboration. I'm very sad he's not around to see this book in print—I know he would be proud. And thanks to my teacher of 20+ years, Judy Abell, who is also gone from this physical plane. I trust they are watching from somewhere...

In terms of this book, specifically, there were so many people who have helped along the way. Most of them read versions of the manuscript (or screenplay) as I wrote and revised: Jane Rice (who read *every version* over the course of several years), Ginny McArthur, Amy Benedict, Donna Ray, Tina Fisher, Donna Thal, Susan Frank, Romy Rosemont, Tom Wiggin, Dash Taylor, Alet Taylor, Andy Taylor for his songwriting advice, and Robert Zoltan for his tireless assistance with the book cover. I'd also like to thank the following writing professionals for their input: Sarah Cornelius, Danny Manus, Mark Malatesta, Philippa Donovan, Jessica Powers, SarahBelle Selig, and fellow Northwestern alum, author Robyn Peterman. Finally, a shout-out to Bobby's Coffee Shop in Woodland Hills, California, where I get some of my best writing done.

I am profoundly grateful to you all.

For my mother Jane Rice
and my son Dash Zane Taylor.
I love you with all my heart.

Contents

1. PROLOGUE 1
2. DAY ONE 6
3. Tuesday Afternoon 7
4. Tuesday Evening 19
5. DAY TWO 27
6. Wednesday Morning 28
7. Wednesday Afternoon 35
8. Wednesday Evening 46
9. DAY THREE 53
10. Thursday Afternoon 54
11. Thursday Evening 65
12. Thursday Night 83

13.	DAY FOUR	90
14.	Friday Morning	91
15.	Friday Afternoon	122
16.	Friday Night	128
17.	DAY FIVE	132
18.	Saturday Morning	133
19.	Saturday Afternoon	138
20.	Saturday Night	151
21.	DAY SIX	161
22.	Sunday Morning	162
23.	Sunday Afternoon	173
24.	Sunday Evening	202
25.	DAY SEVEN	215
26.	Monday Morning	216
27.	Monday Afternoon	225
28.	Monday Evening	248
29.	DAY EIGHT	258
30.	Tuesday Morning	259
ABOUT THE AUTHOR		269

PROLOGUE

*"We have no reliable guarantee
that the afterlife will be any less
exasperating than this one, have we?"*
-Noël Coward

Twenty-two-point-four miles, one Bud Light, and a third of a bottle of Fireball later, they had just passed through Alamo and were approaching Glenwood. Jennifer was trying to concentrate on *anything* other than Sy's unfortunate singing. She was focused intently on the map on her phone. It was only 113.8 more miles to Savannah, though that wasn't much comfort to her considering that the relatively short drive from Milan had been the Longest. Twenty-two-point-four-miles. Ever. Sy's driving had become more "freeform" in direct correlation to his impressive alcohol consumption; and his off-key singing was boring a hole through the temporal lobes in Jennifer's brain. Especially after he insisted on replaying the theme from *Bonanza* seven times in a row (for luck).

Jack rifled through a first aid kit that he found on the floor behind the driver's seat. You know, in case Sy rolled the truck and they needed a Band-Aid or two. Jesse dozed peacefully between Jennifer and Sy. She had fallen asleep almost immediately after leaving Milan.

The theme song from *The Courtship of Eddie's Father* ended and was followed by the theme song from *Gilligan's Island*. Jennifer stared at Jesse resentfully, thinking, *God, I hate her sometimes. How can she sleep through this? Just like always, she sleeps and I'm wide-awake dealing with everything unpleasant. So typical! Stop it, she's pregnant. Jesus, I'm a horrible person. No wonder Sean is cheating on me. No, wait, no, I'm not. They're the problem. I'm—*

Then the song switched again and Sy attempted some ill-timed harmony.

> *"Come and knock on our door...*
> *We've been waiting for you...*
> *Where the kisses are hers and hers and his,*
> *Three's Company too."*

"OH MY GOD, JUST SHOOT ME ALREADY!" yelled Jennifer reflexively.

Sy stopped singing and looked over, Jack glanced up from his triage prep, and Jesse awoke with a start.

"What is it? What's happening?" Jesse asked breathlessly.

Jennifer, embarrassed, replied, "It's nothing. I'm sorry, go back to sleep."

Jack leaned over the seat and said to Sy, "C'mon, friend, why don't you let me drive for a while?" It was the third time he had offered since Milan.

"You got some kind of problem with my driving?"

"No, no, I just, uh, get a little car sick sitting in the back seat," Jack lied. "It helps me if I'm at the wheel."

"I'VE got a problem with your driving!" Jennifer exploded again. Her impulse control was completely shot. "You're weaving down the road like a drunken snake! I don't think you've stayed inside the yellow lines *at all* since we left Milan! AND you're driving seventeen miles over the speed limit!"

The truck was silent for a moment until Sy said, "Damn, you're uptight, woman."

"Tell me about it," mumbled Jesse.

"Shut up!" Jennifer snapped.

"Good God," said Jack. "Does *everything* with you two end up in an argument??"

"Yes!" the two female J's replied in unison.

Jennifer seethed. Jesse yawned. Ronald Reagan drooled on Jack. Before anyone had time to respond and further exacerbate the situation, Sy caught a glimpse of a rusted yellow and white Dodge pickup truck out of the corner of his eye, rapidly passing them across double yellow lines. The man and woman inside were canoodling dangerously in the front seat.

"That *bitch*! I *knew* it!" Sy yelled.

Four hundred yards ahead of them in no time, the other pickup truck turned off Route 280 and onto 2nd Street in Glenwood, heading due south. Sy sped up, turned right, and followed them, burning considerable rubber as he went. His passengers all toppled left when he turned, chaotically shouting over one another.

"What are you doing? Slow down!"

"Where are you going?! This isn't the way to Savannah!"

"I'm serious, Sy, stop the car and let me drive!"

"Are you kidnapping us?!"

"I swear to God, Sy, I've got my finger on the 911 emergency button. I'm about to push it!"

"*Woof!*"

By the time they were speeding past the Glenwood Church of the Holy Mother on their left, the yellow and white pickup truck was disappearing from sight.

"Okay, they're gone now, we lost them, so slow down. You wanna tell us what all of this was about?" Jack asked.

"They're not gone," Sy answered darkly, his foot still on the accelerator. "That was my lying, two-timing, soon-to-be-ex-wife and my ex-best-friend. I know exactly where they're going!"

"You're *married?*" asked Jesse incredulously.

Just before Preacher Ledbetter Road, Sy hung another rubber-burning, two-wheeled turn to the right onto a bumpy, dirt service road that followed Larry Creek. If it weren't for their seatbelts, they'd have hit the roof of the truck cab when they hit the bumps at that speed. It was fortunate for the dogs, who were launched into the air like popcorn, that Jack's reflexes were as quick as they were.

"Oh, my God, I think I'm gonna be sick," Jesse groaned.

"Don't you dare!" yelled Jennifer. "Put your head between your knees and breathe!"

Once Jack had maneuvered the dogs safely onto the floor at his feet, he reached around Sy's neck and put him into a rear naked choke, and said, "You've got a pregnant woman in here, Sy."

"I can't breathe—I can't breathe—" Sy gasped.

"Snap out of it and slow down," Jack continued rapidly, "or I'm going to choke you until you pass out. Jesse, be ready to grab the wheel if he does, so we don't go into the creek."

"No, seriously, I think I'm gonna be sick," Jesse repeated.

"Oh my God oh my God oh my God," whimpered Jennifer. "We're all gonna die... I should've taken Sean's calls..."

DAY ONE

"That would be a good thing for them to cut on my tombstone: Wherever she went, including here, it was against her better judgment."
- Dorothy Parker

Tuesday Afternoon

The aging strip club façade was bleak in the mid-day Chicago sun, with the unusually warm October heat intensifying the smell of urine out by the trash bins in the parking lot. The failing neon sign over the club should have read "LIVE NUDE GIRLS," but the V was out and the R was flickering, though "NUDE" shined oh-so-brightly. "LI E NUDE GI LS." Unrelenting, bad strip music pulsed inside. Yeah, it was "Toxic." Britney Spears didn't want to be there either, not even in musical spirit.

Thirty-nine-year-old aging bartender and freelance tattoo artist Jesse Chasen brushed her shaggy, shoulder-length black hair out of her piercing yellow-green eyes as she paced. She was smoking her fifth Marlboro unfiltered of the day as she spoke on her cell phone, leaving yet another soon-to-be-ignored message for her older sister Jennifer.

Jesse was dressed in a black miniskirt, a Black Keys tank top, strategically torn fishnets, and Doc Martens. Her arms were covered in elaborate tattoos. On her right arm was a large fire-breathing dragon. Its tail wrapped around her wrist and its long, serpentine body climbed her arm to mid-bicep. The fire it breathed extended up from there, enveloping an impressive, jagged scar that began at her right shoulder and extended along her collarbone. The left arm was covered with a colorful phoenix rising from the ashes, but so far, the desire expressed by the tattoo was just wishful thinking on Jesse's part.

Despite her rapid descent into middle age, whip-smart Jesse still took pride in being relatively cute, but in an aging tough-girl, you-wouldn't-hire-her-to-babysit-your-kids kind of way. Like if Joan Jett and Reese Witherspoon had a love child...

"Hi, it's Jesse. Again. Look, I get it, you don't want to lend me any more money, but could you PLEASE just return my calls. I'm in a really bad living situation right now, and I need some help, Jen. I need to—" *Beeeeep*.

Jennifer's voicemail cut her off, just like it had during her previous six messages. Frustrated, Jesse hung up, tossed her cigarette onto the ground, and stomped it out amidst the broken glass that was sparkling like diamonds on the cracked asphalt.

Her break over, she headed back into the club, her mind swirling, desperate to figure out an escape from... well, pretty much every aspect of her current life. Her stomach lurched uncomfortably, probably because all she had eaten so far today was a handful of fluorescent Maraschino cherries from behind the bar, and nicotine didn't count as a food group.

It was dark inside the club, so it took her eyes a few seconds to adjust. The throbbing beat of soul-deadening strip music assaulted her. *God, I hate this place,* she thought to herself for the thousandth time. But it had been the only job she could land after her extremely brief stint in the makeup department at Nordstrom's. She had quickly discovered that the clientele there didn't *really* want a bluntly honest answer to the question, "How does this look on me?" Though it wasn't until she came to work in a sleeveless shirt one day, and her tats frightened the over-sixty crowd, that she was unceremoniously canned by her (over-sixty) boss, Noreen. Not even a free mascara as a parting gift. "Cheap bastards" was the farewell message that she had left in the employee feedback box. "No" was the farewell message they had left on her voicemail after she requested a job reference from them. So... hello "LI E NUDE GI LS."

The sparse, middle-of-the-day Tuesday crowd was watching a stripper who had definitely seen better days absentmindedly going through the motions onstage in the background, thinking about those better days, no doubt. She might as well have been doing her laundry, except that probably would have been sexier. Jesse went back to work behind the bar that perpetually smelled like it had been wiped down with a sour rag. Because it had been.

"Where you been?" slurred one of the drunk Tuesday regulars. "Gimme a shot of Benchmark."

"You got it, hon," she replied with a smile.

"And show me your tits," he added.

Without missing a beat as she reached for the bourbon, Jesse glanced over at Dwayne, the thirty-two-year-old, 300+ pound bar-back who was restocking the glassware.

"Hey, Dwayne, this gentleman wants you to show him your tits."

Dwayne set down the crate he was holding. With a sexy pout at the customer, he lifted up his pit-stained *Simpsons* t-shirt, letting his man boobs and potbelly hang out in all their glory, and started gyrating his hips to the music.

"I's talkin' to *you*, girl," the customer said.

"Aw, I'm just teasin' ya, Barney," she said, winking at him. "And I bumped you up to a double of Bookers, no extra charge."

Jesse was an expert at handling drunks in a way that shut them down without losing her tip.

"Nice!" he responded. With a little difficulty coordinating his stubby, intoxicated fingers, he peeled off a twenty-dollar bill from the sweaty wad of cash in his pocket and set it on the bar. "Keep the change."

"Well, aren't you a sweetheart," she cooed with a smile, as she picked up the cash and slowly slid it into her bra for effect.

The scuffed-up olive-green bar phone on the wall, left over from the seventies but not in an ironic way, began to ring. Jesse didn't answer it because she spotted her friend Tiny Tim, a big, hulking biker with a long ponytail, a handlebar mustache, and menacing neck tats enter through the side door. He whipped off his black leather biker jacket, threw it down on a barstool, and showed Jesse a cursive tattoo on his shoulder that said *Mandy*.

"Can you do something with this, Jess? I came home last night and that bitch was in bed breeding with our dog walker. Our *dog walker*, fercrissakes."

"Hmm," she said studying it. "I think I might be able to turn this into a snake, or maybe a flying—"

"No, a snake would be fucking PERFECT," he said.

THE KEY TO CIRCUS-MOM HIGHWAY 11

Just then a perpetually-gum-chewing, bleached blonde, twenty-three-year-old with Daddy Issues stuck her head out from a side hallway, snapped her wad of cotton candy flavored Bubblicious, and yelled, "Jess! Call for you on line two."

"Take a message. I'm busy," Jesse said.

"You should probably take this call. And Kyle said to tell you to answer the damn phone when it rings."

"Shut up, Amber," she said dismissively, waving her off like she would a mosquito as she walked over to the phone. "I'm off Thursday, Tiny, so maybe then."

Jesse picked up the receiver. "Hello?... Yeah, this is Jesse, who is this?" She listened to the voice on the other end of the line, her anger building. "What the fuck kind of joke is this, asshole? My parents died five years ago in a car cra— ... What?... You're fulla shit! ... Well, then tell me something that proves it was— "

Completely thrown by the information that came next on the other end of the line, Jesse's face went slack and she sunk down into a squatting position behind the bar. Her back was pressed against the wall, the phone cord stretched to its olive-green limit.

"Yes," she said softly. "Yes, I understand... But is it... Yes, I understand." She thrust her hand out in Dwayne's direction. "Pen. I need a pen!"

Dwayne grabbed the chewed-up ballpoint Bic pen from his back pocket and a drink-stained cocktail napkin off of the bar. Jesse took them from him, holding the phone receiver between her ear and her shoulder.

"Okay, go ahead, I'm ready," she continued to the voice on the other end of the line. She set the napkin on her knee and began to write. "Uh huh... uh huh... uh huh... Okay, got it. Thank you."

The only thing that moved was her hand back to the receiver, then it slowly dropped to the floor. Other than that, she stayed frozen in place, staring, unblinking, at the sticky bar floor in front of her. Dwayne and Tiny Tim watched her, concerned.

"You okay, Jess?" Dwayne asked softly.

No response.

She remained motionless, attempting to make sense of her entire life prior to a minute and a half ago—until the phone's off-hook warning kicked in, jarring her back to her current reality. Lost in a daze and moving in slow motion, she stood up, oblivious to the blaring phone receiver still laying on the ground.

"You alright?" asked Tiny. "You look like you seen a ghost."

Completely distracted, Jesse said to Dwayne. "Can you cover for me for a minute?"

Without waiting for his answer, Jesse ducked under the bar and headed down the side hallway to the back office, while Dwayne bent down to retrieve the phone receiver and place it back in its cradle on the wall.

· · · · · · · · · · ·

It was a joke of an office with peeling, fake wood paneling, and stained pumpkin-orange carpeting. There were dirty dishes and crusty, old microwave food containers piled on every surface near the filthy microwave. Pictures of naked women holding guns and/or power tools and sitting on muscle cars covered the walls.

THE KEY TO CIRCUS-MOM HIGHWAY 13

Amber leaned provocatively over strip club owner Kyle, who sat in his desk chair holding the back of her bare leg as she laughed and flirted with him. Amber was on a quest to unseat Jesse as the official *First Lady of "Li e Nude Gi ls."*

"Yea, that'd be dope as fuck, Amber," said Kyle.

No one seemed to know how old Kyle was, including Jesse, because he embodied a disturbing combination of overly greased and thinning salt-and-pepper hair, 1970s sideburns, speech that was constantly peppered with the latest high school slang, and competing scents of BLADE "Wild Temptations" body wash, BLADE "Shockwave" extreme hold hair gel, and BLADE "Caveman" deodorant.

To be fair, the overkill on scented man products was due to the fact that he also had a flatulence problem that he was self-conscious about, due to a problem digesting the dairy products that he refused to give up. Plus, there was the added benefit of concealing the odor of the crusty remnants of decaying, microwaved Salisbury steak with mac and cheese.

Back to the original point, though—however old Kyle was, he looked like shit for his age.

Jesse stood in the doorway watching Amber fawn over the man Jesse had been living with for the past six months. She could feel the frustration with her life in general, and the disturbing call she had just received, coalesce into an angry pulsating mass that looked a lot like her ripping all of Amber's over-processed blonde hair out of her head by its dark roots. Not that she really gave a rat's ass about Amber and Kyle. But that violent image brought a fleeting measure of great joy to her weary, aging-tough-girl heart.

"I need a few days off," Jesse said to Kyle while staring Amber down, not for the first time.

Caught off-guard, Amber's head jerked around toward the door. She glanced back at Kyle and then quickly headed out of the office, not making eye contact with Jesse who intentionally banged into Amber's shoulder as they passed one another.

"I need a few days off," Jesse repeated.

"No, I'm short-staffed this week," he said as he turned his attention to some paperwork on his desk—the "paperwork" being the new issue of *Dirty Polly Want a Cracker: The Magazine for the Discerning Southern Gentleman*.

"Goddamn it, Kyle, I need a few days. How often have I asked for that? I've got an unexpected family... situation that I have to deal with."

He eyed her for a moment then smiled a crooked, coffee-stained smile. (His BLADE "Albino" toothpaste was not working as advertised.) He held out his hand and said, "C'mere."

She reluctantly took a few steps closer to him. He reached out and grabbed her hand and pulled her the rest of the way toward him. He began to unbuckle his painfully cliché Ed Hardy belt with the other hand. Jesse tried to pull away, but Kyle attempted to muscle her lower.

"You do me a favor, I do you a favor. That's the way it works, baby. You know that."

"Stop it. I'm not in the mood, Kyle," snapped Jesse.

"You're my fucking girlfriend. *Get* in the mood."

He started to get a little rougher, trying to push her head down toward his groin. This was the final straw for Jesse with this asshole-boss-boyfriend. She punched him in the crotch, making him convulsively release her from his grip. He howled as he grabbed himself in pain.

The force of the punch also caused his perpetually tightened sphincter muscles to relax, and he let loose a rip-roaring Ben & Jerry's "Chunky Monkey" ice cream fart that he had been holding in since earlier that morning. *Breakfast of Champions*.

"Oh my God," said Amber's disembodied voice from the hallway where she had been lurking.

"I'm done with this, you piece of shit. I quit," Jesse said as she turned and headed for the door.

"Yeah?? Well, you're too old to work here anyway. *And* you're a lousy lay," he said. "You'd better fucking be out of my place tonight when I get home! It'll be a relief not to have to listen to your goddamn shitty guitar playing anymore."

Without looking back, Jesse flipped him the bird over both shoulders as she walked out, passing Amber just outside the door. Without a glance in her direction, Jesse said, "He's all yours, Amber. *Good luck with that...*"

Amber's response to that was a loud snap of her gum as she braced her olfactory senses and headed back in to Kyle. Jesse, holding her stomach, made a beeline for the restroom down the hall where she immediately vomited. Not because of Kyle's internal combustion system, but because the stress of life these past few weeks had been taking a toll on her own internal system.

"Shit," she mumbled as she wiped her mouth with the last three squares of cheap, one-ply toilet paper on the roll.

She rinsed her mouth in the stained porcelain sink, and wiped her face down with a handful of cool, wet paper towels, absentmindedly running her fingers along the scar on her collarbone as she so often did. She stared at herself in the cracked bathroom mirror, her reflection adorned with a crude drawing of a penis and hairy balls that some neighborhood Michelangelo had scratched into the glass at forehead level. She looked like a mutant unicorn from Three Mile Island.

"Now what?" she asked her defeated reflection.

It had been a rough five years since her parents had died. Their sudden deaths had sent her into an escalating tailspin, which is what precipitated the difficulty she began to have holding on to jobs. Her living situation changed almost as frequently, which is the only reason she had ended up living with a creep like Kyle. Par for the course these days. She was repulsed by him, but a girl's gotta do what a girl's gotta do to make ends meet, she figured. Now here she was again, starting back at ground zero. *Do Not Pass Go. Do Not Collect $200*. Not quite the life she had imagined for herself by age almost-forty.

She stared at the scar running along her collarbone. Most people's emotional scars were easily hidden, but she had to look at her emotional scar every time she saw it reflected in a mirror, or a window... *or in the eyes of every single goddamn person I meet,* she thought. She had tried to camouflage it with the fire-breathing dragon tattoo, but all that did was put an enormous spotlight on it. She couldn't win for losing.

Dwayne was busy with a customer and didn't see Jesse when she ducked back behind the bar to hastily grab her personal belongings. On second thought, as she was about to leave, she turned back, grabbed two bottles of the most expensive top-shelf liquor they carried, and set them on the bar in front of some customers.

"Help yourself, fellas. Kyle said it's on him. He's starting 'Free Booze Tuesdays—All You Can Drink.' Tell everyone you know!"

The men practically pounced on the bottles of free tequila and whiskey. Jesse, with a deep breath, headed out the side door into the bright light of day, like a POW exiting captivity.

· · · · • • • • · ·

Jesse climbed three flights of stairs, then unlocked the front door and entered Kyle's third-floor walk-up. His studio apartment was about as nice a place as his dingy office, except for a few touches here and there that made it seem like a woman had at least *attempted* to make it better than a frat boy's dorm room, Chicago Bears bedspread notwithstanding.

Jesse darted around the apartment quickly, gathering her things and shoving her clothes and personal items into an old canvas duffel bag that she pulled down from a shelf in the closet. Once the duffel bag was full, she supplemented with a few plastic grocery bags that she pulled out of a broken kitchen drawer. Her thoughts as she raced around—ranging from anger at Kyle, to relief at being rid of him, to panic about where she could land next—bounced around in her head like a pinball machine, while snippets of her phone conversation replayed in her head on endless repeat mode.

Kyle's puppy, in a dog cage in the corner, watched her curiously, head cocked to the side, wagging his tail as Jesse hurried about, mumbling to herself. He was a mixed-breed puppy that Kyle said he found sleeping in the bushes outside their building. Though Jesse was pretty sure that was code for "I stole him from a neighbor who was distracted doing laundry in the basement."

Kyle had grandiose plans to train it and make money in the underground dogfighting scene in their neighborhood. But since Jesse thought the sweet little thing might actually be part Golden Retriever and part Beanie Baby, she figured the odds weren't good for the success of that business plan in the face of disgruntled Pit Bulls and Rottweilers.

Right on cue, after Jesse mumbled to herself, "What am I forgetting?... What am I forgetting?" the puppy gave a tiny little yelp.

"Ohhhh, sweetie," she purred.

She stood in the middle of the room facing the cage, conflicted, the two of them locked in a staring battle. The puppy won.

"Okay, I don't know where we're going to live, but I'm not leaving you here with that fucker. He doesn't deserve you. Come here, baby," she said as she set her bags down, pulled him out of the cage, and kissed him squarely on his soft, furry, blonde head. Then she set him down on the floor and picked up the dog cage. She carried it across the room where she proceeded to turn it sideways and dump the dog shit out of the cage and onto the center of the bed.

"Who's the shitty lay *now*, Kyle?" she said to no one in particular.

Jesse walked back to the corner, set the cage down, picked up her bags and the puppy, and grabbed her guitar case that was leaning against the wall next to the front door. Then she walked out of Kyle's place for the very last time, stealing his dog as she left.

TUESDAY EVENING

Jesse's forty-one-year-old sister, Jennifer McMahon, lived in the perfectly manicured, upper-middle-class neighborhood of Glenview, Illinois with her perfect doctor husband Sean. Their perfect children, Connor and Maggie, were both attending their dad's alma mater, Northwestern University. Though they lived on campus, they were close enough to bring their laundry home every week.

Glenview was a Chicago suburb where the inner-city problems a mere few miles away were like a story you read in the newspaper about some other country, and about which you could safely exclaim, "Oh, my goodness, that's just awful!" while you finished your kale/banana smoothie and delightfully flaky almond croissant.

Geography was merely one item in the growing list of fundamental differences between the sisters. The scant two years that separated them in age was the closest thing about them these days. After years of Jennifer coming to Jesse's rescue under the banner of "Oh, she's just free-spirited," Jesse's increasing trouble over the last few years in terms of holding down a job or maintaining a stable living situation, and her constant need to be bailed out financially, had put intensifying strain on the already challenging relationship.

Jesse pulled up to the curb in her 1999 Alpine Green Dodge Neon, the left side of her front bumper tied on with nylon rope, with her stolen dog and all her earthly possessions in tow. She turned off the engine and tried to quell her rising sense of inadequacy as she stared at Jennifer's fairytale, Brady-Bunch-on-steroids house.

She took a deep breath, looked at the puppy that was sitting on the passenger seat next to her cell phone, and said, "I'll be right back. Don't make any long-distance calls."

She walked up to the front door, took another fortifying breath, and rang the bell. Jennifer, in all her straitlaced glory, opened the door and stared at her younger sister for what seemed to Jesse like fifteen minutes but was probably more like ten seconds. Jesse ended the standoff by getting right down to the more pressing business at hand.

"I assume you got the same call I got," she said.

"I did," answered Jennifer.

There was another awkward pause.

"You gonna invite me in, Jen? Or should I just break into your neighbor's shed, grab a lawn chair, and make myself at home here on your porch?"

Jennifer wrinkled her nose, sniffed, and said, "You smell like vomit and dog poop."

"Yeah?" Jesse countered, "Well, you smell like judgment and superiority."

No comment from Jennifer. *Here we go again*, she thought to herself.

"Okay, that was harsh. I'm sorry," continued Jesse. "I'm having some stress issues. I think I might have an ulcer. If you'd just let me in, I could clean up a little. Trust me, I'm well aware that I'm not 'minty fresh' at the moment."

Jennifer reluctantly stepped to the side and let Jesse into the McMahon home. It was beautifully decorated in a *Town & Country* beige sort of way and smelled like French vanilla potpourri.

"So what do you make of it all?" Jesse asked.

Jennifer let her guard down a bit. "I don't know. I was a little thrown by it, I have to admit."

"Yeah, me too. I thought maybe we could go to the airport together in the morning?" Jesse suggested.

Jennifer shook her head. "I'm not going. I don't need the money, and I have *no* idea who this woman was. For all I know, she could've made her money in the Blood Diamond trade."

"Well, how abstractly and self-servingly conscientious of you..." Jesse mumbled.

"Besides," continued Jen, "I have some really serious personal stuff happening here right now. I can't go away in the middle of it all. I just can't. I'm sorry."

Jesse wasn't prepared for that response. "You *have* to go! You heard what he said—if both of us aren't there then all of the money is forfeited!"

"I don't see how they can do that," Jennifer mused. "If you show up, I'm sure you'll get your share."

"Of course they can do that! It's a legal document. He was very clear about that, Jen. Look, I know you don't need the money, but I do! I'm not married to Steve

Mnuchin like you are. I haven't had health insurance for four years!"

"Would you *please* stop calling him Steve Mnuchin? That's horrifying. Can't you at least reference a non-Republican with money in your insults?"

Jesse smiled and said, "I could, but where would the fun be in that?"

Yet another awkward pause.

Jesse sighed. "Seriously, you have to go with me, Jen. I just had to quit my job to be able to go to Florida tomorrow, so I have no job now."

"*Again?*"

"I really need this money, Jennifer," Jesse continued. "*Please*. I'm begging you." She paused, debating whether or not this was the best moment to broach the subject. "And I also need a place to stay tonight. When I quit, Kyle kicked me out of his place."

"Jesus," Jennifer responded, shaking her head.

"You know what? Forget it," said Jesse, her self-esteem running on empty. "I'll sleep in my car. I'm sorry I asked."

Jesse turned around to head back outside to her new house on wheels. One glance at Jesse's old beater at the curb and Jennifer's guilt kicked in.

She sighed and said, "Wait... You can sleep in the guest room. But NO SMOKING in there this time! I had to have the curtains and duvet professionally cleaned after your last stay. I know I'm going to regret this, but ... I'll go talk with Sean about heading to Florida with you tomorrow."

Jesse, smiling, turned back and gave Jennifer a hug and a kiss on the cheek. "Thank you *so much*. You're my favorite sister!"

"Shut up," Jen said, trying not to smile. "And *please* go brush your teeth," she added as she headed to Sean's office.

Jesse went to retrieve the entirety of her life from the car.

....

Sean's office was, of course, beautifully furnished. His Northwestern diploma and doctor's degrees were framed on the wall next to an antique oak bookshelf filled with hardback medical texts. The shelves on the adjacent wall displayed an array of Civil War memorabilia that Sean had been collecting over the past couple of years, below a tattered, framed Union flag.

Sean himself was also "beautifully furnished," with a chiseled face framed by a (mostly full) head of wavy brown hair, and a body tanned and muscular from years of tennis and racquetball at their country club. He was the quintessential handsome doctor, the kind that seemed to get better looking with age, a fact that hadn't escaped Jennifer recently while she examined her elephant-skin elbows that seemed to have appeared virtually overnight.

Sean was sitting at his antique oak desk intently focused on his computer screen through his tortoise-shell reading glasses, so he didn't register Jennifer when she stepped into the doorway and watched him for a moment. She tip-toed behind him, encircled his shoulders, and kissed him on the top of his handsome head while trying to peek at the computer screen (allegedly).

He shut his laptop quickly, which wasn't lost on her, but immediately took one of her hands and kissed it tenderly. "You startled me!"

"What are you working on?" she asked lightly and with a smile.

"Nothing interesting. Just answering work emails, going over billing invoices, that kind of thing. What's up?"

"My sister just showed up," said Jen. "Unemployed and homeless."

He chuckled. "So what else is new?"

"I need to ask you a favor," she continued.

He swiveled around and lovingly pulled her in close, wrapping his arms around her waist. "Of course. Anything for you."

"I need to go to Tallahassee with Jesse tomorrow for that meeting with the lawyer."

"I thought you'd decided not to go," he said, surprised.

"I had," continued Jen, "but she knew all the right buttons to push. I need to do it for her. Can you hold down the fort for a couple of days? I'll move a few things around, fly down there for the meeting tomorrow afternoon, and then fly back first thing Thursday morning."

"Of course. Don't worry about me, I'll be fine," he said. "Take as long as you need."

"Thanks," she said, trying to cover the sadness those words triggered in her.

· · · • • • • • · ·

Jennifer walked back into the foyer just as Jesse came through the front door with her guitar case slung over her shoulder, the puppy tucked under her arm, and all of her bags in her other hand.

"What're you... NO. You can't leave a puppy here!" exclaimed Jennifer. "Sean works all day."

"No, I'm taking him with me," Jesse responded. "The airline lets you bring a therapy dog on the flight with you. I already called to check."

"You have to have a legit doctor's note to be able to do that," Jen responded.

"Can't you get Sean to write one for me?" asked Jesse. "He's a legit doctor."

"He's a podiatrist, Jesse."

"Like they're ever gonna know that. He can say I have a life-threatening hammertoe condition that makes me super anxious." She laughed. "Please? Tell Sean if he writes one for me, I'll name the puppy after him."

"Oh, yeah, that'll be huge incentive. Just a dream come true for him." Exasperated, Jennifer headed back out in the direction of the office. "*Sean?...*"

As Jesse started off in the direction of the guest room, one of the plastic grocery bags ripped, sending all of her shoes spilling onto the floor. When she set the puppy down to focus on her "sole retrieval," forcing the scattered shoes into her already overstuffed duffel bag, the puppy peed on the potted palm in the foyer and trotted off.

Jesse stood up trying to balance all of her worldly possessions. Just then, Jennifer's nineteen-year-old son Connor, captain of the Northwestern Men's Lacrosse Team, and her eighteen-year-old daughter Maggie, math whiz and this year's Big 10 Robotics Champion, entered the front door.

"Hey, Aunt Jesse!" said Maggie.

"Hi, guys! What are you freaks doing home?" asked Jesse as she gave them each a hug.

"Laundry," they responded in unison.

"My God, you're getting so tall, Connor, I barely recognized you."

Connor smiled then scrunched his nose as he looked around and sniffed the air. "It smells like piss in here," he said.

"Shit!" mumbled Jesse. "Sean must've peed on the rug. Sean?!..."

She rushed out in search of the errant puppy.

Maggie looked at Connor, confused. "Dad peed on the rug?"

DAY TWO

*"Be prepared to hold your liquor pretty well.
Don't write naughty words on walls
if you can't spell."*
- Tom Lehrer

Wednesday Morning

Okay, so the day was not off to the best of starts. Because Jesse had slept through her alarm (and her backup alarm), she and Jennifer were late leaving for the airport. Then, twenty minutes shy of O'Hare International Airport, Jesse was pulled over for speeding.

"Shit, shit, shit," said Jesse when she saw the flashing red light in her rearview mirror.

"Damn it, Jesse, I told you to slow down!"

Jesse pulled over to the side of the road, pulled out her driver's license, got the registration out of the glove compartment, and rolled down the window.

The State Trooper approached the driver's side window. "License and registration, ma'am." She handed them over. "Do you know how fast you were going?" he continued sternly.

That was when Jesse launched into a positively Oscar-worthy performance. "No, sir, I don't," she said, starting to cry. "I'm sorry. I wasn't looking at the speedometer. We just found out that our mom died, and we're trying to get to the airport to make our flight down to Florida."

She started sobbing, and Jennifer handed her a Kleenex, adding, "We're not sure we're going to make our flight, Officer."

He studied the two of them for a moment, then said, "I'm very sorry about your mom. What time is your flight?"

"It leaves in forty-five minutes!" Jesse sobbed. "We only have fifteen minutes before they start boarding!"

"Okay, I'm going to let you off with a warning this time, but you have to slow down and go the speed limit. You're putting other people at risk by speeding."

He handed Jesse her license and registration.

"Yes, sir, thank you so much," she said, loudly blowing her nose as punctuation.

"Thank you, Officer. We really appreciate this," added Jennifer.

Jesse pulled back onto the highway, turned to Jennifer with a grin, and said, "Yo, Meryl Streep ain't got nothin' on me."

"Just drive," Jen replied.

By the time they reached O'Hare, parked their car, and got to the terminal, they had to have the beleaguered airline employee at the check-in counter call ahead to the gate to have them hold the airplane door. Jennifer, and Jesse carrying Sean in her arms, sprinted the entire way like middle-aged women wearing the wrong type of shoes in a track meet.

The rest of the passengers were already seated on the early morning flight to Tallahassee. Jesse and Jennifer struggled to find enough room in the packed overhead bins to squeeze in their carry-on bags.

"There's no space left anywhere!" complained Jesse.

"Yeah, well, hardly surprising," grumbled Jen. "That's what happens when you barely make your flight."

Jesse spun around to face her sister.

The man in the aisle seat next to her narrowly avoided an elbow-induced head injury, grumbling, "Jesus, lady, watch it!"

"I'm sorry I slept through my alarm, Jen! How many times do I have to keep apologizing??"

The flight attendant came by and helped muscle the bags into a compartment two rows up, and said, "Ladies, we need you to take your seats and fasten your seat belts. We can't take off until everyone is seated."

"I'll take the aisle," Jennifer said to Jesse.

"Oh, *please* let me have the aisle," Jesse begged. "My stomach is a wreck this morning. Please?... In case I have to get to the restroom quickly?"

"Ladies. In your seats!" the flight attendant repeated impatiently. "We're all waiting for you."

"Fine," Jennifer said to Jesse as she tried to maneuver herself to the window seat across the middle seat passenger who wasn't getting up. He was a pervy-looking, paunchy guy with a comb-over, wearing a threadbare blue trench coat and thick glasses. "Excuse me," she said as she slid by him. He watched her Ann Taylor-clad derriere the whole way, as it passed very close to his face.

"Seriously?" she said to him as she caught him leering.

Paunchy Perv quickly looked down at his *In-Flight Magazine*, busted. Jennifer settled in and pulled out her Kindle Fire.

The pilot announced over the intercom, "Flight attendants, prepare for departure."

As a flight attendant moved down the aisle toward her seat in the back of the plane, Jesse said to her, "Excuse me, miss, as soon as we're up, do you think I could get two Bloody Marys?"

"You need to order it on your screen with a credit card," the flight attendant explained.

"But if I—"

"Ma'am. PLEASE," admonished the flight attendant, rolling her eyes and moving off to her seat.

Jesse tried to balance the puppy on her lap while getting her credit card out of her should-be-under-the-seat-by-now purse and then proceeded to navigate the directions on her seat-back screen, putting in her drink order. Jennifer watched Jesse out of the corner of her eye with a mixture of disapproval and concern as only a judgmental older sister can do.

"It's 9:00 a.m.," she said to Jesse.

"Yeah, well, I'm pretty sure it's 9:00 *p.m.* somewhere. Maybe Bangkok. But, hey, thanks for the time update, Siri," Jesse dismissed her sarcastically.

Jennifer shook her head with a snort and went back to her Kindle.

"Look, don't start in with the judgment," Jesse continued. "I just found out my whole life up to this point has been a lie, so you'll have to excuse me if I need a little something to help soften the edges."

"Um, yeah, me too," Jennifer said, not looking up from her reading. "But I'm not living in Bangkok time as a result."

Paunchy Perv, who had been watching the exchange back-and-forth like a tennis match, leered at Jesse. "I love Bangkok. Bang cock..."

Jesse leaned back, closing her eyes to shut him out. "Yeah. Restraining order."

Jennifer looked out the window, lost in thought.

·· • • • • • • • ··

1991

Sixteen-year-old Jennifer was sitting cross-legged in an armchair, leafing through a family photo album she had found on a shelf in the hall closet. Her parents, Jim and Carolyn Chasen, were sitting on the couch near her, absorbed in the newest episode of *Home Improvement*. Jennifer stopped at a photo and studied it.

"Who is this, Mom?" she asked.

"Who is who, honey?"

"This girl holding Jesse," said Jennifer.

Jim and Carolyn both looked over at her as she held up the book and pointed to a photo of a young, sad-eyed woman sitting in a chair holding newborn Jesse. Two-year-old Jennifer was standing at the young woman's knee looking up at the baby. Jim and Carolyn looked at one another in silence.

"What?" asked Jennifer.

Jim began tentatively, "That's..."

"That's your aunt Angie," Carolyn quickly interrupted. "We, uh, we lost her not too long after that picture was taken."

"How?" asked Jennifer. "What happened?"

"It was her heart," Carolyn said. "She went quickly. I don't really want to talk about it." Carolyn got up and left the room.

"I'm sorry," said Jennifer to Jim. "I didn't mean—"

"It's okay, sweetie. It's just a sad topic."

He got up and followed Carolyn out. Jennifer watched him go, then turned her attention back to the album and flipped to the next page. Jim found Carolyn sitting on the edge of the bed in their room.

He sat down next to her and asked, "Why did you lie to her? That was the perfect opening to talk about everything."

"No," Carolyn said. "We're not going to. There's no reason they need to know the ugly details. I don't want to talk about it again."

They locked eyes for a moment, wordlessly, then Jim nodded and said, "Maybe you're right."

· · · • • • • • · · ·

Two Bloody Marys later, Jesse had been sound asleep for several hours. Paunchy Perv in the middle seat had been eyeing her to make sure she was still out cold. He stole a sideways glance at Jennifer and saw she was completely absorbed in her book, *Anatomy of a Cheating Husband*. He slowly inched his hand towards Jesse's sleeping left boob to cop a feel, but Sean jumped up in Jesse's lap and started to growl at him, causing McPervy to withdraw his hand before it had come in for a landing.

Jesse woke up with a start. "Oh God," she blurted.

She reached around Sean for the vomit bag in the seat pocket in front of her and barely got it open before vomiting into it.

"You okay, Jess?" asked Jennifer, honestly concerned. "You know, if you really do think you have an ulcer, you should maybe lay off the alcohol for a while. It'll just make it worse."

Jesse closed and sealed the bag, threw it into the passing flight attendant's garbage collection bag, and popped a piece of *Arctic Ice Storm Gum with Intense Flavor Crystals* into her mouth. She hugged the puppy close, trying not to cry.

The voice of the pilot came over the intercom. "All seat backs and tray tables should be in their upright and locked positions. Flight attendants take your seats. We'll be landing momentarily."

Wednesday Afternoon

In the nondescript lawyer's office reception area, there was nothing except four chairs lined up along the wall, one plastic philodendron in the corner, and a small reception desk that looked like something you'd buy at an office supply store and have to assemble yourself using directions written in Swedish.

The only colorful addition to the setting was the seventy-five-year-old receptionist named Dottie who showcased a hairstyle leftover from the 1950s, wore garishly applied *Baby-Doll at Any Age Makeup with Intense Sparkle Crystals*, and had a slight southern accent. She was busy talking on the phone with her Ladies Bowling League teammate Ronnie Lynn.

"No, he didn't," she drawled. "He got his thumb bit off by the 'gator in his tryout.... I *know*, that's what I told him too!" She saw Jennifer and Jesse enter the office with their suitcases. "I gotta go, honey... You too." She hung up and smiled at the girls. "Can I help you?"

"Yes," said Jennifer. "We're here to see Mr. Tudball. Jennifer McMahon and Jesse Chasen."

"Oh, yes." She pushed a button and spoke into the phone, "The girls are here, Mr. Tudball." Then to Jesse and Jennifer, she added, "You can go on in."

They entered the office which was about as lavishly decorated as the reception area except for a few more artificial plants. They set their bags down on the floor just inside the door and Jesse set Sean down. He immediately took off to explore the new landscape, then lifted his leg and peed on the potted plastic Golden Dieffenbachia.

Mr. Tudball was a short, squat, man in his mid-sixties, with a frizzy fringe of red hair around his balding dome. He spoke with a pronounced lateral lisp which came out as a slushy sound from the sides of his teeth. The slightly "off" color coordination of his suit, tie, and shirt made it seem like he might also be colorblind. The poor bastard was living life behind the eight ball.

He stood up to shake hands with them as they introduced themselves. "Please, have a seat. We need to wait just another minute before we get started," he said.

The women didn't dare look at one another, as it was taking every ounce of self-control they could muster not to start laughing—not specifically at Mr. Tudball, but at this increasingly bizarre situation.

As soon as he spoke, he reminded Jesse of the actor Wallace Shawn, from her favorite movie, *The Princess Bride*. Unbeknownst to them, Mr. Tudball was actually Mr. Shawn's second cousin once removed on his mother's side. He had owned a used car lot in Kissimmee, Florida for almost thirty years until his chronic insomnia found him watching a late-night rerun of *The Love Boat* one balmy night in July, and he saw a commercial for an online law school called U-Sue U. He picked up the phone, registered on the spot with a small deposit on his credit card, and the rest was history.

There was a long pause until Mr. Tudball broke the silence with, "Did you have a good flight?"

Simultaneously, Jennifer said, "Yes," and Jesse said, "Yeah, it was fine."

Another long pause. Mr. Tudball busied himself by straightening papers, adjusting his tie, and brushing some imaginary dust off of the desk in front of him. Jennifer and Jesse glanced at one another, wondering what they were waiting for.

"Can I get you some water?" Mr. Tudball asked.

Jennifer shook her head and Jesse said, "I'm good, thanks."

Mr. Tudball picked up the phone receiver and pressed a button. "Any word from the other party, Dottie?... Hmm, that's unfortunate. Then we'll move to Plan B. Go ahead and make that call to Thibodaux." He hung up.

"Can we possibly get a few more details yet?" asked Jesse, becoming impatient. It had been a long day already.

"Yes, certainly. Let's start from the beginning... As I told you both on the phone, the couple that raised you were not your biological parents. They were your aunt and uncle. The reason they raised you was because your mom, Angela Hartley, Angie, ran away as a teenager about six months after giving birth to Jesse."

"Great," mumbled Jesse. "One more thing that's my fault."

Jennifer reached over and took her hand. "Don't do that, sweetie," she said quietly to Jesse. Then, to the lawyer, she said, "So whose sister was she? Our aunt's or our uncle's?"

"Angie was your aunt's younger sister. Your mom was seventeen when she ran away in the middle of the night, almost forty years ago, leaving only a note for them."

· · · · ● ● ● · · ·

1977

Seventeen-year-old Angie Hartley ran from the front entrance of the apartment building where she had been living with her older sister Carolyn Chasen and her brother-in-law Jim Chasen. She made a beeline to a beat-up orange 1972 Ford Pinto idling at the curb. She carried an old pink canvas duffel bag covered in psychedelic flowers and peace signs, and a couple of plastic bags stuffed with her clothes, shoes, and a few personal mementos too precious to leave behind.

Through the open passenger's side window, she threw her bags into the back seat. When she yanked on the passenger door handle, it stuck, so she quickly climbed through the open window, yelling, "Hurry! Go! Go!" at her friend Patsy in the driver's seat.

The car pulled out, tires squealing, and rounded the corner at the end of the block. And she was gone.

Back in the small apartment, made as homey as possible on very little money, six-month-old Jesse was crying in her crib. Two-and-a-half-year-old Jennifer was standing in the crib next to Jesse under a homemade pink and yellow butterfly mobile, holding on to the railing, also crying. She was calling out, "Mama!... Maaaamaa!!!"

THE KEY TO CIRCUS-MOM HIGHWAY 39

Carolyn came running in to see what the commotion was about and found her teenaged sister gone.

"Angie?" she called out. She spotted a handwritten note folded over the crib railing, and hurried over to get it, trying to comfort the girls while she read it.

After a moment she exclaimed, "Oh, my God... JIM!!"

Jim rushed in. "What the hell is going on??"

She handed him the note. She picked up Jesse and started rocking her, while wiping the tears off of Jennifer's face, telling her, "It's okay, honey. You're okay. You're okay, sweetie."

The note read: *I'm so sorry. I can't do this. I can't do the whole mom thing. I'm so sorry, you guys. Please take care of the girls for me. You be their mom and dad. You'll be much better parents than I ever could be. I'll be in touch when I can, but please don't come looking for me. I mean it. I'll just leave again. –Angie*

Jim started to swear. "Of all the goddamn, selfish—!"

Carolyn cut him off. "Shhh! Not in front of the girls, Jim."

"I want Mama!" cried Jennifer.

Carolyn set now-quiet Jesse back down into her crib and then she picked up Jennifer. She rocked her and softly stroked her hair. "Your mama's not here, baby. Your mama's not here."

"I WANT MAAAAAMAAAA!!" wailed Jennifer, inconsolable.

Carolyn did her best to be soothing, though she was also crying now. "Shhhh... I'm your mama now.... I'm your mama now..."

Jim walked over to Carolyn and put his arms around the two of them, and they stood there in a weeping huddle.

"It's gonna be okay," he said. "We're gonna get through this. We'll figure it out."

Jesse was asleep again in her crib, blissfully unaware.

·········

Back in the lawyer's office, Jennifer and Jesse sat there staring blankly at Mr. Tudball who had just finished giving them the details.

"Oh, my God," Jennifer said quietly, "I have that dream all the time. That really happened? I remember that... Why are we just now finding this out, after all this time?"

"Yeah," added Jesse, "this is really screwed up. Why all this drama opening these old wounds? Wounds I didn't even know I had until now! Thanks for that."

"I can't tell you why your aunt and uncle never told you. I don't know the answer to that. But as I told you on the phone, there is a significant amount of money that was left to you."

"Like how much is a 'significant amount'?" asked Jesse.

"Enough to be worth opening old wounds, I should think. There's 1.2 million dollars in the estate, minus my fee, to be divided among her children."

They stared blankly at him again, stunned, as they assimilated that new piece of information.

"What the fuck?" said Jesse. "Did she rob banks for a living??"

Mr. Tudball ignored the question.

"What did she die of?" asked Jennifer.

He paused for a moment, considering the wording. "Your mother had colon cancer."

"Shit," said Jesse quietly. Then responding to their unappreciative looks, she added, "No pun intended."

"So how does this all work now?" asked Jennifer.

"Okay, I have to tell you that there are some unusual conditions in terms of collecting the money. It will be paid only after you complete a little 'journey' of sorts where you'll be given more information that will help you get to know both your mother and your family a little better. It will answer a lot of the questions you might have. All of your expenses during your travel time will be covered."

"Wait. We have to go on a *scavenger hunt* to collect our inheritance?" asked Jennifer incredulously. "You can't possibly be serious."

"Yes. Completely serious," he said.

Jesse threw her head back and guffawed. "Oh, my God, that's fucking hilarious! This is the best thing I've heard in a long time."

"That's really easy for you to say, Jesse," said Jennifer, pretty damn irritated with the whole thing by this point. "You don't have a life to get back to."

"Nice," Jesse responded, more hurt than she let on at that bluntly worded truth. "And what exactly do *you* have to do? An important meeting of the Glenview Garden Club? Or are you and The Girls getting your assholes bleached?"

"You know what," began Jen, "I don't appreciate the sarcasm. You have absolutely no idea of what's going on in my life right now, so don't pretend like you do."

"Well, maybe if you returned my calls once in a while I would," Jesse shot back.

"Yeah. Uh huh. Except that I don't recall you ever asking about *me* when you call. Just you *telling me* what you need *me* to do to bail *you* out."

Jesse had no response to that because she realized it was probably true (though she couldn't remember the exact details). *My bad*, she responded... in her head.

Mr. Tudball, who had been checking his watch as this fun little exchange played out, interrupted, "Okay! Let's keep going with this, please. You have somewhere you need to be this evening... You will be given an envelope in each location, which will have the information about your next destination, as well as food and expense money. The journey has to be completed within one week from today, or the money in the estate will be donated to charity."

"This is going to take an entire week?!" Jennifer exclaimed.

"We only have *one week* or it's donated to *charity*?" asked Jesse. "That is fucked up. Who abandons their kids, then only gives them a week or their inheritance is donated to charity?"

"NO. I don't have a week," continued Jen. "I have to get home. I can't be away for that long right now!"

"Oh, my God! Jennifer! You know, if you could relax your sphincter for just a minute, who knows what magical things might happen. You might start shitting faeries and leprechauns."

Jennifer grabbed her purse. "That's it. I've had it with you, Jesse. I don't need this bullshit from you or from some control-freak, dead-beat bitch of a mom. And *I* don't need the money. I came here as a favor to YOU. But you know what? I'm done." She grabbed her Dooney and Bourke carry-on overnight bag at the door.

"Wait! I didn't mean—" But Jesse was cut off by the slamming of the door as Jennifer exited. Jesse looked defeated, knowing she had royally fucked up, once again pushing away someone who was earnestly trying to help her. "Goddamn it," she said quietly to herself. "Why can't I just keep my mouth shut?"

"Good question," Mr. Tudball agreed.

After a moment of silence, Jesse asked, "I don't suppose I could make the trip by myself?"

"Nope. Sorry. The will is very clear," he said.

She took a deep breath and exhaled loudly. "Well, I guess we're done here then."

Before Jesse could stand up, the door to Mr. Tudball's office reopened. Jennifer threw her bag down with an exasperated groan, narrowly missing Sean who was camped out by the plastic Ficus tree. She took her seat again. Despite all current outward appearances, she really did love her kid sister.

"Fine. What do we need to do?" Jen said brusquely.

Jesse reached over and took her sister's hand, kissed it, and very sincerely said, "Thank you. I'm sorry. Really I am."

Without looking at her, Jennifer said, "Whatever." She shook her head with a tiny hint of a smile. To Mr. Tudball, she added, "This is the most ridiculous thing I've ever heard. A scavenger hunt..."

"Hey, I don't make the rules, I just follow them," he replied.

"Wow, was that your quote in your high school yearbook? Sweet!" said Jesse (because she really *couldn't* stop her mouth).

Mr. Tudball ignored her once again. He handed Envelope #1 to Jennifer along with a single sheet of paper, bypassing Jesse's outstretched hand.

"The paper has your hotel info printed on it. One night already paid for. The envelope has an address and a time written on the outside. That's where you'll be going tonight. Leave the dog at the hotel. Arrive at least fifteen minutes before the time on the envelope. You're not to open the actual envelope until you get there. Is that clear?"

"Yeth. YES," said Jennifer, mortified by her inadvertent faux-pas-lisp.

Jesse stifled a laugh.

Mr. Tudball handed Jennifer another set of paperwork, and said, "This is the paperwork for your rental car. The Enterprise is two doors down from this building to your right as you exit. It's already been paid for in full for one week."

"Does it turn into a pumpkin at the stroke of midnight at that point?" Jesse asked.

"As far as you're concerned, yes."

· · · · ● · ● · · ·

The women exited the Enterprise office and headed across the parking lot to their brand-spanking-new white Chevy Impala, their "pumpkin-carriage" for the week.

Jesse held her hand out and said, "Lemme have the keys. I'll drive us to the hotel."

"No, you drove us to the airport this morning, and look how that turned out," Jennifer said.

"C'mon, Jen, there were extenuating circumstances!"

"Plus," continued Jennifer, "you had two Bloody Marys on the plane."

"Oh, my God," said Jesse, "are you serious? That was *hours* ago."

"I'm driving," Jennifer persisted.

"Fine, you can drive this leg. But you can't be a control freak and drive the entire trip."

Jesse went around to the passenger side, lifted Sean into the back seat, and parked herself up front. Jennifer familiarized herself with all of the buttons and switches and bells and whistles on the dashboard and steering wheel. She pulled the car to the exit, but she couldn't see around the van that was parked on the street and was blocking her view of oncoming traffic.

"I can't see what's coming, Jess. Can you tell me when it's clear?"

Jesse leaned forward as far as she could and craned her neck around. "Okay, as soon as the big blue truck passes, you have a very small window. You'll have to move fast."

They waited for two cars to pass first before the Waste Management truck blew by.

"Hurry! Go! Go!" Jesse yelled at Jennifer. The car pulled out, tires squealing, and rounded the corner at the end of the block. And they were gone.

Wednesday Evening

The women sat in their rental car, minus the puppy, staring at a giant candy-striped circus tent at the far end of the crowded parking lot. THE CLANCY BROTHERS CIRCUS was emblazoned in enormous, brightly colored letters across the Big Top between a sprinkling of multicolored triangular flags.

"Check the address again. This can't be right," said Jennifer.

"I've checked it three times, Jen. This is it."

"Open the envelope," said Jennifer.

Jesse tore it open and pulled out a pair of yellow, red, and blue Clancy Brothers tickets, and said, "Yep. Apparently, Mom's taking us to the circus. I guess we're living out the childhood with her that we were deprived of. Well, *that* makes up for everything."

They stepped out of the car and joined the throng of patrons ambling toward the Big Top.

"Good grief, who are all these people that go to the circus on a Wednesday night?" Jennifer wondered.

THE KEY TO CIRCUS-MOM HIGHWAY

"Umm... the fun people?" Jesse suggested.

"Let me see that," said Jennifer, reaching for the envelope. She pulled out the piece of paper that accompanied their two tickets. "Okay, it says to stay in our seats after the show ends and a woman named Marjorie will come out with further instructions for us."

As they approached the entrance of the tent, a clown dressed in black and white, more like a traditional mime, snuck up behind Jennifer while she looked down and was intently reading the instructions. His black and white painted face peered over her shoulder as he pretended to read with her. Startled, Jennifer swung around and punched him in the chest. Her reflexive (and completely out-of-proportion) response knocked the wind out of him.

"Jesus! Get away from me!" she exclaimed.

The clown/mime, coughing, moved away with a great flourish of dramatic indignation, taking a puff on the asthma inhaler he pulled out of his clown pants pocket.

"God, I hate mimes," she grumbled.

· · · · ● · ● · · · ·

1982

Five-year-old Jesse and seven-year-old Jennifer were leisurely strolling in Lincoln Park with their mom and dad on a beautiful, sunny, perfect Saturday afternoon in May. Jesse was between Carolyn and Jim, being hoisted in the air by her hands with squeals of delight. Jennifer held on to Jim's other hand, carefully and methodically licking a melting chocolate chip ice cream cone with rainbow sprinkles.

Jennifer looked off to the side where a street mime near them "fell off a wire" he was pretending to walk across. He lay there on the grass, unmoving. Jennifer screamed as though she had just witnessed a murder. Her ice cream cone landed upside down on the ground next to her black patent leather Mary Jane-shod feet with a loud *splat!*

••••••••••

They handed their tickets to a circus worker in a Harlequin costume as they went in, and Jesse laughed, "That's so cliché. You mime-hater, you."

"Fuck you," Jennifer said with a smile.

"I *love* how much you're swearing these days, Jen!" Jesse teased. "I mean, the downside is that you'll probably go to hell now, but at least there'll be a lot of sailors there with you that you can exchange salty stories with."

"Yeah, well, you have a special talent for bringing that out in me," said Jennifer.

"You are welcome," grinned Jesse. She put her arm around Jennifer's shoulders and gave her a squeeze. Jennifer shook her head and smiled. Sisters...

By the time they had purchased refreshments and various accouterments and had entered the large arena to find their seats, music was playing and the pre-show had begun. Members of the troupe moved through the almost sold-out crowd, incorporating unwitting audience members into the act. Jesse, embracing the experience like a kid, was decked out in her colorful new jester hat with jingle bells; and she carried a big bag of popcorn and a jumbo-sized cup of (unappetizingly named) Clown Juice. She had a Collector's Edition show program tucked under her arm. It was the most relaxed and carefree she had felt in quite some time.

They found their seats toward the back of the Big Top on Aisle B. Jennifer went in first and parked herself next to a lone empty seat. Jesse took the aisle seat. They didn't notice the clown that had been working his way along the row behind them, climbing across audience members' laps.

"Aw, c'mon," encouraged Jesse. "This'll be fun! I mean, we're here, we might as well enjoy it, right? Thanks, Dead-Mom!"

As they settled in, the traveling clown was now directly behind them. He reached around Jennifer (because when it rains it pours) and placed a bulbous, red, rubber nose on an elastic string around her face with his rubber-gloved, but surprisingly dexterous, hands. She screamed, swung around, and beaned him in the head with her tasteful, French navy blue Tory Burch purse. Her reflexes were positively ninja-like.

He went down hard onto the already sticky floor. There was uproarious laughter from the crowd around them, including Jesse. Two big, rubber clown hands reached up and grabbed the back of Jesse's seat. He pulled himself up to standing.

"And I thought the kids were bad. They don't pay me enough for this shit," he mumbled to himself as he walked off slowly, holding his head in a daze.

Jesse looked back at Jennifer and laughed. "Well, I don't think any more clown-mimes will be bothering you after that."

They spent the next two hours watching choreographed magic acts, a precision gymnastics team on giant balls filled with flashing lights, daring feats performed by conjoined twins on a high-wire, and the Adonis-on-a-Rope performing aerial silk tricks. Well, Jennifer mostly watched, though she was quite distracted, repeatedly checking her phone for messages that never appeared.

The one exception to her lack of focus was during the lone animal act which involved a woman dressed in a gossamer angel costume performing acrobatic tricks on horseback. At the end of her act, a projected line of text flashed on the back of the stage that said "Angie Was Here." It happened so quickly that they almost missed it.

Jennifer looked at Jesse and said, "Did you see that?!"

"Yeah," Jesse replied. "What was that? Was that for us?"

"I don't know. It doesn't seem to have anything to do with the horse act, so... yeah... maybe? I don't know. Look it up in your program," urged Jennifer.

"Well, well, look who's glad now that I waited in line and sprung for the deluxe program!" said Jesse with a smirk.

She pulled it out and looked up the horse act to see if the performer's name was Angie. But the horse acrobat was a Poli Sci graduate from U.C. Santa Barbara named Stephanie Lynn Riggobutti, whose hobbies included deep-sea fishing and knitting rainbow sweaters for gay cats that she sold on Etsy in honor of her great-aunt Philip, the founder of LAGSOA (Lesbians Against the Gender Stereotyping of Animals). Her name was not Angie. No mention of any "Angie" whatsoever, and nothing else like that one message appeared for the remainder of the show.

At the show's conclusion, they stayed in their seats as instructed for what seemed an eternity. Almost everyone in the audience had left, and workers were busy sweeping up the spectacular amount of garbage strewn all over the ground. Jesse, still wearing her jester's hat, had fallen asleep sitting up. Her head was resting precariously on her hand, periodically falling forward until she caught herself, all while asleep.

Jennifer was checking her phone for perhaps the eighty-seventh time, increasingly irritated that she had to waste her entire evening at the circus for no apparent reason, when Marjorie came rushing up Aisle B, Envelope #2 in her hand.

Marjorie was a Little Person originally from Duluth, Minnesota who had been discovered by a Clancy Brothers Circus scout when he was in town for his Uncle Shem's third wedding. He saw a photo of Marjorie in a local Duluth advertising flyer modeling clothes for the now-defunct He-Sells-She-Sells Children's School Uniform Store at the mall, and he tracked her down. Pointing out that she was an embarrassing thirty years older than her fellow models, he offered her a modest raise, health insurance, and better show business exposure than she was getting in *The Land of 10,000 Lakes*.

"Hi, ladies, I'm Marjorie. I'm SO sorry I took so long!" she apologized breathlessly. "We had an emergency situation backstage after the show with The Flying Finnegans, and I had to act as a surrogate marriage counselor. Again. Long story. I won't bore you. Anyway, here are your directions for tomorrow along with money for expenses."

She handed the envelope to Jennifer.

As Jesse began to wake up, rather out of it from a Clown Juice sugar coma, Jennifer asked Marjorie, "Wait, why did we have to be here tonight? And what was that 'Angie was here' message? Was that for us?"

"Oh. Yes! Sorry," apologized Marjorie. "I'm supposed to tell you that your mom worked here for two years."

"She worked here? Doing what?" Jennifer asked incredulously.

"You'll find out more about that tomorrow," Marjorie explained.

Jennifer threw up her hands in exasperation.

"You'll need to leave early," Marjorie continued. "You have a long drive. It's about six-and-a-half hours."

"A six-and-a-half hour drive?! Where are we going? Happyland, Oklahoma?" Jennifer asked sarcastically.

"No, that's actually fourteen hours from here. Your drive'll be easy-peasy compared to that!" Marjorie answered, Jennifer's sarcasm going (easily) right over her head. "You'll be going to the Thibodaux, Louisiana area at the edge of the Atchafalaya Basin. It's about four hundred and forty miles, give or take, and you'll want to get there during daylight because the place you're going to is a little tricky to find. That's why you need to leave early. You'll be going to the home of Poppy and Harville Poupard. Have a safe trip!" And with that, she rushed off to continue her domestic circus mediation.

Jennifer turned to Jesse. "Poppy Poupard?"

Jesse yawned. "I love that kind of mustard."

DAY THREE

*"Never let anyone drive you crazy;
it is nearby anyway
and the walk is good for you."
-Lewis Carroll*

Thursday Afternoon

Jesse and Jennifer slowly climbed out of the punishing confines of their Chevy Impala to stretch their weary, stiff, aging legs and to fill the tank at a rickety old gas station along a Thibodaux, Louisiana back road. It had been a long drive. Jesse put the nozzle in the gas tank and then got Sean out of the car, while a frustrated Jennifer, brow furrowed, reread the paper with the directions to the Poupard house.

Jennifer said, "I think we must've missed a turn somewhere back there. That GPS is worthless. I need to go and ask someone about these directions." She looked up at Jesse and the puppy. "You need a friggin' leash for that thing..."

"Oh, she didn't mean that. You're not a 'thing,'" Jesse said to Sean before kissing him on the mouth.

"Oh, my God, that's disgusting!" said Jennifer. "Do you have any idea where that dog's mouth has been? He licks his own balls."

Jesse shrugged. "Eh, I've licked worse."

THE KEY TO CIRCUS-MOM HIGHWAY 55

Jennifer cringed. "Please don't elaborate."

"Lemme have some cash," Jesse said, holding her hand out, the puppy tucked under the other arm. "I'll see if they have a leash for him in there."

The shack-like, wooden storefront looked like something out of the Old West. You could almost hear spurs jangling as they walked over, though it was probably just the bell that jingled when Jesse pushed open the front door. The tiny store smelled like a mix of tobacco, ranch-flavored corn nuts, and... and something else... She couldn't quite put her finger on it until she saw the woman at the cash register with hair that had been flat-ironed within an inch of its life.

She immediately flashed back to a traumatic curling iron mishap in the eighth grade that had left a large patch of hair on the left side of her head only one inch long, which she then had to turn into a "styling choice" for the Homecoming Dance. So that was it, tobacco, ranch-flavored corn nuts, and burnt hair.

She wandered past the adjacent displays of venison jerky strips, candy cigarettes, and hunting knives, and asked the woman at the cash register, "I'm guessing you guys don't have dog leashes, do you?"

Outside, Jennifer approached an old man in his late eighties. He was wearing a plaid flannel shirt and baggy pants, sitting on a small wooden chair off to the side of the storefront door. He had a black patch over one eye, a few teeth missing, and he was chewing tobacco, occasionally spitting into an old Dr Pepper can.

"Excuse me. Hi," began Jennifer. "I was wondering if you could help me. These directions we got are a little confusing, and I'm wondering if we're in the right place."

Looking at her warily, he said, "Catch me dat," and took the paper out of her hand. He did his best to read it with his one good eye, his finger sliding along the typed words very slowly. As in *very, very* slowly.

In a thick, rapidly spoken Cajun dialect that she couldn't follow well, he said, "Dis plain as day. You couyon filles gone ri' pass da turn. Turn 'round go bag dare haf mile ta dis sign wi' dis picture on't." He pointed to the paper where there was a little voodoo protection symbol.

Jesse came out of the store at this point, sucking on a big red, white, and blue Bomb Pop. She was leading Sean on a makeshift leash she had crafted out of three connected bungee cords. She joined Jennifer and listened to the rest of the old man's directions.

"Da road not peeve. Go fie hunnert feet down da dirt to da fork to da chicken bone cross onna wood stake, and go right. Still not peeve. Der ohm bout a haf mile down da lef."

"Um... okaaay," said Jennifer, trying to decipher that. "So... left here?" She pointed at the symbol. "And then left at something with a chicken bone??"

She was taken aback when he reached out and thumped her on the forehead with his finger and said, "No, not lef, you couyon, you! You brainless? Not lef! Ah don be sayin' dat, me. Git it into you had! Right, right!" Then he mumbled to himself, "Stupid touriss."

Laughing at the conversation debacle she had just witnessed, Jesse said, "Okay, thank you!" and she quickly pulled Jennifer back toward the car.

He dismissively waved them away with a scowl, and under his breath said, "Yea, beck moi tchew..."

THE KEY TO CIRCUS-MOM HIGHWAY 57

"That crazy old man! Did you get *any* of that??" asked Jennifer.

"Yeah, I think so. I had to decipher drunk people at work who might as well have been speaking Cajun. You learn to get the gist of things."

They got into the car and pulled back out onto the road in the direction they had just come from. Jesse handed Jennifer a Bomb Pop.

"Here, this is for you," she said. "Do you remember these from when we were little?"

Smiling at the memory, Jennifer said, "Oh my God, I loved these."

"Me too," agreed Jesse. "Remember we used to get 'em from that Wonko's ice cream truck that inched through the neighborhood every weekend playing 'Mary Had a Little Lamb' on an endless loop?"

"Mr. Peterson! Oh, my God, I had that stupid song stuck in my head until I was about twenty-three," laughed Jennifer.

"We'd have blue lips for days!" recalled Jesse. "And we'd take 'em to that fort we built in those juniper bushes out back, and we'd talk about all the adventures we were going to have." Then softly, staring ahead, she added, "I miss that."

Jennifer looked over at her. "Yeah, me too... Well, here we are on an adventure together."

"Yep, here we are. *Some* of us kicking and screaming a little more than others," Jesse said, poking Jennifer's arm.

"Nah, not too much kicking..." corrected Jen. "Hey, better late than never, right?"

"Right," agreed Jesse.

"Oh, look, there it is! That symbol," said Jennifer, pointing. "We go left here. I did get that part."

They turned left and went slowly down the dirt road until they approached the fork.

"Okay," Jen continued, "there's a horrifying chicken bone cross. Were we supposed to go left again here?"

Jesse reached over and thumped Jennifer on the forehead. "You brainless? He don be sayin' dat, him. Do NOT go lef! Go right, right! Stupid touriss!" said Jesse. Her imitation of the old Cajun pirate was spot-on.

"Wow, you *do* have a good ear!" Shaking her head, Jennifer mused, "My God, what have we gotten ourselves into?"

Jennifer turned "right, right" and continued along the dirt road for a bit. They eventually approached a petite house sitting back about fifty feet from the edge of Bayou Lafourche.

Jesse checked the address on the paper. "Yep. This is the place," she said.

They pulled up, parked, and got out of the car, with Sean on his brand-new bungee-leash. Then they headed up onto the porch, swatting mosquitoes as they went. Loud Zydeco music was playing inside. Jesse knocked but there was no answer. She knocked again, a little louder this time. When there was still no answer, she started to open the door.

"What are you doing?" asked Jennifer. "We can't just barge in!"

"Okay, well, I'll let you keep your little Zika-infected friends company out here," said Jesse. "I'm going in."

Jennifer followed.

THE KEY TO CIRCUS-MOM HIGHWAY 59

"Hello?" Jesse called out, as she cracked the front door open.

They stepped farther into the large, open kitchen/living room area. The room was bursting with color, filled with rustic, homemade crafts, paintings, and fresh flowers. It was the kind of home that feels good to step into, one that wraps you in a warm and welcoming embrace.

Harville Poupard, a tall, strapping man in his early sixties, was standing at the stove with his back to them, putting the finishing touches on a pot of crawfish etouffee. He was dancing and singing along with the song "Ya Ya," completely bare-assed. Harville was naked except for a chest-to-thigh, pink ruffled apron that only covered him in front, with a lopsided bow in the back at his waist.

"Oh!" exclaimed Jesse. "I'm so sorry! We're looking fo—"

Poppy Poupard, also in her early sixties, entered just then. She was a good two feet shorter than Harville and was very slight of build. The comical pairing looked like an NBA player had married a jockey.

"Good Lord, Harville, turn down the music and put some pants on. *Put some pants on!* We have guests!" she admonished.

Surprised by the sudden audience, he said, "Oh! They weren't supposed to be here for another hour! My apologies, ladies." He noticed the puppy and added, "I'd keep that critter inside if I was you. This is 'gator country." Then he exited to pantsify himself.

"Well," said Jennifer, pointing at her sister, "this one drove like a bat out of hell for the first half of the trip, so we made good time."

"Shhh," said Poppy quietly. "Best not speak about bats around here. Bats have a different meaning here... That over there is my mother Eulalie." She indicated an extremely old woman with cloudy eyes and long grey hair pulled back in a bun. She was sitting in a far corner making something out of the plant leaves in her lap. They hadn't noticed her before, what with Harville's dancing bare ass and all.

"Oh, now where are my manners?" she continued. "I'm Poppy. Welcome! *Welcome!* Can I get you girls some sweet tea? You must be parched after your long drive."

"Yes, please," answered Jesse.

"That'd be nice. Thank you," echoed Jennifer.

"Y'all have a seat on the couch. Have a seat and I'll bring it to you."

They walked over and sat down on the old, worn, blue velvet couch. It had years' worth of cultivated butt indentations in the seat cushions, and large crocheted doilies were draped over the back. Jesse glanced over at the old-as-shit woman named Eulalie. She had a string of large beads and some kind of animal teeth around her neck, and she appeared to be blind. She didn't seem to ever look down as she worked with the plant leaves and roots. Instead, she stared straight ahead out of unblinking, milky blue eyes, working by feel.

Poppy came over with iced sweet tea in two glass jelly jars and handed them to the sisters. She sat down in a chair across from them and said, "I need to talk to you girls."

"*Finally*," said Jennifer, "some information."

"Well, no. I'm so sorry to have to tell you this after driving all day, *so sorry*, but before I can give you any information about your mom, y'all have to do something else."

They groaned.

"Now what??" asked Jesse.

"I don't mean to be rude, Poppy, but this is getting extremely frustrating," said Jennifer. "We got virtually no information last night. We were told we'd get information when we got to your place."

"I completely understand. Let me explain. The lawyer's office called us yesterday while you were there. There was one other person who was supposed to be at that meeting with you, but he didn't show." She paused, not sure how to break this next piece of information. "Well, I guess I'll just come right out and say it. Y'all have a brother."

They stared at her, dumbfounded.

"I'm sorry, what?" asked Jennifer, not quite sure she heard that correctly.

"A *brother??*" asked Jesse.

"Yes. His name is Jack Babineaux and he lives in New Orleans. Y'all have to go get him and bring him back with you. The will clearly states that all children have to be present on the journey to collect the inheritance. *All children.* If he doesn't come, the journey ends here, so if I were you, I would find a way to get him here."

Jesse groaned again.

"I know, *I know.* I'm sorry. I wish I had better news for you. I want so badly to be able to tell you about Angie. Y'all remind me so much of her."

"Why didn't the lawyer tell us this when we were right there in his office?" snapped Jennifer, her patience worn thin.

"We thought it might be better to wait until you had already made the drive to Louisiana since Jack is close by here anyway. We were afraid that if he told y'all this in Tallahassee, you might not have come."

Poppy stood up and walked back over to the kitchen area to retrieve a piece of paper that was sitting on the woodblock island. Jesse and Jennifer were quiet for a moment after this latest bombshell.

Jesse turned to Jennifer. "A fucking *brother??*" she whispered. "What, was she just traveling around the country squirting out soon-to-be-abandoned kids everywhere she went?"

At that moment, Jennifer's considerable talent for compartmentalizing her emotions kicked in, and for the first time on their trip, she calmly took charge. "Okay. Well. This is the adventure we always wanted... Alright, maybe not specifically *this* one. But..." She turned to Poppy. "Where do we need to go?" she asked matter-of-factly.

Jesse began to feel queasy again. She jumped up. "Oh, no! Restroom?!"

"Down the hall, first door on your left," Poppy said quickly, pointing down the hallway past the living room.

Jesse ran.

"Here," said Poppy, as she walked back to Jennifer and sat down on the couch next to her. "I've drawn y'all a map."

Jennifer slid closer to her and looked at the map as Poppy began to explain the directions. Jesse walked back in slowly, wiping her mouth with her t-shirt. She glanced over at Eulalie who motioned for Jesse to come over. Jesse looked around, not sure if the gesture was meant for her. Eulalie motioned again. Jesse cautiously approached the tiny woman who had otherworldly eyes and a face that was a roadmap of wrinkles. Poppy and Jennifer continued talking in the background.

"Y'ain't feelin' well," Eulalie rasped. It wasn't a question.

"No, I'm not," confirmed Jesse.

"You ain't got no idea what's goin' on with y'self, do you, child?"

"Umm... an ulcer?" Jesse asked tentatively.

Eulalie cackled with delight at that. "Child, you ain't got no ulcer. Unless that's the baby's *name!*"

INFORMATION OVERLOAD. A brother *and* a baby? Jesse's head was swimming.

"Pregnant?" she asked weakly. "No... No, how could you even know something like that?"

"Honey-baby, I can *see* it in you plain as day. You almost two months along now. S'a girl."

At this point, silent Jesse was forcing back tears.

"Go along now with your sister," Eulalie continued. "When you come back, I'll have some medicine made for you 'n that ulcer-baby." She cackled again at her own joke.

Jesse stood there in silence, staring at her.

"Go on now!" admonished Eulalie. "Y'all got bizniss ta take care of."

Jesse walked slowly back over to Jennifer who had all of Jack's address information by this point. Poppy was holding Sean in her lap.

"Aww, little cher bébé," Poppy cooed, stroking his head.

"Poppy said they'll take care of the dog while we're gone. I'll drive," said Jen.

"Okay," Jesse answered quietly.

They started to head out the front door when Jennifer turned back to Poppy and said, "Can you give us just one small piece of information to tide us over? Like how you two knew our mom?"

Poppy smiled sympathetically at them and acquiesced. "Okay, just one little piece. Harville and I knew Angie because we worked in the circus with her... Now go and bring Jack back."

The sisters headed out the front door and got in the car just as Harville re-entered the living room.

"Where'd they go?" he asked. "Did I put pants on for nothin'?"

THURSDAY EVENING

Jennifer and Jesse stood at the front door of an old, red-brick townhouse with yellow trim and black shutters. The townhouse was a block off of Bourbon Street in the French Quarter. It was during that transitional time of day when the daylight was shifting to evening. The types of people on the street were beginning to shift as well. They knocked on the door several times but there was no answer. A neighbor was smoking a cigarette on his scrolled iron balcony. He was one door down on the second floor and had been watching them, sizing them up.

"Y'all lookin' for Sydney?" he called down to them.

"No," said Jennifer. "We're looking for Jack Babineaux."

He eyed them suspiciously. "What for? You bill collectors?"

"Bill collectors?" Jennifer asked, confused by the question.

"No," Jesse assured his neighbor. "Just relatives in for the evening. We wanted to say hello." She flashed him her most charming of smiles.

"He's already left for work," said the neighbor.

"Where is that?" asked Jennifer.

He eyed them suspiciously again. "Y'all must not be very close relatives if you don't know *that*."

"Oh, we've been out of touch for a few years," offered Jesse.

"Hmm," he considered, taking a slow drag off of his cigarette while sizing them up. "Okay. You'll find him at Lucky Peter's. It's a couple of blocks to the left down Bourbon Street, opposite side, on the corner of St. Peter Street."

Jesse turned to Jennifer. "That's right where we're parked!"

"Thank you very much," Jennifer said to the neighbor with a wave.

It was a short walk to Bourbon Street. As soon as they turned left, they found themselves in front of a shop filled with all the glorious, cheap-ass, shiny tourist crap an out-of-towner could ever dream of wasting their money on. It beckoned to Jennifer. She grabbed Jesse's arm.

"Wait, can we stop in here really quickly? I want to pick up some souvenirs for the family. They can at least get something fun out of this, and I'm sure we won't have time to stop afterward."

She veered into the shop. Jesse followed her.

"You mean aside from the obvious gift of having you out of their hair for a week?" said Jesse.

"*There's* the Jesse I know!" teased Jennifer. "You were so quiet the whole way here. Not a single insult at all since we left Poppy and Harville's. I was starting to worry about you."

Jesse smiled. "I'm good. Just thinking."

At this point, New-Orleans-Jennifer had completely embraced the experience. She went nuts with the trinkets, and t-shirts, and hats, and mugs, and mass-produced Voodoo statuettes wearing colorful outfits, and necklaces made of plastic penises hung on Mardi Gras beads that Glenview-Jennifer never would have bought. She glanced back at Jesse who was lost in quiet contemplation.

"You're not getting anything?" she asked Jesse.

Jesse shrugged and shook her head.

"Because we have plenty of cash if you're worried about that," Jennifer continued as she picked up a replica of a Civil War Remington Army Revolver.

"Jesus, you're buying a gun?" asked Jesse.

"It's not real. Sean's a Civil War buff, so I thought this might be fun to get him," she said as she dumped her mountain of treasure on the counter to check out.

"Since when is he a Civil War buff?" asked Jesse.

"Since he went on HelpMeFindMyAncestors.com to research his genealogy two years ago. He discovered he was distantly related to some Civil War Union officer—a great-great-great-uncle-twice-removed, or something like that. He became obsessed to the point that I had to start tuning him out when he talked about it. It got really annoying. I don't even know how much he's spent on memorabilia at this point. I stopped asking."

"Oh God," groaned Jesse. "Please don't tell me he does those ridiculous Civil War reenactments. I will never be able to look at him with a straight face again."

"I know, right?" Jennifer agreed. "Honestly, he did a couple of them, but I shamed him into stopping after the last one where he got killed almost immediately and had to lie there completely still for four hours. The fake blood was made out of corn syrup, and it attracted ants. He was bitten over 100 times. I gave him such a hard time about it that he never did another one. I feel kind of bad that I was so mean about it. I was kind of a bitch."

Jesse gasped, feigning shock. "NO. Really?"

"Very funny," said Jen. "Anyway, this'll be my attempt at an apology for that. I think he'll appreciate it."

Jennifer completed her purchase and they stepped back into the growing evening crowd on Bourbon Street. They walked in silence for a moment, passing an old nun riding a bicycle with training wheels down the center of Bourbon Street. The bike was covered in hand-painted signs preaching doomsday prophecies. Next, they passed a man wearing a gold lamé unitard, and after that, a family of five from Nebraska wearing matching burgundy corduroy outfits.

"Seriously, why have you been so quiet?" asked Jen. "Are you okay? I mean, aside from the obvious?"

Jesse stopped walking, considering whether to share the news. The pedestrians behind them were forced to weave around her. She looked at Jennifer who was watching her, concerned.

"Miss Eulalie says I'm pregnant," she announced.

"...What?... Miss EULALIE... That old, half-blind bat in the corner wearing animal teeth?"

"We're not supposed to talk about bats down here... for some fucking reason," Jesse reminded her.

Jennifer burst out laughing. It was the first time she had laughed that hard during the entire trip.

"It's not funny!" protested Jesse.

"Yes, it is. It's hilarious. She's your OB-GYN medical source? I wouldn't worry about it, Jesse. You DO use protection, don't you?"

"Yeah... Usually..." Jesse closed her eyes, remembering a drunken night in August that was *not* included in that "usually" response. She clasped her hands on the sides of her head and yelled, "Fuuuuck!"

"Oh my God, Jesse, wait here. I'll be right back."

Jennifer ran back to the corner and turned down a side street to a little pharmacy she had spotted on their walk over, leaving Jesse to wait on the street by herself. Jesse didn't notice the man in a grey pin-striped business suit who glanced over at her as he passed by. She didn't see him the second time he passed her going the other direction. Not until he came up next to her and whispered, "How much you chargin' for your services, sweetheart?"

"My serv—?" she began. Jesse realized he had mistaken her for a hooker waiting on the street for a john. Needing someone to take her immense frustration out on, she decided to mess with his head. "I'm pregnant, asshole. Hey, are YOU my baby-daddy? Yeah, I remember you from last month! You're my baby-daddy! *You're my baby-daddy!*"

She continued calling after him as he waved her off and ran away as quickly as his Hugo Boss shoes would carry him. He almost knocked Jennifer flat on her ass as she rounded the corner. She had added a small, white paper pharmacy bag to her growing list of purchases.

"What'd you get?" asked Jesse.

"I got you a home pregnancy test to put your mind at ease, so you can go back to the angry, acerbic Jesse I know and love. You can use it when we get to the club."

"Okay. Thank you, Jen."

They walked the last short distance to Lucky Peter's, listening to the dueling music styles as they passed consecutive music clubs, each trying to lure the Bourbon Street foot traffic into their lair.

Lucky Peter's was a bustling place, filled with a wide array of patrons in terms of gender and lifestyle—gay and straight, men in drag, and tourists from Minnesota who had heard about the club from the cousin of a friend of a friend and who wanted an "exotic" story to take home to their provincial Midwestern lives. It was lavishly decorated in rich jewel tones, expensive fabrics, chandeliers, faux marble tabletops, and animal print chairs. There was a stage in the main room next to the dark and moody-chic bar area. If King Louis XIV owned a drag club on Bourbon Street, this would be it. Though, distracted by the current issue at hand, Jesse and Jennifer didn't notice at first what this place was all about.

"That'll be fifteen dollars each," the doorman told them.

"Fifteen dollars each just to walk into a bar?!" exclaimed Jesse. "Holy cover charge, Batman!"

"Don't talk about bats," he responded as he took their cash. "Enjoy the show."

As they entered the club, a man dressed as Cher was onstage finishing up a lip-synched rendition of "If I Could Turn Back Time" to wild applause, whistles, and cheers.

"We're going to put your mind at rest," said Jennifer, "because we're going to find the ladies' room and you're going to use this thing." She grabbed a passing cocktail waitress. "Excuse me, we're looking for Jack Babineaux. We were told he works here."

"Yeah. Grab a seat and I'll go look for him," the waitress said.

"Where's your ladies' room?" Jesse added.

"The unisex bathroom is down there to the right," answered the waitress, pointing in the direction of a side hallway. It was illuminated by soft, blue, recessed ceiling lights, under a sign that said "Blue Light District."

"Okay, thanks," Jesse responded. "We'll be right back."

During this time, it finally dawned on Jennifer that most of the men working at the club were dressed as women. "Oh, my God, Jesse, this is a drag club."

"No shit, Sherlock. What gave it away? The five o'clock shadow on our waitress?" Jesse grabbed her hand and pulled her toward the glowing blue hallway. "You're coming with me for this. I need emotional support."

The walls of the bathroom were painted in the same rich jewel tones, decorated with street-art-style paintings of iconic female popstars and movie stars. There were three stalls, two of which were occupied. A man dressed as Dolly Parton was washing up at one of the sinks. Jennifer glanced over at Dolly, fascinated, as they walked in and headed over to the empty stall together. They passed Cher coming out of the adjacent stall.

It was a tight fit in there with two bodies and a large shopping bag filled with tourist crap. Jesse attempted to open the box, but struggled with the child-proof wrapping.

"I can't get this damn thing open," she said.

"Here, let me do it," said Jen, taking the box from her. She opened the wrapper as Jesse unzipped her pants and sat down on the toilet. "Now just hold it under there while you pee," Jen continued.

Cher and Dolly looked at each other uncomfortably during this exchange they were inadvertently privy to. Dolly shrugged and walked out.

"Be careful!" Jennifer cautioned. "Make sure you get it directly under the stream of urine."

"I'm trying, Jen! I haven't done this in a really long time."

Cher put her hands on her hips, and in a deep, baritone voice said, "Uh, ladies, no funny stuff in the restroom. We pride ourselves on being a respectable business here. We have five stars on Yelp."

From out of the stall, Jesse's voice responded, "Back off, RuPaul! I'm having a female emergency."

"Yeah, who isn't?..." mumbled Cher, heading back into the club.

The sisters emerged from the stall, Jesse carrying the urine-drenched stick, and Jennifer saying, "Be careful with that. Make sure you keep it level."

"How long do we wait?" asked Jesse, setting the stick down on the faux marble sink ledge while she washed her hands.

"I don't remember. It's been a while." Jennifer read the directions on the back of the box. "Here it is. Two minutes."

Jesse dried her hands, picked up the stick, and started to head out to the main room.

"Wait, where are you going with that?!" called Jennifer.

"I'm not gonna hang out in the bathroom waiting around. I'm taking it to the table with me. I want to watch the show."

"Oh, my God, that's disgusting, Jesse. It's covered in urine!"

"Fine," said Jesse, walking back into the stall. "I'll wrap it in some toilet paper." She re-emerged, wrapping the pregnancy stick like a mummy. "Tell me when the time is up," she added.

They headed back out into the main room and found a small table that was available in the back. Jesse set the toilet paper cocoon down as the waitress came back over.

"There you are, I've been looking for you. You're in luck, Jack is up next. What can I get you to drink?"

"Oh, nothing for me, thanks," said Jennifer.

"Lady, there's a two-drink minimum if you're watching the show."

Jesse said, "Uh... I'll have..."

She glanced over at the stage, and was temporarily distracted by the current performer who was dressed as Barbara Streisand, in a slinky black dress with plunging neckline, lip-synching to the Fanny Brice song "My Man".

> *"I just like to dream*
> *Of a cottage by a stream*
> *With my man.*
> *Where a few flowers grew*
> *And perhaps a kid or two*
> *Like my man."*

"Tick tock, ma'am," said the waitress. "I've got other tables to get to."

"She'll have a Shirley Temple," said Jennifer. "I'll have a Shirley Temple too. Shirley Temples all around! We're goin' NUTS tonight!"

The whiskered waitress walked away with a "God, I hate fucking tourists" look on her face.

The emcee came back onstage. "Mes dames et monsieurs! Laydeez und gentlemen!" he called out, like the emcee from *Cabaret*. "Y'all are in for a treat..."

"How much longer?" Jesse whispered to Jennifer.

"...our next act is one of our country's most beloved icons..." continued the emcee.

Jennifer looked at her watch. "Oh, it's time!"

"...performing the song 'Jackie Onassis'..."

Jesse took a deep breath and began the de-mummification process.

"... Here she is! Our very own *Jackie, Oh!*" the emcee concluded.

That's when Jesse saw the big red "+" sign in the window on the stick. "Goddamn it!" she yelled.

The people at the surrounding tables turned to look at her, not quite sure why she was so upset about *Jackie, Oh!* But Jesse didn't notice them, or the show, or much of anything in this space-time continuum outside of that flashing neon sign in her hand screaming YOU'RE HAVING A BABY! YOU'RE HAVING A BABY!

"Let me guess," whispered Jennifer.

"Shit," Jesse said to herself as she buried her face in her hands.

The waitress set their Shirley Temples down on the table and announced, "That'll be twenty-four dollars." Jennifer handed her the money.

THE KEY TO CIRCUS-MOM HIGHWAY

Jesse looked up, mid existential crisis, to watch thirty-seven-year-old Jack Babineaux slink onto the stage in a full-length blue sequin gown, giant sunglasses, and a perfectly coiffed, take-me-seriously-I'm-a-brunette Jackie wig. He was accompanied by an impressive cadre of backup performers taking photos, asking for autographs, and lip-synching the backing vocals. He launched into his drag-queen-fabulous, lip-synched version of "Jackie Onassis," an early song by the 1980s New Wave band Human Sexual Response. The song was from their album *Fig.15*, which also contained the songs "Anne Frank Story" and the utterly delightful crowd favorite "Butt F**k".

> *"I want to be Jackie Onassis.*
> *I want to wear a pair of dark sunglasses.*
> *I want to be Jackie Onassis, oh yeah.*
> *I want bodyguards all around.*
> *I'm anxious to avoid an autograph hound.*
> *Just let me be Jackie Onassis, oh yeah..."*

Monetary transaction complete, Jennifer also began to watch the show. "I'm... so confused," she said. "Is that—?"

"Our brother the drag queen," said Jesse. "I love it!" She turned to Jennifer. "Why do you sound upset? At least he's not a mime."

"I don't know," Jennifer lamented. "He's not really singing, so I think *technically* he is."

Jesse began to laugh. "This damn day just keeps getting better and better!" She attempted to stop laughing, but for the life of her, she couldn't squelch it. The harder she tried, the harder she laughed, until Jennifer began laughing too. It was like laughing in church.

When *Jackie, Oh!*'s number was over and their hysteria had subsided, they made their way over to a person off to the side of the stage who seemed to have a stage manager vibe.

"Hi!" said Jennifer, pouring on her Glenview charm. "We're Jack Babineaux's sisters. He told us we should come and find him after he finished his act."

Too busy to deal with them, the stage manager quickly replied, "Okay, yeah. He's back in the second dressing room to the left."

They headed backstage, passing Marilyn Monroe, Barbara Streisand, Lady Gaga, and, surprisingly, Ruth Bader Ginsberg "The Notorious RBG." She was waiting to go on next to perform "Mama He's Crazy" by The Judds.

The dressing room was crowded with men in various stages of dress, wigs, and makeup. They spotted Jack, a masculine version of Jesse, in the far corner at a mirror taking off his makeup. His wig was already off, just a bobby-pinned stocking cap over his hair. They made their way over to him.

"Jack?" said Jennifer.

"Yes?" he said, looking at them blankly.

"We're the people you fucking stood up yesterday!" said Jesse, off to a roaring bad start.

Jennifer motioned for her to cease and desist. "What my sister Jesse means is... Hi. We're your sisters. I'm Jennifer."

Jack, not at all happy that this was happening, said, "Look. I'm sure y'all are very nice ladies, but I'm not interested. I didn't show up at the lawyer's office yesterday because *fuck our mom*. If she didn't want to keep me, then I'm not interested in anything she's associated with. As far as I'm concerned, she never existed." He went back to makeup and hair deconstruction.

"No," corrected Jesse, "that doesn't work for us. If we don't bring you back with us tonight, then we don't get our inheritance either."

"Sorry," he shrugged. "I don't know what to tell you. I'm not going. I have a very nice family here in New Orleans. End of story."

"Isn't there any way we—" began Jennifer.

"Dale!" Jack called out to a very large man dressed as Diana Ross, seated near the door. "Can you see these ladies out for me? They were just leaving."

Dale stood up, but Jennifer said, "That's okay. We can find our own way out. C'mon, Jesse."

Jesse shook her head in frustration and started to follow Jennifer. Then over her shoulder to Jack, she said, "Yeah, well, you look about as much like Jackie Onassis as I do!"

"I'm devastated," he said with deadpan delivery into the mirror as he continued his makeup removal.

· · · · ●●●●● · · ·

Out on the street, Jesse and Jennifer stood on the corner, off to the side of the entrance. Jennifer was lost in thought. Jesse pulled out a cigarette, lit it, and started pacing.

"What do we do now?" she asked, the desperation beginning to kick in.

"I'm not sure there *is* anything else we can do," answered Jennifer.

"I'm not going home, Jen. Not after everything we've already been through. That fucker is coming with us!"

"And exactly how do you propose we convince him?" asked Jen skeptically.

"I'm not sure yet." Jesse paused to think. "We could rufie a drink and send it back to him," she offered.

"Yeah?" said Jennifer. "You always carry a dose of that on you, Jesse, for just such an occasion?"

Jesse was quiet as she watched some of the performers come out the side door of the club onto the side street. Jennifer watched Jesse smoking.

"You know," Jennifer delicately broached, "you might want to rethink the smoking now that you've found out that you're pregna—"

Jesse cut her off. "I don't want to talk about it! Let me see that bag of tourist crap. What do you have in there? Here, hold this for a second," she said, handing Jennifer the lit cigarette.

Jesse grabbed the bag, and Jennifer bent over to extinguish the cigarette on the sidewalk. Not one to litter, she looked around for a garbage can but didn't see one in the near vicinity, so she gingerly wrapped the cigarette stub in a tissue from her purse, and put the little nicotine-scented nugget into a side pocket. By this point, Jesse had squatted down with the bag of treasure and was rummaging through it. She grabbed a New Orleans "The Big Easy" t-shirt, sunglasses, and a NOLA baseball cap and shoved them at Jennifer.

"Put these on," she instructed. "And put your hair up under the cap." Then she pulled out a leftover Mardi Gras t-shirt with a pair of bare breasts that said *These are the only boobs of mine that you people will be seeing today* and held it up. "Really, Jen?..."

She pulled it on quickly, then pulled out a colorful Mardi Gras wig, and a floppy sun hat to complete her own disguise.

"Um, what exactly is the plan here?" asked the now bespectacled "Big Easy" Jennifer.

"We're gonna kidnap him," Jesse announced matter-of-factly.

"We're gonna *what?* Are you crazy? And just exactly how are we—"

"Just get your hat on and come over here!" Jesse said. "We need to be disguised by the time he comes out, which could be any second. We'll only have one shot at this, so follow my lead, and don't blow our cover!"

They finished putting on the clothes and nonchalantly moved over to the side door on St. Peter Street just as the door opened and a couple of not-Jack people came out.

"This is ridiculous!" whispered Jennifer.

"Be quiet, Jen!" said Jesse as she lit up another cigarette.

The side door opened again and this time Jack came out with one other guy. He had his dress on a hanger in one hand, and the wig and sunglasses on a Styrofoam head in the other. "See you tomorrow, Bill."

Jack turned toward Bourbon Street and Bill headed in the opposite direction toward Royal Street.

Jesse hugged Jennifer, pretending to cry, sobbing in a bad Southern accent, "But ah don know whut ta dooo. I luv him sooo muuuch."

Jack looked down at the sidewalk when he walked by them. As soon as he passed them, Jesse tossed her cigarette on the ground and reached under her bare boob t-shirt. She pulled the replica Civil War Remington Army Revolver out of the waistband of her pants and stuck it in the center of his back.

"Make a sound, motherfucker, and I'll blow a hole right through you," she said, as menacingly as she could.

"What—?" he began.

"Jesse, what are you doing?!" cried Jennifer.

"Oh, Christ," he said. "*You two again?* What about the word NO don't you understand?"

"I'm not kidding," Jesse warned. "You're coming with us, Jack. Keep walking or I WILL shoot you."

"Oh my God oh my God oh my God," Jennifer whimpered to herself, panicking.

"You're bluffing. You wouldn't shoot me in the middle of a crowded area."

"Yeah?" Jesse said. "You wanna test that theory? You have no idea how desperate I am at this moment in time." She ushered him a half a block down and across St. Peter Street to where their rental car was parked. "Now get in the goddamn car!" she ordered.

Jennifer was fumbling nervously with the car keys. She electronically unlocked the doors and climbed into the driver's seat. Jesse forced Jack into the front passenger seat.

"Hey! Watch the wig and dress, you lunatic!" he yelled at Jesse as he climbed in.

She closed his door, then got into the seat behind him. At this point, he was more annoyed than afraid.

"Hurry! Go! Go!" Jesse yelled at Jennifer, tires squealing as they pulled out. "And just remember I've got a gun pointed at your head, Jack, so don't try anything stupid. Put the child lock on the doors, Jen, so he can't try to jump out."

THE KEY TO CIRCUS-MOM HIGHWAY 81

He shook his head in disbelief that this was happening. They drove in silence for a few minutes. The only voice was a British woman named "Penelope" that Jesse had chosen in the GPS settings, oh-so-pleasantly giving them directions back onto the freeway.

Jack broke their silence. "Where are you crazy-ass people taking me?"

"You don't need to know that," answered Jesse.

He glanced at Jennifer then turned and looked back at Jesse, still in their ridiculous disguises, and said, "You know that if you cross state lines with me, that's a federal kidnapping charge, right?"

"Shut up and turn around!" ordered Jesse.

He turned to Jennifer again. "She has brain damage, doesn't she?"

Jennifer shrugged. "Possibly."

"That's not funny, Jen!"

They drove in silence for another couple of minutes until Jack said, "I have people who are going to come looking for me when I don't come home tonight."

No response.

A few minutes later, with the lights of the city behind them and darkness having settled in for the night, Jesse noticed a light down low between Jack's seat and door. She saw that he was trying to text someone. She rolled down her window, reached up, snatched his phone, and threw it out the open window before he could grab it back. It shattered into hundreds of tiny pieces as it hit the freeway behind them. "Jesus Christ! That was a brand-new iPhone, you psychopath!"

"Shut up and turn around," ordered Jesse.

"You owe me twelve-hundred dollars," he said. He glanced at the gun in her right hand before he turned to face front.

"Yeah, good luck collecting on that," Jennifer mumbled quietly.

"I'm right here, Jen. I can hear you!"

As they drove in silence again for a few more minutes, he worked out in his head what his next move would be. He didn't say or do anything else for a while, waiting until he felt Jesse had let her guard down a bit. Then suddenly, in one deft move, he ducked his head to the left as he twisted right, reached his left hand over his right shoulder, and grabbed the gun out of her hand. Jennifer screamed, swerving the car, as she tried to simultaneously watch him and keep her eyes on the road. Jesse, suddenly disarmed, never saw it coming.

"Hey!" she protested lamely.

Jack was beyond annoyed as he looked down at the gun in his hand. "Are you kidding me? A plastic Civil War gun? You people are fucking insane."

"I'm so sorry," Jennifer softly apologized.

Jack shook his head in disbelief. They all stared at the road ahead and drove off into the dark and stormy (metaphorically speaking) night.

THURSDAY NIGHT

The car pulled to a stop in front of Poppy and Harville's place. Jennifer, Jesse, and Jack got out of the car, exhausted from their evening ordeal.

Jack, still irritated, turned to them and shrugged. "Now what? Why are we here?"

They headed to the front door and Jennifer responded, "Honestly? We're not sure ourselves yet. It's why you had to come. We weren't getting any more information from Poppy and Harville about our mom unless we brought you back with us."

"And who the hell are Poppy and Harville?" he asked.

"Our mom worked in the circus with them," answered Jesse. "That's all we know so far."

"What? The circus?"

Poppy opened the door, grinned at Jack, and vigorously shook his hand with both of hers. "Hi, Jack, I'm Poppy." Normally, she would've gone in for a big hug, but he most definitely had an air of "hug non-receptivity" about him at the moment. She turned to Jennifer and Jesse, beaming,

"Good job, ladies! *Good job!* Come on in, I'll show y'all where you'll be sleeping."

"Wait, we're going to sleep?" asked Jack incredulously. "Isn't someone going to give me a reason about why I'm here first?" He turned to Poppy. "Do you have any idea what these women have put me through tonight??"

"Well, we had hoped y'all would be back sooner. Harville fell asleep about an hour ago, and he needs to help me tell you the story. So I'm afraid we'll have to talk to you about your mom in the morning after we've all had a good night's rest."

Three foldaway cots with colorful, threadbare, handmade quilts had been set up in the living room. The room was now softly lit by old, knobby, milk glass lamps on several end tables. The puppy ran up to Jesse, wagging his entire body.

"Hi, Sean!" she exclaimed, scooping him up and kissing him all over his furry little head.

"Oh, well, look who appears to have a heart," said Jack.

"You're not really going to call him Sean, are you?" Jennifer asked her.

"Of course I am."

"We're a little short on beds here," Poppy interjected, "so we set up some cots for y'all. We weren't sure if you'd be coming back with them or not, Jack, but we set one up for you too, just in case. Our fingers were crossed! I hope you'll all be comfortable. There's a bathroom down the hall to the left where you can change. I've set out some extra towels for y'all in there."

"Unfortunately, I don't have anything to change into," said Jack. With an angry glance at Jesse, he added, "I wasn't expecting to be going anywhere tonight."

"No worries," said Poppy. "I'll get you some of Harville's old pajamas."

"You don't, by any chance, have an extra toothbrush, do you? And I'd prefer not to use Harville's."

Poppy laughed. "I think I can find you something."

Poppy went off to locate supplies for Jack, while Jennifer went to her suitcase, pulled out a nightgown and her toiletries, and headed to the bathroom. The door shut and the sound of the shower came on.

"This is ridiculous," he mumbled under his breath.

Jesse faced off with Jack. "Look, just give us one day. Let's hear what Poppy and Harville have to tell us. If you still don't want to go with us the rest of the way after that, we'll drive you back home tomorrow. Deal?"

"'The rest of the way?' I don't even know what that means. So, yeah, I can guarantee you that I'm going home tomorrow."

"'The rest of the way' means we have one week to go on this stupid, fucking journey to find out who our stupid, fucking mom was and why she made the stupid, fucking choices she made. That's the only way we get our inheritance." Jesse paused. "Just give us the day before you decide. Please."

Jack looked at her for a moment, considering it. Her wording resonated with him. "Okay. Deal. I really do need to call home though. Sydney is going to call the police if I don't come back home and don't call."

Jesse pulled out her phone. "What's the number? I'll send a text for you."

"Just give me the damn phone. I can't say 'come and get me' because I have no idea where we are."

Jesse realized that was true. "Yeah, okay, you're right."

She punched in her password to unlock the phone and handed it to Jack. He wandered over to Eulalie's chair in the far corner of the room and sat down, talking to Sydney in hushed tones. Bits and pieces of phrases floated over to Jesse as he recounted the events of the evening, but the gist of the talk was about how he was still expecting to be home the next day.

"What's the number on this phone?" he called over to Jesse.

"Why?"

"Oh my God, paranoid much? Is every conversation with you like pulling teeth?"

"Yes!" Jennifer called from the bathroom, out of the shower now.

"I want to give Sydney a contact number, in case of emergency. Is that okay with you, Warden?"

She recited her cell number which he relayed to Sydney. Poppy re-entered the living room carrying a pair of Harville's funky Budweiser pajamas and an unopened toothbrush and set them on Jack's cot. Then Poppy grabbed a covered glass of liquid from the butcher block island that divided the kitchen and living room areas and brought it to Jesse.

"Eulalie said you're to drink this whole thing. There's a pitcher of it in the fridge so you have some for tomorrow too. Y'all fais do-do now. Sweet dreams. See you in the morning."

"Goodnight. Thank you," they both said.

Jesse drank her magic Eulalie potion as Jennifer came back in a tasteful, conservative, lace-trimmed, satin nightgown (beige of course). Her face was freshly scrubbed. Jack headed to the bathroom next and turned on the shower. Jesse whipped off the bare boob t-shirt, wriggled out of her jeans, and took off her bra without taking off her Rolling Stones t-shirt. It was a skill she became adept at during her sophomore year of high school. She slid into bed in her skimpy black lace underwear and t-shirt and snuggled in for the night with Sean.

Jennifer sat down on the edge of her cot, pulled her phone out of her purse, and dialed her home number. There was no answer, so she tried Sean's cell phone. Straight to voicemail. She quietly left a message.

"Hi, it's me. Again. Still trying to reach you. I'll call again in the morning." She hung up, stared at the empty space in front of her, then put her phone away.

"Pretty late for him to be out on a Thursday night, isn't it?" Jesse asked.

"He's probably already asleep," said Jen nonchalantly.

Jennifer climbed under the covers and rolled over so that her back was to Jesse, but Jesse could tell that her sister was disturbed by her husband's unavailability.

"Goodnight, Jesse."

"G'night, Jen."

Jesse absentmindedly stroked Sean's puppy-dream-filled head as she lay there in bed thinking. Jack came back into the room and walked by her, swimming in Harville's baggy Budweiser pajamas, and carrying a glass of water. Jesse broke out laughing.

"Nice. Jackie Onassis in her redneck phase."

No response from Jack. She watched as he took a couple of pills out of two prescription bottles that were in his man purse, downed them with his glass of water, and climbed into his cot.

"What're those for?" Jesse asked.

"Not that it's any of your business, Nancy Drew, but I have an anxiety disorder. Which you've helped with sooo much tonight. Thanks for that."

"Okay, okay, I'm sorry about the whole gun thing," she said.

"Whatever. Lunatic."

"Ha!" Jesse laughed. "Welcome to the family!"

Jack didn't respond, so Jesse got back out of bed with the puppy and set him down on the cot next to Jack, and in her best Al Pacino impression from *Scarface*, she said, "Say hello to my leetle friend."

"Very funny," he responded.

Jesse smiled at her gun joke, climbed back into bed, and reached over to the little table lamp on the coffee table next to her cot. "Goodnight, John Boy," she said as she turned out the light.

Jack smiled in the dark in spite of himself, then pulled Sean in close and shut his eyes.

· · · · • • • • · ·

Jesse woke up to a rough, wet puppy tongue licking the hand that was hanging off her cot. There was noise coming from the brightly lit kitchen area. Jesse propped herself up, squinting in the light, and watched Jack as he finished making pancakes and started to eat them.

"It's 3 a.m.," she said, looking at the old clock on the wall above the stove. "What're you doing?" He didn't seem to hear her. "Jack?... You okay?..."

Still no response from him. She lost interest in Jack, picked up Sean, and covered her face with her pillow to block the light so she could fall back asleep. Jennifer slept through it all.

DAY FOUR

"He would make a lovely corpse."
-Charles Dickens

Friday Morning

Jesse and Jennifer were awakened Friday morning to the sound of clattering dishes and silverware in the kitchen area, and the smell of freshly brewed chicory coffee. Poppy and Harville were finishing their breakfast preparations. Jack wasn't stirring.

"G'morning!" said Harville when he saw the girls awake.

"Good morning, girls, did you sleep okay?" asked Poppy.

"Mostly..." responded Jesse.

"I slept like a rock, thank you," said Jennifer.

"Who made pancakes last night?" asked Harville.

"Chef Boy-R-Dee over there," said Jesse, indicating the still-sleeping Jack. He was wrapped in his blankets like a mummy.

"Well, breakfast is almost ready," announced Poppy. "I hope eggs, grits, and alligator sausage is okay."

The sisters looked at each other and shrugged.

"I've never had alligator sausage, but I'm game. Pun intended," Jesse said with a smile.

"I'm sure whatever you've made will be delicious. Thank you so much," said Jennifer.

"Here's some more of Eulalie's tea for you, Jesse," Poppy said as she held out a glass filled to the brim.

"Thanks, Poppy. Where *is* Eulalie this morning?"

"Oh, she's been up since before six. She's out in the side room working with her people already. She's a pretty well-known local healer," explained Poppy. "The gift runs in her family. Never a shortage of folks comin' by to see her, that's fer darn tootin'."

Harville nodded in agreement as he wiped his hands on his pink ruffled apron (butt covered this morning). Then he said, "Somebody wake Jack up. Food's ready."

Harville served up plates with all the fixins and set them on the butcher block island. Poppy carried a tray of glasses and a pitcher of orange juice out the back screen door. Jennifer grabbed her clothes from her overnight bag next to her cot and went into the bathroom to quickly change. Jesse stuck her legs out from under the covers, slipped on her pants, and took Sean over to Jack's bed to let him lick Jack awake.

Jesse nudged Jack's arm a few times. "Rise and shine, Sleeping Beauty."

Jack groaned. "No, it's too early. I'm exhausted."

"Yeah, I'll bet. But breakfast is ready. If you're even hungry yet after your one-man 3 a.m. Pancake Social."

"What the hell are you talking about? I wasn't up at 3 a.m."

"Okaaaayy... Whatever you say," she responded, not sure whether he was lying or really didn't remember.

The screen door banged shut as Poppy re-entered the kitchen to help Harville carry plates out to the porch.

"We're going to eat on the back porch, and I thought we could start the talk about your mom," Poppy announced.

Jesse gave Jack a harder shove. "C'mon, hurry up, Jack, get dressed. It's showtime!"

He groaned again. Jesse, with Sean at her heels, headed outside with Jennifer, Harville, and Poppy. Jack dragged himself out of bed, grabbed his clothes from the night before and his non-Harville toothbrush, and headed for the bathroom.

The open-sided back porch was a generous size, covered by a tin awning roof. Hung at the corner was a handcrafted wind chime made from alternating metal Budweiser bottles and sections of hollow, aluminum tubing from the hardware store, suspended from an old hubcap. The porch faced the backyard which was filled with oak and pecan trees, and extended to the edge of Bayou Lafourche. It was marshy with cattails at the water's edge, and a Spanish Moss-covered cypress tree extended out over the water.

Jennifer and Jesse followed Harville and Poppy to a large square coffee table where all the food was set up. The coffee table was surrounded by two large, white wicker chairs with faded, floral print cushions, and two matching wicker loveseats.

Harville glanced at Sean. "Best put that little critter on a leash if he's coming out here."

Jesse headed back inside with Sean to get his bungee-leash. Harville and Jennifer settled into the chairs, and Poppy sat down on one of the loveseats. Next to her was an old purple velour drawstring bag filled with lumps of something. It was sitting on top of an old scrapbook with the edges of yellowing newspaper clippings poking out from the sides. There was also an open shoebox containing what appeared to be a collection of brightly colored programs and postcards.

The front cover of the scrapbook was made out of blue jean material, with a large jean pocket in the center. It was covered in hand-drawn hearts and flowers, and stickers that said things like "Keep on Truckin'," "Jive Talkin'," and "Stayin' Alive"—clearly illustrating that nobody needed that pesky final "g" in the freewheelin' 1970s. There was an old strip of silver duct tape holding the frayed binding together.

Jesse came back out with Sean in her arms, putting on his bungee-leash. Jack followed them, tentatively, not quite sure what was in store. The two of them headed to the empty spaces on the other loveseat, and Jesse attached Sean's leash to one of the loveseat legs.

Before Jack sat down, Harville extended his tanned and calloused hand. "The name's Harville, son. Good to finally meet you."

"Nice to meet you too," said Jack as he shook Harville's hand. "How's it going?"

"Hangin' in there like a hair on a biscuit," said Harville.

Jack laughed at that and took a seat, adding, "Oh, and thanks for the pajamas last night."

"Not a problem. Personally, don't wear 'em anymore. I like to let 'the boys' breathe, you know..."

Jesse leaned her head over to Jack and said, "We're lucky he's wearing pants at all right now."

Harville laughed good-naturedly.

"I thought we could talk while we eat," Poppy said, "if that's alright with you three."

They all nodded in agreement, got their plates of food situated on their laps, and dug in.

"Well, okay then," she continued. "So Harville and I met your mom Angie in..." She looked at Harville. "I don't know why I can't ever seem to remember this. '75? '76?"

"It was 1977," he said. "Just after the Bicentennial."

"Oh, yes, that's right," she said, giving herself a thud on the ol' noggin. "We were working with the Clancy Brothers Circus. It was based out of Tuscaloosa, Alabama, but we toured on a circuit through all of the southeastern states."

"Poppy and I were the high wire act."

"We were driving back to Tuscaloosa from here," she continued, "after we'd had a few days off..."

· · · · · · · · · ·

1977

Poppy and Harville, in their mid-twenties, were driving along I-59 in their beat-up yellow 1968 Chevy El Camino when they saw solitary seventeen-year-old Angie standing on the side of the road, thumb out. She was dressed in short-shorts; a red, white, and blue poncho; a tank top; and blue-striped tube socks with sneakers. Her dark hair was pulled back in a high, slightly askew ponytail. Harville pulled the car to the side of the road just past her, and Angie picked up her bag and ran up to Poppy's open passenger window.

Leaning forward in the driver's seat, Harville asked, "Where ya headed, miss?"

Angie leaned on the open window frame. "Where are *you* headed?" she responded.

"Back to work in Tuscaloosa," said Poppy.

"Then that's where I'm headed too," Angie said with a grin.

Poppy looked over at Harville and nodded.

"Okay then," he said. "Just throw your stuff in the pickup bed and hop on in."

She tossed her bag into the El Camino's flatbed, Poppy opened the passenger door, and Angie squeezed in next to her.

"Not so safe for a little thing like you to be out here hitchin' rides all by yourself," cautioned Harville.

Angie shrugged and chose not to respond.

・・・●●●・・・・

"Didn't give much information about herself at first," Poppy continued, "other than saying she was on her own and looking for a place to land. So we brought her with us. We figured if nothing else, we could at least get her a free meal. Poor thing hadn't eaten more'n a few bites for a couple a days, and she told us she'd been looking for unlocked cars to sleep in at night."

"We got there, to Tuscaloosa, I mean," added Harville, "and it turned out one of our workers had been picked up on a parole violation while we were on break, and they were looking for a new person to muck out animal stalls and do odd jobs in exchange for food and a place to sleep. So Angie signed on."

"I can't believe our mom *literally* ran away and joined the circus," Jesse said.

"I thought that was an urban myth. I didn't think people really did that," added Jack.

"Apparently they do," said Harville. "Your mom toured around with us for about six months before she started apprenticing with Shelley, the girl who did acrobatics on horseback."

Jesse and Jennifer exchanged a look.

"She was about to get married and move on," he continued, "and the company was having a hard time finding someone to replace her."

・・・・・・・・・・

1977

Shelley, the female horse acrobat, was a tiny little thing in her late twenties, with honey-colored hair and a light spray of freckles across the bridge of her nose. She was demonstrating a moving dismount stunt. After she remounted the horse, they circled back to Angie, and Shelley hopped off. Angie deftly mounted the horse and urged it into a slow canter.

"Now remember," Shelley coached her, "when you hop up onto the saddle, get your knees up under you, wait until you feel the rhythm of the horse, and move with that. Then, holding on to the rings, tuck your head down to his left, and then just like a front walk-over, one leg after the other."

Angie tried, but she let go of the saddle rings too early and didn't have her feet directly underneath her on the ground. She went down in the dirt, flat on her ass. Angie coughed as she breathed in the puff of dirt that rose into the air around her, and the horse trotted off. Shelley jogged over, grabbed his bridle, and lead him back over to Angie as she stood up and brushed herself off.

"Not too bad. Way better than you did yesterday!" Shelley said encouragingly.

Angie shook her head and climbed back up into the saddle. The horse shook his head and pawed at the ground.

"Don't let go of the saddle ring before you feel your feet on the ground directly underneath you," continued Shelley, "and then *immediately* arch up to standing. Your head comes up last."

Angie urged the horse into another slow canter and gave it another shot. She waited until her feet were solidly on the ground, and then she let go of the rings. But she was a fraction of a second too late. The momentum forward sent her flat on her face this time. Shelley couldn't help but laugh.

"Ow! Goddamn it!" yelled Angie, spitting out dirt. "I think I just swallowed a little piece of horse manure."

"You almost had it! You did everything right. You just have to be ready to take a few running steps forward out of it. Easy as pie! Otherwise, it's a face plant."

"Yeah, I figured that one out already, Shelley. Thanks."

"Don't be frustrated. You'll get it." Shelley led the horse back over to Angie again. "One more time, Angel Heart."

・・・・・・・・・・

"Everybody had a show name," explained Harville. "Your mom already had the nickname 'Angel Heart' from her name, Angela Hartley, so that's what she went by in the show."

Poppy picked up the blue jean scrapbook with the yellowed newspaper clippings, and said, "She got to be pretty darned good. Did y'all know she was a gymnast in Jr. High School?"

"How would we possibly know that? We didn't even know she existed until four days ago," said Jennifer.

"So that'd be a 'no' on the gymnastics," Jesse added with a hint of bitterness.

"Oh, yes, what was I thinking? *What was I thinking?* I'm so sorry."

Jack looked from Jennifer to Jesse. "Are you serious? Why didn't your parents tell you before this?"

"I dunno, Perry Mason. I wish they had, but they're dead, so it's kind of hard to ask them that now," said Jesse in her trademark punch-in-the-face delivery. "Guess we just weren't as lucky as you."

··········

1997

Eighteen-year-old Jack sat on the couch between his mom and dad. His mom was holding one of his hands in both of hers, and his dad's arm was around his shoulders. Jack was looking at the ground in front of him. He turned to his dad and asked, "Why did you wait so long to tell me?"

"Well, son, your mom and I decided early on that we were going to wait until you were older. We thought it would be easier to process the information by then."

"And now that you've turned eighteen," his mom continued, "you can legally contact her and meet if you want to. That was part of the adoption agreement we made when we were blessed to have you come into our lives."

Jack didn't respond immediately.

"We love you very much," she continued, "and we want you to know that you have our full support whatever you choose to do."

He looked at each one of them and said, "I don't want to meet her. And I don't want to know anything else about her."

"You won't hurt our feelings if you want to meet her, son. We would totally understand," said his dad. "So if you change your mind later, you just let us know."

"Thank you for that. But... you two are my parents. You're the only parents I've ever known, and the only ones I need."

··········

"I'm so sorry about your folks," said Jack to his sisters. "How did they—?"

Jesse cut him off before he could finish the question. "Do we really have to talk about this right now?"

Everyone was quiet, not quite sure what to say. Jesse reached down to pet Sean and focused all her attention on him. Jack silently mouthed "I'm sorry" again to Jennifer. She shook her head to signal that it wasn't a good subject matter to bring up. Poppy turned to Harville to change tack, attempting to redirect the conversation away from the awkward moment.

"Would you clear some of the plates, dear, so the kids can have their hands free?"

Harville stood up and began collecting the empty breakfast plates from everyone. As he took them into the house, Poppy passed Jennifer the blue jean scrapbook with the old, yellowed newspaper clippings.

"There are some articles in there from your mom's Jr. High School newspaper, some of her at her school gymnastic meets, some pictures of her as a cheerleader, and some old Polaroids of her hanging out with friends. A few of them are from a little later. They're of her with each of you when you were babies. She brought this little scrapbook with her when she left home. I imagine it was a comfort to her when she was feeling alone."

Jennifer shifted her gaze from the articles to her sister. "She looks exactly like you, Jesse."

Jesse looked up, her attention diverted away from the puppy. Poppy picked up the shoebox next to her and passed it to Jack and Jesse on the loveseat.

"That box is filled with pictures and old programs from her time in the circus, and postcards she collected from all of the towns we performed in."

They examined the contents of the box, hungrily gathering these new pieces of the puzzle in front of them.

Harville had rejoined them by this point, adding, "That girl saved everything!"

"Well, I can think of *three* exceptions..." mumbled Jesse as she continued looking at the programs and postcards.

Choosing not to respond to Jesse's comment, Poppy picked up the velour bag and laughed, "This is a bag of rocks she used to collect."

Jack looked up. "Did you just say 'rocks'?"

"Yep. All smooth, flat ones. She used to pick them up everywhere she went. She called them her 'wishing stones.'"

"We'd see her talking to herself sometimes," Harville added, "skipping stones on whatever water we happened to be near at the time. She said the more times it skipped, the more likely her wish would come true."

· · · · ● ● ● · · · ·

1977

Angie was down by the riverside near the circus grounds. A soft breeze was gently lifting her hair and billowing the calico peasant dress she was wearing. She was holding a smooth, flat "wishing stone" and whispering into her clasped hands. Then she tossed the rock at an angle on the water and it skipped four times before it sank. She laid down on the grass looking up at the pale blue sky. The sun kept peeking out from behind the softly drifting puffs of clouds.

Poppy had been watching her from a short distance away. She ambled over and laid down next to Angie and smiled. "Here you are."

"Hi," said Angie.

Together they silently watched the clouds meander across the sky, like boats traveling down a wide blue river, shapeshifting from boats to animals to faces and whatever else was lurking in their young imaginations.

"You always look so sad out here, Angie... When you talk into your hands like that, are you praying?"

"No. Just making some wishes for some people," she answered.

"Well, that's kind of like praying. In a way," said Poppy.

Angie furrowed her brow in thought. She clearly wanted to say something, but she was hesitant. She turned her head to face Poppy.

"I did something that wasn't good, Poppy. If I tell you what it is, do you promise you won't think badly of me?"

Poppy, concerned, reached over and took Angie's hand in hers and said, "I promise."

・・・・●・・●・・・・

"That's the first time she opened up to me about her mom dying and about leaving you two girls."

No one spoke, so Harville finally said, "Lotta information to take in. Do y'all have any questions for us at this point? Or do we need to take a break for a few minutes?"

"No break, please!" implored Jack. "We're just getting started."

"I do have a question," said Jennifer. "Did she tell you who our dad was?"

Poppy and Harville exchanged a "here we go" look, and Poppy said, "Yes, she did."

"You know, why don't we take that break first," suggested Harville. "Sorry, Jack, but I need one before this next part of the story. I gotta pee like a racehorse. Y'all get up and stretch for a minute too. Do a body good."

He stood up and went inside, the screen door banging shut behind him. Jack and Jennifer helped Poppy collect the rest of the dishes and silverware and followed Harville in. Jesse unhooked Sean's bungee-leash from the leg of the loveseat. She led him down into the backyard to relieve himself. After a moment, Jennifer, Jack, and Poppy meandered back onto the porch and sat down.

Unseen by all four of them, a stealthy, six-foot alligator climbed out of Bayou Lafourche and into the soggy brush at the water's edge. It began to lumber into the yard just in time for Harville to come back out on the porch and spot it.

"'Gator! Everyone inside! Move!"

The three on the porch got up and quickly moved toward the screen door. Jennifer looked back at Jesse who was lost in thought and hadn't heard Harville.

"Jesse! Alligator!" she yelled.

Jesse snapped to attention and saw the alligator moving faster toward them, heading straight for the puppy. She jerked hard on the bungee-leash and had to scramble to collect Sean as he flew past her like an involuntary, horizontal bungee jumper.

"What do I do? What do I do?" she yelled.

A cacophony of simultaneous answers came.

"Run!" screamed Jennifer.

"Don't just stand there!" yelled Jack.

"Run, girl!" said Poppy.

"RUN IN A ZIG-ZAG PATTERN!" yelled Harville, fortunately, in a louder voice than all the others.

Away from the noise in the backyard, Eulalie had her hands on a client who was laying on a "healing table" under an animal skin. A bundle of sage burned in a shell on a side table. There were animal artifacts, dried plants, and jars of roots soaking in liquid, lined up on shelves on the wall. Eulalie had collected straws of prelle to boil into a tea for blood infections, saw palmetto fruit for prostate problems, plantain leaves to make a salve for poison ivy and skin swelling, bon blanc for colicky babies, turkey grass for kidney and liver trouble, groundsel tree for inflamed kidneys and flu, bright red mamou seeds for pneumonia, and cocklebur leaves for headache and fever.

Eulalie's grandfather had been a local healer, a traiteur, and had taught her when she was a young girl about all the indigenous healing practices. But it wasn't until she was older, and started to see things that were unseen, and know things she had no way of knowing, that she accepted the gift she had for healing.

Her head suddenly jerked up to full attention at something unheard by the naked ear.

"I'll be right back," she said to the person on the table. "Stay relaxed and keep focused on your breathing."

She moved quickly to a side table and opened the drawer.

Back in the yard, Jesse, with Sean in her arms, ran toward the porch, zigzagging back and forth now, but the alligator was very fast. It looked like she wasn't going to make it when Eulalie appeared from around the side of the house where she had been working. She pointed a big .44 Magnum, like Clint Eastwood's in *Dirty Harry*, calmly took aim past zigzagging Jesse, and shot the alligator dead in its tracks.

"Yep. The most powerful gun in the world," she said to herself.

Then she disappeared around the side of the house. Just like a superhero, she saved the day and was gone. *Poof!*

Jesse, frozen in place, panting, stared at the dead alligator. "Jesus Christ!"

"Amen," said Poppy and Harville.

"Looks like we have supper," Harville added.

Jesse ran up onto the porch, clutching Sean. Jennifer grabbed them both in a bear hug. Harville took a big knife out of a sheath on his belt.

"Papa, why don't you take it on around to the side. I don't think the kids are gonna want to watch that."

He re-sheathed the knife and grabbed some leather work gloves that were sitting on the edge of the porch. Then he stepped off the porch, walked over to the alligator, and dragged it out of sight by the tail so he could break it down while the others talked. The rest of them returned to their seats, Jesse still clutching Sean, visibly shaken.

"Well... that was fun," said Jack.

"I didn't even think Eulalie could see," Jennifer said to Poppy.

"She's legally blind, but, well... she has her own way of seeing," Poppy answered vaguely.

"You've gotta be *kidding* me," said Jesse upon hearing that a gun had just been fired in her direction by a "legally blind" senior citizen.

"Let's get back to your dad while Harville works on the 'gator," said Poppy, changing the subject. "He doesn't like this part of the story much." She looked at the sisters and continued on to the next surprising part of the tale. "So... I don't know how else to say this except to just dive right in and tell you."

"Oh, no, now what?" groaned Jesse.

"You two, Jennifer and Jesse, have different fathers."

"What?" asked Jesse, not quite believing what she just heard.

"We're not full sisters?" asked Jennifer.

Jesse looked at Jennifer and said quietly, "Well, that kind of explains a lot."

"Your mom," continued Poppy, "had just turned fifteen when she got pregnant by a boy in school she had been going steady with since she was thirteen. His name was

Danny McAllister. When the pregnancy was a few months along, she left school and finished the year from home, and the McAllister family suddenly moved away."

"What a bunch of assholes," mumbled Jesse. "The McAsshole family flees the scene of the crime."

Poppy pressed on. "She went back the following year, and your grandmama took care of the baby—you, Jennifer—during the day; but everyone knew what had happened, and school was never quite the same for her after that. People weren't so nice to her, even her old friends if you can believe it. She got a reputation for being 'easy' even though that wasn't the case. She had loved that boy." She paused for a moment, watching a wave of sadness cross Jennifer's face, before pressing on with the next part. "Then when she was sixteen-and-a-half, there was an older boy named Scott Breen, who was out of school by then..."

· · · · ● ● ● ● · · ·

1976

Angie stood by herself, eating a handful of pretzels, unconsciously picking at a loose thread on the side of her navy-blue corduroy skirt. Rufus and Chaka Khan's "Sweet Thing" played in the background of the party at the ranch-style house of her classmate Stacey Winkleman. She watched other high school classmates talk loudly, laugh, and spill beer on the wall-to-wall shag carpeting. Stacey's frequent parties were always a hit because of the hands-off policy of her parents. They would lock themselves in their own bedroom upstairs armed with several bottles of Cold Duck and Boone's Farm for their own little private party.

She felt like an outsider in the group of people that used to be her good friends. She pulled her Bonne Bell root beer-flavored lip gloss out of her back pocket, absentmindedly applied it, and made the sudden decision to leave. She headed into Stacey's bedroom, grabbed her blue and white satin baseball jacket and purse from the pile on the bed, and headed back out toward the telephone near the front door to call her mom.

Twenty-year-old Scott Breen, the loser older guy who would hang out with underaged teens, buy beer for them, and sell them weed so he could feel important, had been watching her intently. He headed her off at the door.

"You're not leaving, are you? The party's just getting started, and you're probably the only interesting person here." He grinned at her.

"Yeah, I'm gonna head home. I'm not feeling well," she said.

"Aw, that's too bad. Do you need a ride? I could give you one."

She hesitated. "Um..."

"Seriously, I don't mind at all," he continued. "Especially if you're not feeling well."

"Yeah, okay, sure. Thanks."

They walked to his 1972 Dodge Charger parked on the street out front. He opened the passenger door for her like a gentleman, then hopped in the driver's side, and they drove off. He kept her talking, so she wasn't paying much attention to the route they were going, until she realized they had turned down a road that was more deserted, with no houses nearby.

"Wait, what are you doing? Where are we?"

He pulled the car off to the side of the road and parked. "You weren't having a good time at that party, so I'm gonna show you a good time," he said as he slid across the long bench seat and pulled her towards him.

"What? No!"

She struggled to get away as he started to kiss her.

"Get off of me!!" she screamed, as he maneuvered her down onto the wide front bench seat. *"HELP!"* she screamed again, continuing to struggle against him.

He covered her mouth with one hand as he pinned her down with his legs and body. Then he reached under her skirt and pulled her underwear down with his other hand.

"Stop yelling. You don't have to pretend with me. I know all about how you put out, Angie Hartley. Just relax and we'll have a good time."

・・・●●●●・・・

"Oh, my God," said Jesse. "She was *raped? That's* who my father is?"

"Yes, hon, she was raped," Poppy said gently. "After you were born, Jesse, is when your grandmama died unexpectedly from a brain aneurysm, and your mom moved in with your Aunt Carolyn and Uncle Jim. It was such a hard time for her. She tried her best to finish school, but it was all too much."

Poppy paused to gauge their reactions. Jennifer and Jack were focused on Jesse.

"So, you see, it's not that she didn't love you girls, but with two little ones and *then* losing her mom, she just... couldn't do it. That's when she left home and headed south and met us."

It was so quiet around the table you could hear a pin drop. Jesse was trying to hold back tears.

"You okay, hon?" Poppy asked.

Jesse shook her head and tried to speak. "I... I... Every new piece of information I get on this trip is more... I don't know. Now I don't even have the sister I thought I had."

"Stop that," said Jennifer. "Of *course* you do." She stood up, slid Harville's empty chair closer to Jesse, and sat down and took her hand. "Two asshole dads don't change that. I am still the same annoying, judgmental older sister that you love to hate."

Jesse laughed at that, in spite of herself, as Jennifer turned to Poppy.

"Did they ever catch the guy?" asked Jennifer.

"I'm getting to that part," Poppy answered.

"And what about my dad? Did she say who he was?" Jack asked. "My parents didn't have any information about him. Although the way this story is going, I'm not sure I want to know," he added. "Except the competitive part of me is kind of hoping I win the award for *The Most Outrageously Shitty Father Story*."

Poppy took a deep breath and continued, "That's part of what I'm getting to. Your mom had been on tour with us for a little over a year. We had just finished a week outside of Breaux Bridge and we had a day off, so we decided we were going to come home and see Eulalie. But first, we went out after our show with some of the other circus performers."

· · · · ● · ● · · ·

1978

The final show outside of Breaux Bridge had just ended, and the roustabouts were breaking down the colorful tents, getting ready to move to the next location about thirty miles north of Baton Rouge.

Poppy, Harville, and Angie had already headed over to The Hair of the Dog Saloon with their fellow circus performers to decompress now that they had the next day off. The bar was noisy and crowded with the local regulars. Loretta Lynn's song "Out of My Head and Back in My Bed" played on the jukebox. Their group was laughing and talking over a few pitchers of beer, just having a grand ol' time. Harville was holding court, sharing slightly embellished funny stories about each of his co-workers in turn.

Standing at the bar was a group of four guys that included Scott Breen, now twenty-two. They were pounding back shots of cheap whiskey and scoping out the local girls in the bar.

Scott had left Illinois and had drifted around a bit trying to find easy-money jobs. He and his friend Jerry eventually ended up in Beaumont, Texas, following a lead Jerry had gotten about an underground gambling scene where they thought they could make some easy money. When that didn't pan out, because that particular scene was harder to break into than they had anticipated, they got a lead on some construction jobs just over the border in Lafayette, Louisiana. They headed over and landed themselves some regular employment. That's where they were now living.

As the guys were checking out the pack of local fillies, Scott spotted Angie at the table with her friends. "Well, holy shit, look who it is," he said to himself with a smile.

Then he got distracted as the bartender set down another round of shots for the guys.

"That is SO not true!" Angie laughed as Harville finished telling a story about her mucking out stalls during her first week on the job. "I think *you* were the one who—"

She stopped mid-sentence with a sharp inhalation when she saw someone over Harville's shoulder that, in profile, looked a lot like Scott Breen, though she couldn't be sure. The color drained from her face. She quickly looked down and turned her head away from Scott's direction to keep him from seeing her.

"Excuse me," she said to the group as she hurriedly got up from the table. She pulled her hair forward to shield her face and walked quickly to the ladies' room.

Poppy glanced at Harville with a puzzled expression and then followed Angie. She knocked on the restroom door.

"Angie?... You okay in there?"

Angie opened the door just a crack and motioned for Poppy to come inside quickly.

"What happened out there?" Poppy continued. "Was it something Harville said? He was just teasing you, honey."

"No, no, I'm sorry, I just thought I saw someone at the bar that I used to know. It took me by surprise. Can you check for me and see if he's still there? He has brown hair, and he's wearing a white baseball cap and a blue plaid shirt. Don't let him see you looking!"

"Of course."

Angie's heart was racing so fast that she thought she might pass out. She waited in the restroom taking slow, deep breaths, while Poppy stepped back out and did some quick surveillance.

When she reentered the restroom, she said, "I didn't see him at the bar, hon, so I walked around the whole place. I didn't see him anywhere."

"Do you think we could go?" Angie asked. "I'm sorry, Poppy, I really don't want to run into him. He's not a good guy."

"Absolutely. We'll just tell people you aren't feeling well. No one will ask questions that way."

Angie kept her head down as they left the restroom, surreptitiously glancing around to double-check that he wasn't there. His drinking buddies were still at the bar, but Scott was nowhere to be seen. They reached the table, made their excuses, and exited. Poppy, Harville, and Angie headed for the old El Camino with Angie in the lead, moving very quickly. When they piled into the El Camino and headed off, Angie visibly relaxed.

Scott had been sitting in his car drinking a lukewarm can of Colt 45. He watched them drive off, pulled his car out onto the road, and followed them at a distance into the dark Louisiana night.

··········

"We were talkin' the whole way back," Poppy continued. "She filled us in on all the details of who Scott was and what he had done to her, so we didn't notice that someone had been following us back to Eulalie's. He must've been sittin' outside here for a good two hours until we all went to bed. That's when your mom came out onto the back porch. She loved listening to the sounds of the bayou in the quiet of the night. She said it soothed her."

· · · · • • • · · ·

1978

Angie sat alone on the back porch listening to the dreamlike, nocturnal sounds of the birds and insects. Then, suddenly, from out of the shadows, came the drunken lyrics to the song "Angie" by the Rolling Stones. She had always loved that song. Until now. *This* particular rendition made the hair on the back of Angie's neck stand up on end. She bolted upright in her chair, gripped by fear at the sound of that voice from her not-so-distant past that she immediately recognized. It *was* him that she had seen at the bar. She tried to speak, but no words came out. She tried to stand, but she couldn't move. She was literally frozen in place.

He emerged from the dark, his gait slightly unsteady. He was carrying a bottle of cheap whiskey that he had been drinking in his car while he waited near the house until he saw the lights go out. He leered at Angie.

"How did you—how did you find me here?" she asked in a faint whisper, her head spinning, eyes darting around, looking for a path to escape.

"Saw you at that bar lookin' really fine, pretty lady," he slurred. "Couldn't believe my good luck that you followed me down here! Thought it'd be nice to have a reunion, so I followed you. I always wondered whatever happened to you. We had that fun night together and then you pretty much disappeared."

"*Fun night?*" she said angrily. "You *raped* me!"

"Raped you? Yeah, I don't think so." He laughed. "I seem to recall you coming on to me pretty strong when I was driving you home from that party," he slurred.

Her head was spinning in confusion from his gaslighting. She remained paralyzed in place as he moved towards her, blocking her way to the back door. He continued the song, singing about whispering in her ear.

When he whispered, *"Angie..."* her fight or flight response kicked in and overrode her temporary paralysis. Angie jumped up, attempting to keep furniture between them.

"Stop it!" she said.

"Angie..." he whispered again.

"Get away from me, Scott. I'm not kidding! *Leave*!"

The chase around the furniture began. She used objects to block him. He was laughing, thinking it was all a game, and stumbling a bit because of his intoxication level.

"You're still a feisty little thing. That's *so hot*."

She bolted into the yard, hoping to make it to the door on the far side of the house, but he pursued her and managed to grab her arm before she could get away.

"Let me go!" she yelled.

She tore her arm away from his grip, but he was able to grab a corner of her shirt, and he pulled her down to the ground as the scene from two years prior nightmarishly began to play out once again.

Her full voice returned, and she screamed, "HELLLP! Harville! Popp—"

"Shut the fuck up," he said, clamping his hand over her mouth to keep her quiet. "You know you've missed me. You *know* we had a good time together. I don't know why you're lying about that now."

Her continued cries for help were muffled by his hand as he had her pinned on the ground, fighting him like a trapped animal. He unzipped his pants.

·····••••··

"You're telling me that shit-bag rapist is my dad too?" asked Jack.

"I'm sorry, but, yes, that's what I'm telling you," confirmed Poppy. "You and Jesse have the same mom *and* dad."

"Welcome to my stagnant gene pool," said Jesse mirthlessly. Jesse and Jack stared at one another as though they were seeing each other for the very first time. Then Jesse added, "So I guess that means we tie in *The Worst Father Competition*."

"I guess so," he said. Then, with a nod in Jennifer's direction, he continued, "All *she* has is some cowardly Irish dude."

"Hey," Jesse said to Jennifer, "maybe your dad Riverdances."

"Free tickets," offered Jennifer.

"I don't suppose a rousing chorus of 'Oh Danny Boy' would be appropriate right about now, would it?" asked Jack.

Harville was standing in the doorway by this point. "Y'all are gettin' a little ahead of the story."

All eyes turned to him.

"There's a little bit more that happened before Jack arrived." To Poppy, he added, "I'll finish cuttin' the 'gator tail up after we're done here, so you can soak it in buttermilk."

"Thank you, hon. I'm sorry, I was really hoping to have this next part told before you came back."

"That's okay. I should be the one to tell it anyway," he said as he walked around to Jennifer's old seat and sat down across from them.

··········

1978

Angie was struggling under Scott, trying to shake his hand off of her mouth so she could scream again. Poppy and Harville, awakened by that first cry for help, rushed outside and saw what was happening. Harville was carrying Eulalie's .44 Magnum.

"You let her go!" Poppy screamed at Scott.

Scott released Angie and she crawled away, sobbing. Poppy rushed over to her and helped her to her feet. Scott was still on the ground, fumbling with his zipper, and trying to calculate his next move through his alcohol stupor.

"You've got about ten seconds to get off my property, or my face is the last thing you'll ever see," warned Harville.

"Hey, hey, there's no problem here." Scott smiled at Harville. "We were just having some fun. Like old times. Angie invited me—"

"You're a *liar!!*" screamed Angie, cutting him off. "I never invited you, you piece of shit."

Scott, now standing, impulsively lunged at Angie who was next to Poppy, and a shot rang out. Without a moment's hesitation, Harville had pulled the trigger. Scott collapsed to the ground like a deflated blow-up doll. They all froze, staring wordlessly at the crumpled, dead body on the ground in the middle of them all.

After a long pause, Angie said, "Good." And she spit on his lifeless body for good measure.

Poppy turned to Harville, "What do we do with him now?"

"Shouldn't we call the police?" Angie asked.

Eulalie appeared in the doorway of the back porch. "No police. You gotta get rid of the body. Get him in the back of the pickup, and dump him in the bayou. Let the 'gators take care of it."

Harville was on it. "Get some meat and twine, Eulalie. We'll tie it to his body as bait."

Poppy put her arm around Angie's shoulders and said, "Let's get you inside and get you cleaned up, hon. You can stay here at the house with Eulalie. We'll take care of this. Don't you worry about it."

"No, I'm going with you." Angie was resolute. "I wanna watch that fucker go down."

Poppy considered that for a moment. "Well, okay then. Let's drag him out front and get him into the truck."

Harville took one foot, Poppy and Angie grabbed the other one, and they dragged him around the side of the house. Eulalie was waiting by the truck in the driveway with some raw chicken meat and twine.

They attempted to hoist Scott's body into the back of the El Camino, but the limp, dead body was heavy and they dropped him a few times before they were able to maneuver him into the truck bed.

Harville said, "There's a car over there in the trees with Illinois plates. You follow us in it, Poppy, and we'll put it into the bayou too."

"Go down the road to the abandoned Robichaux dock," said Eulalie. "It's overgrown so you'll be hidden while you work."

Once they had the body situated in the truck bed, Harville tied the bait meat to Scott's body to attract the alligators while Poppy headed over to Scott's car and found the keys still in the ignition. She backed his car out and sat there idling until Harville and Angie pulled out and headed down the road, and then she followed close behind. About a quarter of a mile down the road, they pulled into the area around the old, abandoned dock. Harville backed the El Camino up, diagonal to the dock, and turned off the headlights. Poppy drove Scott's car past the El Camino and onto the dock itself. The three of them maneuvered Scott's body out of the El Camino and onto the ground. Then they dragged him to the front of Scott's car at the edge of the dock.

"Why did you tie meat to him?" asked Angie.

"The 'gators generally won't go after a dead human body without some kind of meat tied on as bait, and we want all traces of him gone," Harville responded matter-of-factly.

"And why do you know that?" Angie asked tentatively.

"Oh, if these bayous could talk..." he answered cryptically.

Harville took hold of Scott's wrists and Poppy and Angie each grabbed an ankle.

"We need to get some momentum to get him out there in the water," said Harville, "so let's swing him back first, and then out toward the water so the weight of his body carries him out there farther."

But they found that was easier said than done. Poppy and Angie dropped his feet on the first backswing, causing Harville to lose his grip as well. Scott's body landed on the dock with a dull thud.

"He's a slippery little shit," said Poppy.

They picked him up again and attempted the same backswing, but this time on the forward swing, he flew out over the water, his limbs flapping in the air like a rag doll, and he went in with a splash. They stood there silently and watched the body being swallowed whole by the dark, hungry water. Within seconds, several previously unseen alligators began to swim toward the spot where he went in.

"Okay," said Harville, "let's get his car in now. Give the damn bastard a speedier ride to hell."

•••••••••

A stunned Jesse, Jack, and Jennifer stared at Harville and Poppy, slack-jawed.

"Holy shit," said Jack quietly.

Jesse turned to him and said, "Right??"

"You killed our dad," continued Jack, "and fed him to the 'gators? Jesus."

"Amen," said Poppy.

"Didn't really have a choice son, all things considered. Not when he lunged at your mama after he was already warned," said Harville. "But I am sorry it went down that way."

Jennifer leaned forward, her elbows resting on her knees. "Did anyone ever come looking for him?" she asked.

THE KEY TO CIRCUS-MOM HIGHWAY 121

"We did see one Missing Person flyer that someone had put up on a bulletin board outside the grocery store in Henderson," said Poppy. "And one small mention about a Missing Person in the *Daily Comet* a few weeks later, but no one ever came around here asking about him."

"After that night, we *never* told another person what had happened here," added Harville. "Until right now."

Jesse turned to Jack and said, "How long do alligators live? I mean, what are the chances that the alligator we're eating for dinner is one of the ones that ate our dad? Isn't that a disturbing thought?"

"I dunno," he responded, "a little cannibalism seems like the logical next part of this damn story."

"That's disgusting, you guys," Jennifer chimed in.

"Naw," said Harville, responding to Jesse's comment, "that gator'd be much bigger by now. Or dead."

Jennifer said to Poppy, "So what happened next? And whatever happened to my dad? Did she ever hear from him again?"

"I'm afraid that's all the information we have for you today, hon," answered Poppy. "You'll hear the next part tomorrow when you get to your next stop in Bessemer, Alabama."

Jesse looked at Jack and raised her eyebrows questioningly. They locked eyes. It was bad enough to find out he was one hundred percent related to her, but the idea of being stuck in a car with his kidnapper for a week was God-awful. A Hamlettian battle raged in his brain. *To go or not to go, that is the question. Whether 'tis nobler in the mind to suffer the slings and arrows of outrageous... family... blah, blah, blah, whatever.*

"Goddamn it," he said. "Yeah, okay. I'm in."

FRIDAY AFTERNOON

The three J's were sitting together on the covered back porch, the afternoon rain falling softly on the grass in the yard and pattering on the tin awning overhead. Jack was shucking corn on the cob and Jennifer was snapping the tips off of a small pile of string beans. They were tossing the discarded food parts into a brown paper grocery bag on the floor between them. Jesse sat in a chair next to them studying the photos and school newspaper articles in Angie's blue jean scrapbook. Poppy, in the kitchen with Harville, craned her neck in an attempt to unobtrusively peek out onto the porch.

"Do they seem okay?" asked Harville.

"I can't tell. They're still not talking. Poor things."

"Well, let's just leave 'em be for now," suggested Harville. "That was a lot to take in this morning."

The three siblings continued to work in silence for a few more minutes, lost in their own thoughts, until Jack blurted out, "Jesus, that story got dark. I don't even know how to process it all."

Jennifer looked up, met his gaze, and nodded. "Yeah," she said quietly.

They went back to their food prep chores, in silence once again.

After another minute Jesse said, "She looked so happy in all of these pictures. It's strange to look at them now knowing what was going to happen to her so soon after these were taken." She closed the book, set it aside, and continued, "Do you ever think about that? How some random thing can send your life suddenly in a completely different direction, and from that moment on, life isn't anything like how you thought it was going to be?"

Jennifer, knowing what Jesse was referring to, nodded.

"Yep," said Jack quietly, intently focused on the ear of corn in his hands. "I think about that all the time…"

"It's hard not to feel a little bit sorry for her after hearing everything that happened," Jennifer added.

"Seriously, Jen?" Jesse said. "You would abandon your kids because some bad things happened to you? Please."

"No, I'm not saying that. I can't imagine *ever* doing something like that. But I'm not her. You don't have to make the same choices as someone to have a little compassion for them."

Jesse leaned back and turned her head to watch the rain falling into a large, muddy puddle just off the side of the porch. Jennifer turned her attention once again to the string beans.

"Uh… Are we never going to talk about our dad getting murdered and fed to the alligators? By our *hosts* here?" asked Jack. "That's some stone-cold, crazy gangster shit right there, people."

"I don't really know what to say about it," said Jennifer.

"Well, what about you?" he said to Jesse. "He's your dad too. You didn't find that a little disturbing?"

Jesse shrugged without emotion and said, "He had it coming."

"That's it? C'mon. If I can't talk about it with you guys, who am I gonna talk about it with? My parents are both in law enforcement, so it's not exactly gonna be good post-church Sunday dinner conversation when I get back home."

"What kind of law enforcement?" asked Jennifer.

"Police department. My dad's in Homicide, so of course, this whole thing pushes my buttons in regard to what I was always taught about the rule of law and order. But... my mom works in the Special Victims Unit and has worked a lot of sex crimes through the years, so I've heard countless stories about the volume of people that get away with those, while the victim's life is changed forever."

"Yeah, go with that second one," said Jesse.

"I agree," said Jennifer. "And these are just the times that we *know* about him doing it."

"If he did it twice, you know he would've done it again. That fucker didn't even think that first time was rape!" added Jesse. "So do I wish I had a better dad in this story? Hell, yeah, I do. Tom Hanks would've been nice. But as far as I'm concerned, Harville stopped a serial rapist in the making. So, thank you, Harville. And adios, good riddance, and fuck you, Dad."

"We all have to agree not to talk about this with anyone after we leave here," said Jennifer. "It doesn't matter how long ago this happened, Poppy and Harville would be in serious trouble if word got out."

THE KEY TO CIRCUS-MOM HIGHWAY 125

"And how do we explain where our dad is?" asked Jack. "I know my parents and Sydney are going to ask about him."

"Fishing accident," Jesse suggested. "He was in a boat out in the swamp fishing with friends. They were drunk, he stood up to pee over the side of the boat, he fell overboard, and the alligators got him. I'm sure that must happen all the time down here, right? Beyond that, we just say that those are the only details we know."

"That works for me," said Jennifer. "Are we all agreed?" she added, looking directly at Jack.

"Yeah. Agreed," he responded.

"Not to mention the happy ecological twist in all of this," Jesse added as an afterthought.

Jack and Jennifer stared at her, waiting for her to elaborate on that one.

"What?" she shrugged. "Poppy and Harville kept some wildlife fed and thriving. That's just good karma."

• • • • • • • • • •

Meanwhile, back in Illinois...

Ever since Sean (the human) had stumbled upon his distant Civil War connection, he'd become somewhat obsessed with amassing a collection of authentic Civil War-era Union Army artifacts. He had, in fact, purchased so many items through eBay over the last couple of years that he had become one of their "Official Distinguished Customers." Not that he really got anything for that other than a *20% Off* coupon for one item and a generic certificate with his name misspelled.

He had been using his doctor's office as a clandestine landing place for his smaller purchases so that Jennifer wouldn't know the extent of his newly acquired ~~shopping addiction~~ hobby. He'd slowly bring them back to his home office where he'd covertly slip them into his existing display cases. That was easy enough with smaller items like coins, Union flag tokens, buttons off of Union uniforms, excavated Union bullets, and the like. But the framed, antique, thirty-four-star Union flag circa 1861 had to be shipped to the house. It had cost him over $10,000 which set him back quite a few bunion surgeries and plantar wart removals.

He had managed to avoid revealing the actual cost of the flag to Jennifer by vaguely answering her question with, "I was surprised at how much *less* it cost than I thought it was going to." Then he quickly changed the subject to the sweet old widow from Kankakee, Illinois that sold it to him to pay for her cataract removal and breast lift.

His mistake, however, had been later that night when they were about to have their Weekly Wednesday Night Sex. He was so excited about the arrival of the damn flag, that he inadvertently blurted out some newly acquired trivia while kissing her neck, mid-coitus.

"Do you know there was no official star configuration on the United States flag until 1912?"

She immediately disengaged, got out of bed, and threw on her bathrobe, yelling, "No! And I don't want to! In fact, I don't ever want to hear about the goddamn Civil War again, Sean Bertram McMahon! Please rejoin the twenty-first century!"

And with that, she headed downstairs, whipped up a Croque Monsieur sandwich for herself, and settled in to watch Meryl Streep in *It's Complicated* for the twenty-fourth time, stress-eating her feelings until she drifted off to sleep on their beige couch.

Jennifer-free for the week, Sean had taken off work early to get ready for his bachelor weekend plans. He finished dusting his framed flag, dusted his framed letters from Union Officers, and then carefully hung on the wall his newest treasure, a tintype he located of Major General Stephen Augustus Hurlbut, his actual distant relative. *"Oh, frabjous day! Callooh! Callay! He chortled in his joy."*

He was also talking on his Bluetooth headset while he worked. "Yeah, it's amazing. Do you want to see it?... Okay, then we can head out from here... Tuesday or Wednesday, I think. She's gone at least a few more days... I know, we're going to have some fun... Yes, please wear that! Hold on, that's my other line... Definitely. I'll see you in a few hours. Bye." He switched over to the other call. "Hello?... Yes, this is Sean McMahon... I am. Who is this?... Are you serious?"

He slowly sat down.

"Let me grab a pen."

Friday Night

With the other members of the Poupard slumber party soundly asleep, Jesse had been sitting by herself on the back porch in the dark, in just her t-shirt and underwear, occasionally slapping at a thirsty mosquito. She strummed her guitar and softly worked on some lyrics she was writing.

> *"When you don't know the players,*
> *and don't recognize the game,*
> *When the road before you changes,*
> *and your scars don't have a name..."*

She paused, then set the guitar down and leaned back in her chair, feeling the dampness of the mist that had settled in. Listening to the dreamlike, nocturnal sounds of the bayou, she was looking for a way to connect with the mother she never knew. She thought what an odd thing it was to be looking to nocturnal insects for a sense of family and belonging. Jennifer had her husband and children, and Jack had Sydney and his adoptive parents; but with her aunt and uncle and now newly discovered birth mother no longer living, Jesse felt as though she was the only one who had lost a link to any sense of family history and continuity. She felt adrift.

She looked out into the misty darkness and listened to the sounds of crickets and frogs, the occasional bellow of a distant alligator, the hypnotic sing-song of the whip-poor-will, and the call-and-response hooting of two owls. She inhaled the scent of decaying leaves, perpetually damp from the almost daily afternoon rains, and closed her eyes.

Inside, Jennifer and Jack were nestled all snug in their beds, while visions of cheating husbands and men in drag danced in their heads. Sean was curled up nearby in Eulalie's chair, snoring his little puppy snore, dreaming his little puppy dreams, when Jack suddenly sat up, eyes wide open, speaking loudly as though he was in danger. "Oh my God! Kellem! Drabinsky! Can you hear me?!"

Jennifer woke with a start. "Wh-what's wrong, Jack?"

Jesse was pulled out of her bayou reverie and rushed inside from the back porch to see what the loud talking was about. That was when Jack threw back his covers and jumped out of bed, frantically looking for something unseen and mumbling breathlessly to himself, "Where is it? Where is it? Hang in there, Winters! Stay with me!"

"He did something like this last night too, but without the talking," said Jesse, "where he seemed to be awake but he couldn't hear me when I spoke to him. It's like he's sleepwalking. He said he has an anxiety disorder," she said as she grabbed Jack's man-purse from the floor next to his cot and pulled out his prescription bottles to look at the labels. "He's taking Ambien and Xanax," she said.

Then, like a flash, Jack took off out the front door, staying one step ahead of his midnight monsters.

"Shit!" said Jesse.

"We've gotta follow him to make sure he doesn't get lost out there, or hurt himself," said Jennifer.

With no time to throw on clothes, they took off after Jack. Sean followed at their heels, barely making it through the front door before it closed.

Out in the driveway, Jennifer asked, "Which direction??"

Jesse spun around and spotted a flash of fast-moving Budweiser logos disappearing into the fog about fifty yards down the road and pointed. "There he is! Jaaaack!"

Sean sprinted past them and ran in Jack's direction.

"Oh my God," said Jennifer, alarmed. "Your damn dog is loose! Why did you let him out? Now we've got to save both of them!"

"Stop yelling at me, Jen! I didn't know he followed us out!"

Jesse and Jennifer ran as fast as their tender bare city feet would carry them. Jack suddenly darted off the road into the trees and tall grass, and Sean followed him.

"Ow! Goddamn it!" yelled Jesse as she stepped on a piece of gravel, causing her to lose a bit of ground as she limp-ran the rest of the way.

When they got near to the place where they had seen him run into the brush, they heard one sharp little bark from Sean. They pulled to a stop and spied Jack squatting down near a tree next to an overgrown dock. He was looking around, totally confused. Sean stood in front of him, panting and wagging his tail.

Jennifer called to him, "Jack?"

"Jennifer, look at the dock!" said Jesse. "Do you think this could be the same one?"

Jennifer shrugged. They both moved slowly toward Jack.

"Hey, Jack," said Jesse softly. "It's Jesse and Jennifer."

"Wh-what happened?" he asked, reaching down to pet Sean.

"Shhhh, everything's alright," Jennifer assured him in her soft calm mom voice, the one she used to use when Connor or Maggie had a childhood nightmare.

"We're gonna help you home now, okay?" said Jesse.

He nodded as they held out their hands to him and, working in concert, pulled him up to standing. He bent down, scooped up Sean, and snuggled the puppy into the crook of his neck. They each put an arm around Jack in the center. The four of them formed an interesting family tableau as they made their way back to the Poupard house—Jack in his oversized Budweiser pajamas; Jennifer in her tasteful, conservative nightgown; Jesse, limp-walking in her Rolling Stones t-shirt and underwear; and Sean licking Jack's ear.

"I'm so sorry, you guys," he said. "I should've warned you."

"It's okay. Don't worry about it," Jennifer responded, soothingly.

"Yeah," added Jesse with a smile, "we had *just* said to each other how we needed to get outside for a little fresh air and a midnight jog."

DAY FIVE

"Anyone can slay a dragon, he told me, but try waking up every morning & loving the world all over again. That's what takes a real hero."
-Kai Skye (as Brian Andreas)

Saturday Morning

Bright and early the following morning, after a hearty breakfast of couche couche, fried eggs over boudin, and sweet potato biscuits, the siblings loaded their bags, Jesse's guitar, Angie's memorabilia, and the puppy into the car.

"Oh, no..." said Jesse, clutching her stomach. She darted back into the house.

"Poor thing," said Poppy as they watched Jesse disappear inside. She turned to Jennifer and handed her the next envelope. "The directions to Bessemer are easy. It's a pretty straight shot. It's all in there."

"Del's a good man," Harville told them. "Been a family friend for a very long time. You'll like him. Though you might want to warn Jesse to hold off on the cussin' while you're at his place. Del's pretty religious and doesn't like that."

The screen door slammed behind Jesse as she stepped out of the house. She was definitely dragging this morning.

Poppy handed her a beverage container, saying, "Make sure you keep taking this medicine from Eulalie. It'll make you feel better. I promise."

"I will," Jesse assured her. "Please tell her how much I appreciate it. And thank you, both of you, for everything."

"You are very welcome. *Very welcome!*" said Poppy, as she hugged Jesse.

"It's been our pleasure," said Harville. "Good luck on the rest of your journey. We hope y'all find what you're lookin' for."

They all hugged goodbye. When Jesse walked around to the driver's side, she spotted a round, flat rock in the driveway. With a furtive glance at the others, she picked it up and slipped it into her back pocket before sliding in behind the wheel for her driving shift. Jack climbed in behind her with the puppy, and Jennifer rode shotgun. They pulled out and took off, calling out the window and waving as they drove away.

Traveling north on Highway 59, Jesse was quiet as she drove.

"How's your stomach, Jess? You feeling okay?" asked Jennifer.

"I don't want to talk about it," was Jesse's curt response.

Jesse glanced in the rearview mirror at Jack who was looking profoundly tired in the back seat. He was petting Sean and staring blankly out the car window.

Jennifer turned around to face him and asked, "Does that happen a lot? The sleepwalking, I mean?"

"So I'm told," he said. "I often don't remember. Sydney keeps an eye on me when it happens."

"Have you thought about changing your medications?" she asked. "It could be the combination."

"Yeah, but those seem to be the best ones at keeping the nightmares at bay, usually, and helping me sleep."

"If you can call that sleep..." Jennifer added.

Jesse glanced back at him again. "So why do you have anxiety problems and nightmares?" she asked bluntly.

Jack hesitated for a moment, weighing whether or not he wanted to open that topic for discussion. "It, uh, started when I got back from serving two years in Afghanistan."

It wasn't quite the answer Jesse was expecting from her Drag Queen brother. "You were in the military?"

"Yep. I enlisted after 9/11."

Jennifer said, "Wow, did you—"

"I don't really want to talk about it if that's okay," he said.

"Of course," she responded softly. She turned back around and faced forward, watching the road slip by.

"Was that what your nightmare was about last night? Do you think that murder story yesterday triggered it?" Jesse continued.

"I don't know. Look, I really don't want to talk about this!" he snapped. He immediately regretted telling them.

"Jeez, you don't have to bite my head off!" Jesse snapped back.

"Seriously, don't make me sorry I said yes to coming on this trip," he said.

"Oh, my God, you guys, stop it. You're worse than my kids were when they were... kids," said Jennifer. "We have a long drive ahead of us. Don't make me turn this car around."

"You can't say that when you're not driving, Jen," said Jesse. "It makes no sense."

"I know! I was kidding!" She let out an exasperated sigh.

Jack stroked Sean's head and returned to staring darkly out the window at the passing scenery. Jesse eyed him surreptitiously in the mirror.

Over the next hour, Jennifer occasionally attempted some small talk to ease the tension, but no one was having it. Nerves were frayed and tempers were short after too little sleep the previous night. Not to mention the disturbing story from the previous day that they were all still attempting to process.

After another hour, Jennifer couldn't stand the crypt-like silence anymore. She reached for the radio, asking the others what they wanted to listen to. Jack answered, "Country," as Jesse simultaneously said, "Anything but Country."

"What's wrong with Country??" he roared. "They're the best damn storytellers in the music business!"

"If you have to even *ask* that question," said Jesse, "then it's pointless in even responding to you."

"Good! I don't wanna hear it!"

"Fine!" Jesse snapped.

"Fine!" he snapped back.

"Fine!"

"Fine!"

Jennifer was morbidly curious to see how long they'd keep that call-and-response going, but after three more rounds of "Fine!" she yelled, "SHUT UP! I don't want to hear another word out of either one of you for the rest of this drive."

That seemed to do the trick.

That is, until Jesse mumbled, "You're not the boss of us..."

Jennifer threw up her hands in frustration then turned to stare out her own window for the remaining four hours of the drive. Four *very. Long. Hours.*

SATURDAY AFTERNOON

Their bright and shiny rental car drove through a very poor section of town. Old people on makeshift front stoops and children playing in grassless yards watched them as they slowly drove by, looking for house numbers that were virtually nonexistent in this neighborhood.

Their comically out-of-place British GPS woman "Penelope" suddenly announced, "You have arrived at your destination." They pulled onto the expanse of dirt outside of a small, rundown, powder-blue house with a tar paper roof. They came to a stop next to a rusted car with no tires, a smattering of old car parts, and half of a prehistoric air conditioning unit that inhabited the yard.

Jesse put the car in park, turned off the ignition, and they all got out and stretched. Jesse put the bungee-leash on Sean and walked him around the side of the house to take a peek into the backyard.

"Is this it?" asked Jennifer. "I thought they said it was a juke joint."

"Is this not like all the upper-middle-class, suburban juke joints you frequent?" Jack laughed.

"Very funny," she said.

"Yeah, this is it," Jesse called over. "There are some picnic tables back here next to a little tin shack that says 'Del's Joint.' This looks awesome."

"Should we go ahead and get our stuff out now," asked Jennifer, "or wait until after we say hello?"

"Might as well get it out now. One less trip," Jack answered.

As Jack and Jennifer collected their few bags from the trunk, and Jesse's guitar from the backseat, Jesse picked up a round, flat stone from the side of the house and stuck it in her pocket, then she and Sean joined the others at the front door. Jack's knock was answered by a soft-spoken Black man in his late eighties, with bowed legs, a weathered face, and kind brown eyes.

Del had worked in the oil fields in his teens, and spent a couple of years in his late forties as a roustabout with the *Clancy Brothers Circus* where he met and befriended young Poppy and Harville; but for most of his adult life, both before and after his short stint with the circus, he had made his living as a gravedigger in the greater Birmingham area. It was during those lonely midnight shifts at the graveyard when he taught himself to play the harmonica. He had always been a fan of the music of Little Walter, Sonny Boy Williamson II, Howlin' Wolf, and Sonny Terry; so when he came across an old harmonica at a local church fundraiser when he was twenty-eight—buried in the middle of some knitted baby booties and "gently used" potholders—teaching himself to play had become his mission. He liked to think that there might be some spirits of crotchety, old bluesmen guiding him along during those solitary nighttime practice sessions in the graveyard. Though he was always careful not to accidentally make one of those "Robert Johnson at the Crossroads" bargains in his desire to play well.

Music had been a passion, but when his wife Hattie died during an outbreak of scarlet fever at the young age of forty-three, it also became his solace. It was also after her death, when his grief was so immense that he couldn't bear to be in the home they had built together, that he up and left. That was when he had stumbled upon the *Clancy Brothers Circus* during one of their two-week stops just outside of Mobile, and he signed on for the next two years. He had stayed away until his heart had mended enough to go home.

Once he was back in Bessemer, he converted his old tin garage and workshop into a makeshift juke joint. Despite noise and parking complaints from the neighbors to the City Council, he had managed to keep the doors open for decades by not calling it a business, but rather, "a Saturday night music party for friends and others (donations gladly accepted)."

"C'mon in, kids. C'mon in," Del said, ushering them through the front door.

They followed him in and set their belongings by the entrance.

"I'm Delbert Morris, but you can call me Del," he said as he extended a hand weathered by years of hard manual labor. They introduced themselves, Jesse last. Del smiled and took her hand, shaking his head in amazement. "Well, if you ain't the spittin' image of your mama."

THE KEY TO CIRCUS-MOM HIGHWAY 141

Again with that comparison. Jesse still didn't know quite how to respond to it.

"I... it's... nice to meet you," was all she said.

"Well, thank the Good Lord for guiding you all here. You girls'll be sharin' the bed in the back bedroom. I hope you're okay with that. And, Jack, I'm afraid you'll be out here on the couch."

"Not a problem, sir," Jack assured him. "We appreciate you making room for us here."

"Can I get you all anything?" Del asked the trio.

Jack and Jennifer declined the offer.

Jesse said, "Not for me, but if you have a bowl that I could use for some water for Sean here, that would be really great. Thank you."

As Del headed to the kitchen for a bowl of water, the three J's headed to the living room. It looked like the furniture hadn't changed since the sixties or seventies. It wasn't cool, retro furniture. It was modest, generic furniture from places like *Sears* and *Levitz,* a little worse for wear. On the walls hung religious pictures and a wooden Jesus on a cross. On the little table next to the couch there were some old and faded family photos in simple frames.

The three of them parked themselves on the green and brown plaid couch where a short stack of folded sheets, a pillow, and a thin wool blanket were balanced on the arm. In front of them was a low wooden coffee table that held three photo albums, one with each of their names written on the front. Del came back with a bowl of water for Sean that he set down on the mat inside the front door. He then joined the others in the living room, and slowly lowered himself down onto his brown Easy-Boy recliner across from them.

"What are these?" Jennifer asked him, referencing the photo albums.

"I'll get to those shortly." He smiled. "Just leave 'em be for the moment though. I imagine y'all are probably anxious to hear the next part of the story." They nodded. "Alrighty then, let's have at it.

"Angie, your mama, came to me after she left Eulalie's. Poppy and Harville told me she needed a safe place to stay because a bad man had been after her. Didn't tell me much more than that, but they said she needed a hiding place right urgent. So she come here and stayed in that back bedroom you girls are in. She helped me out with the music nights here on Saturdays, checkin' people in, cleanin' up, whatever needed to be done. She was a good girl. After about a month, she said she was gettin' the feelin' to move on, but right around then she found out she was with child. She weren't none too happy about it either."

Jesse stared at the ground in front of her, thinking about her own newly discovered mama-drama situation that "she weren't none too happy about."

"Said it was the bad man she was gettin' away from," continued Del. "Now, I know not everybody agrees with this, but the way I see it, the Lord blesses you with a child, you treat it as a gift. You was that gift, Jack."

"You think rape is—" Jesse began.

"So, um, did she move on from here then?" asked Jennifer quickly. She cut Jesse off before she could start a heated debate about the theological beliefs surrounding reproduction with an eighty-nine-year-old man sitting underneath a large wooden carving of the Crucifixion.

"No ma'am! I weren't gonna let her leave and be on her own then. Especially the way she was feelin' about it. I talked her into stayin'. Started teachin' her some music to take her mind offa things. She got pretty good after a while."

· · · · ● ● ● ● · · ·

<u>*1979*</u>

The juke joint was small and packed with mismatched tables and chairs. There was a very tiny dancing area in front of the low stage. The walls were covered floor-to-ceiling with blues posters and signed photographs of Del with guest musicians. Year-round Christmas lights, tinsel, and colorful strands of beads were strung everywhere. If you wandered in here on a Saturday night with a case of the blues, you most definitely wouldn't leave with one.

Del, in his late fifties, was on the small, raised stage area, looking very dapper in a button-down shirt, brown slacks, and a diamond crown straw fedora. Sitting on a wooden chair behind a mike stand, he finished a song on his harmonica to the appreciative applause of the packed-in crowd of all ages.

He leaned into the mike and said, "Now I got a special treat. Some of y'all know Angie from around here. She's gonna join me on this next one. She's gotten pretty darn good on the blues harp, so I'm sure you're gonna like this."

Nineteen-year-old Angie, now about seven months pregnant, stepped onto the stage with a metal folding chair and set it up next to Del. He put his harmonica in his shirt pocket and picked up his guitar from the floor next to his chair. She pulled out her harmonica, took a deep breath, and signaled to him that she was ready. The two of them launched into the old "Big Bill" Broonzy number "Key to the Highway," not too fast or too difficult a song for the harmonica. A drummer and keyboard player sitting upstage of the duo joined in. Del launched into the lyrics as Jesse played.

> *"I've got the key to the highway,*
> *billed out and born to go."*

He looked at Angie.

> *"I'm gonna leave here runnin'*
> *because walkin' is much too slow.*
> *I'm goin' back to the border.*
> *Baby, where I'm better known.*
> *Because you ain't done nothin' baby..."*

· · · · · • • • · · ·

"When Angie got the first signs she might be goin' inta labor, Poppy drove out here right quick to be with her and then to help take the baby back to Louisiana. Your mama felt like she weren't in a position to care for a baby the way it should be cared for, so Poppy and Harville helped her set up a private adoption with a nice couple in the New Orleans area that couldn't have children of their own. Good people as I understand it, Jack."

"Yes, they are," Jack confirmed.

"So did she stay here a while longer after that?" asked Jennifer.

"Nope. I tried my hardest," said Del, "but I couldn't talk her inta stayin'. Left almost right away."

Jesse let out a mirthless laugh. "Of *course* she did. Don't wanna stay too long with the new baby. Just have 'em and leave 'em and never look back." In a sarcastically perky voice, she said to Jennifer, "At least she's consistent, am I right, partial-sister? High-five for Dead-Mom!" She held up her hand to Jennifer who didn't respond. "No?..." She held her high-five hand up to Jack. "Brand new surprise brother?" He didn't respond either. "No?..."

"Stop," Jennifer admonished quietly.

"Now, now," Del frowned. "'Judge not lest ye be judged.' It may seem like that's what happened from where you're sittin', but she didn't leave and put you out of her mind. Not even close to that. There's a book for each of you there. Go ahead and take a look at those now."

They each picked up the book that had their name on the cover and began to leaf through the photo-covered pages.

"Oh my gosh," said Jennifer as she flipped through her album. "My entire life is in here."

"How did she get all of this?" asked Jack.

"Well, your mama kept in touch with her friend Patsy all those years. Patsy was the only one who knew where Angie was." He turned to Jesse and Jennifer. "Patsy would send her clippings from your school newspapers, and pictures from your after-school events. She went to all of them while you were growing up. She even got photos of you with your family when no one noticed her taking 'em."

"Well, that's not stalker-ish at all..." Jesse mumbled, not looking up from her album.

Del's speech began to slow. "She'd send them to Angie... wherever Angie was... at the... time..."

Then his speech stopped completely, his body slumped, and his head dropped softly forward onto his chest. Jack and Jennifer immediately sat up at attention, not knowing what exactly had happened to him. No reaction at all from Jesse who just looked numb.

"Del?..." said Jennifer tentatively. "*DEL*?!..." No response. "Oh my God, oh my God, not another dead person in this story!"

"We don't know that he's dead," said Jack, who jumped up and went to put his head near Del's face.

"What are you doing?" Jennifer asked him.

"I'm trying to see if he's breathing. I can't tell."

Jesse, oddly unfazed through all of this, went back to leafing through her photo album, which Jennifer and Jack didn't seem to notice.

"Hold on," said Jennifer. She quickly rifled through her purse until she found a metal spoon and held it out to Jack. "Here. Hold this in front of his nose and mouth to see if he's breathing."

He took the spoon with a confused look on his face. "Who carries silverware in their purse? Is that a Midwestern thing? That's just weird."

Before Jack could check the spoon for a foggy sign of life, Del came out of his narcoleptic episode with a sharp inhalation that startled Jack and Jennifer. They quickly moved back to their seats, glancing sideways at one another, as Del continued his talk from exactly where he left off.

"... And for you, Jack, part of the agreement your adoptive parents made was that they would send photos and updates about you as long as she didn't make contact with you herself. That would be up to you when you were old enough to choose. They sent everything to your mom care of Patsy's address, and then Patsy would forward them on to her."

He paused to let them continue looking through the books. They commented on the rediscovered memories they found in front of them: Jack as a Cub Scout, Jesse's first tragic attempt at cutting her own bangs when she was six, Jennifer in a full set of braces and headgear (not a fun two year stretch during junior high school), twelve years of Jack's official school portraits in front of cheesy scenic backdrops, Jesse looking miserable in her junior high school prom photo with her next-door neighbor Gary Shermlin who was eight inches shorter than she was, school plays, swim meets, soccer games, graduations, slightly blurry Chasen family picnics shot from a distance, and a photo of Jack in uniform just before he was deployed. It was a bit mind-boggling, seeing how complete the records of their lives were on the pages of these albums, especially for the women, because somehow Patsy had been able to infiltrate their lives without their knowledge.

"So you see, you were always in your mama's heart. She kept you close all the time through these books."

"It's incredible," said Jesse.

"Yes, it is," agreed Del.

"No. I mean that she knew where we were, and what we were doing all these years, and she never *once* picked up the phone and tried to make contact. This whole time never once tried to re-establish a relationship with us. And now we're supposed to just look at these books and say 'Awww, wasn't that sweet of her? Wasn't she just a great runaway Circus-Mom?'"

Jesse abruptly stood up, stormed out of the living room, and grabbed her guitar still sitting by the front door. She left the house with it and slammed the front door.

Jack looked at Jennifer. "Should we go after her? And when I say 'we' I, of course, mean 'you.'"

"No, let her have some space," said Jennifer. "She's always worked out her emotions with that guitar."

"Sounds about right," said Del to no one in particular. "That's what they call playin' the blues."

"She just found out she's pregnant," Jennifer continued softly to Jack.

Del frowned to himself. The obvious parallel with Angie didn't escape him. How could it?

"The night we were at your show, actually," continued Jennifer. "Right after we found out about you, two days after we found out about our mom, and about twelve hours before she found out her dad was a rapist. So... yeah. It's been a week full of fun surprises."

"Good times..." said Jack. "So why do *you* seem fine with everything?"

She shrugged. "I'm emotionally repressed. It's pretty helpful at times."

· · · · · • • • • ·

Jesse sat at the bottom of the wooden steps leading from Del's back door to the bottom of his steep driveway. She strummed her guitar and sang softly, working out lyrics that were too quiet for Del to discern as he peeked around the side of the house and watched her for a moment. His eighty-nine-year-old bowed legs carried him quietly over to her and he joined her on the steps.

"Nice tune. You write that?" he asked.

She nodded and then went back to her playing, minus the quiet singing.

"Can you play that in the Key of E?" he asked. "It'll give it a more bluesy sound."

She answered him by deftly changing the key. He pulled a Key of A harmonica out of his shirt pocket and played it in the cross-harp position, in the key of E, improvising as he followed her lead. Through the music, it didn't take long to pull Jesse out of her funk. They jammed together for a couple of minutes, building to a big finish.

They both laughed, and Del said kindly, "There you go now. Ain't nothin' a little music can't heal."

"Sounds good in theory," she said dubiously.

"No 'theory' about it. S'a fact."

Jesse smiled at him. "How long does it take to learn to play that thing?" she asked.

"To play it well? I'm still working on it." He laughed. "But to play a few easier things passably, about six to nine months give-or-take if you practice every day. That's how long it took your mama."

No response to that.

"Once she knew she was havin' a baby, and she was stuck here, I taught her. To help take her mind offa complainin'."

Still no response from a pensive Jesse.

"Well, you sit out here and play as long as you want. But I could use a hand in about an hour or so if you're up for it. I got my son Chester coming to get the bar-b-que started. People gonna start showin' up about six for food and conversation. Then the music'll start at about seven or so. I'll need some help with the setup. Not as spry as I used to be in my seventies!"

Jesse laughed.

"There you go!" he said with a grandfatherly pat on her shoulder. He pulled himself up to standing with the help of the stair handrail and took a few steps up the driveway before turning around to face her again. "Hey, why don't you sit in with us onstage tonight? Just for one song if that's all you want to do."

"No, thank you," she demurred. "I don't think I'm up for it tonight."

"It'll do you a world of good. Don't argue with your elders, young lady."

Jesse smiled. How could she argue with that? "Yes, sir. Okay, one song."

He gave her an "it's settled then" nod, and turned to continue his walk back up to the front of the house. She propped her elbow on her knee and rested her cheek in her hand as she watched him make his slow pilgrimage up the driveway incline. Then she went back to her playing, working out more lyrics.

> *"When you don't know the players,*
> *And don't recognize the game,*
> *When the road before you changes,*
> *And your scars don't have a name,*
> *When the ground beneath you keeps on shifting,*
> *Anchorless you keep on drifting...."*

SATURDAY NIGHT

Dusk had fallen, and the strands of Del's year-round Christmas lights made the patio area outside the tin-roofed shack come to life. Del's sixty-five-year-old son Chester was getting the grill started for the hotdogs, burgers, and pulled pork sliders they sold on the side. A group of the "early bird" regulars arrived to hang out, talk, and share potluck side dishes before the evening of music officially started.

Jack and Jesse were following whatever orders Del was giving them—moving picnic tables, unfolding chairs, sweeping off the tiny dance floor. There were even more strands of Christmas lights inside than there were outside. A few of the musicians joked around with one another as they set up on stage and began to warm up. Jennifer was off to the side, just past the grill area, one finger plugging her free ear as she paced and talked on her cell phone. She was trying to keep her voice down but Jesse setting up nearby could hear that she was upset.

"Every night I've been gone you've had to be out that late?... Yeah, well, I don't believe you... No, don't change the subject. You know I have to be here for whatever the hell this is!... Okay, you know what, I can't do this with you right now. I'll call you tomorrow." She hung up with a dark, distracted look on her face as Del passed by.

"Jennifer, can you give Jack a hand over there getting the window propped open?" he asked her as he passed.

"Of course," she said. She headed over to help him raise and prop open the primitively constructed, wooden flap that covered the wide, open, rectangular window hole.

"You got your guitar down here?" he asked as he crossed to Jesse.

"No, it's in my room."

"Well, go on and get it. You can play that song you were working on."

"No, please, not that one!" implored Jesse.

He ignored her response. "But you'll need to go over it once with the other musicians, so they can join in and back you up."

She hesitated, then decided not to "argue with her elders," and headed into the house to get her guitar. Del went back to greeting his weekly regulars.

· · · · ● · ● · · · ·

The raucous music inside was in full swing now. The dance floor was packed with about seven laughing, chatting couples, the maximum number that could fit in the small area. Jesse sat off to the side at one of the tiny round tables with Jennifer and Jack. Little vases of humble plastic flowers decorated the center of each table. The people who arrived too late to grab a coveted seat inside were leaning on their forearms in the open side window.

They were listening to Del play and sing with the guest band from his chair in the front corner of the stage.

That corner seat was where Del parked himself every Saturday night after his opening prayer, the singing of "Amazing Grace," and his talk about racial unity that preceded the music every week. His final words were always, "Okay, now, let's give a big hand for the Lord!" And then the evening was off and running (until 11 p.m. sharp.)

After a particularly complicated riff on his harmonica, Del nodded off again in his chair.

"God, it freaks me out when he does that," said Jennifer, shaking her head.

"Narcolepsy," posited Jack.

"Either that," said Jesse, "or just being two hundred years old."

The song ended, and right on cue, Del woke up and leaned into the mike. "Alright, alright! Let's show these musicians some love!" There were cheers and applause from the crowd. "And now come on up here, Jesse." She stood up and went to get her guitar from the side of the stage as he continued, "We got a treat for y'all tonight, yes we do. A couple of you old-timers might remember Angie who worked here a lotta years ago. Well, this here is Angie's little girl Jesse who gonna be doin' a song she wrote herself, so welcome her to the stage."

There was polite applause from the crowd, but whistles and loud whoops from Jennifer and Jack, making Jesse grin as she got her chair and guitar situated, and adjusted the mike lower. Jack stood up and extended his hand, inviting Jennifer to dance.

"Oh, no. I'm SO not a dancer!"

"Don't be silly. I'm a fantastic lead," he said.

He pulled her up and deftly spun her around as Jesse leaned into the mike and said, "Okay, I'm doing this completely against my will. This is still a work in progress. I call it 'The Finding-My-Family Blues.' So... here goes."

> *"When you don't know the players,*
> *And don't recognize the game,*
> *When the road before you changes,*
> *And your scars don't have a name,*
>
> *When the ground beneath you keeps on shifting,*
> *Anchorless you keep on drifting,*
> *Solo in your heavy lifting,*
> *Then assigning blame..."*

At this point, the other musicians joined in on bass, keyboard, drums, and harmonica. The woman on the keyboard began to add improvised background vocals which helped pick up the pace and lighten the mood, prompting more people to move out on the dance floor. Every now and then a particular lyric would hit home and Jennifer and Jesse would lock eyes.

> *"When the dragon's got you in its sights,*
> *Your life is full of lies,*
> *You're burning up inside the flame,*
> *No one to hear your cries,*
>
> *When you climb beyond the crippling shame,*
> *That's kept you down and made you lame,*
> *Like a phoenix from the ashes came,*

You'll rise, yes, you will rise.

*It's the... Circus Mother, Long-lost Brother,
Daddy Traitor, Hungry 'Gator,
Sister Drama, Hitchhikin' Mama,
Finding-my-family Blues.*

*Your family isn't always one
that's just defined by bloodline.
Sometimes you find them while you search
for meaning in this lifetime.*

*Sometimes a stranger pulls you
from the mud and sets you free.
You know those people are the ones
your family's meant to be.*

*It's the... Circus Mother, Long-lost Brother,
Daddy Traitor, Hungry 'Gator,
Sister Drama, Hitchhikin' Mama,
Finding-my-family Blues.*

*It's the... Fake Revolver, Problem-solver,
Sibling Ragin', Bare-assed Cajun,
"Bud" Pajamas, Midnight Traumas,
Finding-my-family Blues."*

By the end of the song, Jack and Jennifer had stopped dancing and stood still in the middle of the pack of whirling dancers. They stood, watching Jesse, listening to the lyrics about their journey together searching for their unexpected family.

After the song ended to the applause of the crowd, Jesse stepped to the side of the stage area where Jack and Jennifer met her. The musicians launched into their next song, a rollicking cover of Little Milton's song "Your Wife's Been Cheatin' On Us."

"That was really beautiful," said Jack. "I never in a million years would've guessed you to be a such poet."

She smiled. "Thanks."

"I'm mean, you're no *Jackie, Oh!* That's for sure," he teased.

"So few of us are." She laughed.

Jennifer reached for Jesse's hand and said, "I'm so sorry. I didn't— I didn't know what you've been going through."

Jesse shrugged. "It's okay."

They held a look. It was probably the deepest level of understanding that Jennifer had of Jesse's internal world over the last few years.

"Well..." began Jennifer, at a total loss for any other words. "I think I'm going to head to bed. Especially if we have another early travel day tomorrow. You guys coming?"

"I am," said Jack. "I feel like *The Walking Dead*."

"I think I'm gonna stay out here for a while," said Jesse. "Maybe sit in and play some more."

"Okay," said Jennifer. She paused. "That really was a beautiful song, Jess... You're very gifted."

"Thank you, Jen."

Jennifer suddenly gave Jesse a big, unexpected bear hug. "Don't stay up too long."

"I won't. Goodnight, you guys."

Jack and Jennifer exited and headed up to the house while Jesse headed back onto the stage area with

THE KEY TO CIRCUS-MOM HIGHWAY 157

her guitar. Jack assembled his makeshift couch-bed in the living room; while Jennifer headed back to the girls' room, got changed, and climbed into the lumpy, decades-old double-bed she would be sharing with Jesse. She lay there trying to imagine her nineteen-year-old mother staring at these same four walls and ceiling, and she wondered about the thoughts that inhabited her nineteen-and-pregnant-again mind until Jennifer gradually drifted off to sleep.

··········

Several hours later, it was pitch dark in the girls' room—the kind of inky, middle-of-the-night darkness that you only get out in the country (or in a sensory deprivation tank). Suddenly the overhead light came on and an agitated Del rushed to the side of the bed and urgently shook Jennifer's shoulder.

"Jennifer, wake up!"

"What's wrong?" she asked, completely disoriented. "What's happening??"

"You and Jack need to come right now. Jesse's in trouble."

Jennifer leaped out of bed and threw a light jacket on over her gown. They rushed into the living room where Jack was sleeping with Sean curled up next to him on the couch.

"This is all my fault," Del lamented as Jennifer reached for Jack's shoulder. Del was beside himself with worry. "I must've dozed off. I didn't see her drinking. She's with two young men I don't recognize."

"Wake up, Jack!" she said, nudging his shoulder. "Jesse needs our help!"

Jack sprung out of bed, instantaneously alert and on task. Not a normal human response time. "Where is she?"

"They were out in the food area," said Del. "I had to kick these two young men out for being drunk and disorderly, and they were tryin' to get her to come with them."

They all rushed out the back door and down the wooden steps leading to the bottom of the driveway. The crowd had waned, but there were a few patrons standing around chatting. They didn't see Jesse, so they spun around and rushed up the driveway to the front yard, Jack in the lead. Del tried his best to keep up, moving as quickly as his bowed, antiquated legs would carry him.

They rounded the corner of the house and headed for the dirt parking area out front. Two drunk guys in their early thirties, Chet and Aaron, were trying to coax an intoxicated Jesse into their black pickup truck with not-cheesy-at-all (totally cheesy) flame decals running along the sides. Chet had one of her hands and was pulling her. She was smiling but trying to pull away.

"Noooo, you guys, I can't go," she slurred. "I have to leave early in the morning."

"Oh, c'mon." Chet smiled. "Just for a little while. There's a good bar near here. One without so many rules. I promise we'll get you back soon."

"No, seriously. You guys are really cute, but I have to go to bed."

Laughing, Aaron said to his buddy quietly, "Yeah, that's the plan."

"Take your hands off of her," said Jack, rushing over.

Chet blew him off. "Hit the road, Jack."

"How do you know his name?" slurred Jesse.

"It's all good, man," said Aaron. "My friend's girlfriend here had a little too much to drink. We're taking her back home."

A dark shadow passed across Jack's face as his entire countenance shifted. "I'm not gonna ask you again. Take. Your hands. Off of her."

Chet looked at his buddy, clearly thinking the two of them could take Jack in a fight, no problem, and said sarcastically, "Oooh, he's not gonna ask me again! He's gonna —ughkk—"

Before they had time to react, Jack hit Chet in the throat and took him to the ground. His face was pinned down in the dirt and he was coughing. Jennifer rushed over to Jesse and pulled her away.

"Jesus Christ, man!" yelled Aaron.

Del became even more agitated as the situation escalated and he turned back to the house, moving as quickly as he was able, yelling over his shoulder, "I'm calling the police!"

Aaron panicked. "No! Don't do that, sir! No police! We're leaving, we're leaving. Get the fuck up, Chet! I'm on probation."

"Yeah, get the fuck up, Chet," repeated Jack as he released his grip, "or I won't be so gentle next time."

Chet scrambled up, holding his throat, still coughing. They flung themselves into the pickup, slammed the doors, and squealed away in a cloud of dust. On this particular midnight stroll, Jesse, hair messy and mascara a little smudged, had her arms around Jack and Jennifer's shoulders as they helped her back to the house.

"I'm sorry," she mumbled.

"No worries," said Jack. "It's all good. Let's just get you inside."

"I don't feel so good," she added.

"Really? Because you look *suuuper* pretty," Jennifer teased.

"Awww," said Jesse smiling, leaning her head on Jennifer's shoulder. "Fuck you, partial sister."

Jennifer leaned her head on Jesse's, and responded, "Fuck you too."

"For a big sister," said Jack, "you're setting a horrible example for me, just so you know."

"Ohhh," said Jesse, still smiling, switching her head over to Jack's shoulder. "Fuck you too, surprise brother."

He returned the smile, and the head lean. "Yeah, we're all fucked."

As they headed inside the front door, Jennifer said, "You guys are killing me with these middle-of-the-night adventures. It's like herding ferrets in the dark."

DAY SIX

*"Security is mostly a superstition.
It does not exist in nature, nor do the children of men as a whole experience it. Avoiding danger is no safer in the long run than outright exposure. Life is a daring adventure or nothing at all."*
-Helen Keller

Sunday Morning

Out in the driveway, Jack carefully moved his *Jackie, Oh!* wig and wardrobe to the side so he could load their bags into the trunk without any further hairdo or sequin damage. It was getting crowded back there what with their accumulating treasure trove of mom items that Jennifer was adding to the trunk—the scrapbook, the box of programs, the sack of rocks from Poppy and Harville, and the three photo albums they received from Del.

Jesse was wearing dark sunglasses because it was painfully bright out and she had a *wicked* hangover. She stood nearby with her guitar slung over her shoulder and Sean on his bungee-leash. Del approached her. Jennifer and Jack, in the background, talked through the directions that were in the new envelope they had just been given. Del handed Jesse a glass of Alabama H2O and some Tylenol.

"Take these and drink all the water." He watched her as she downed the whole glass without taking a breath, like a woman who had been wandering in the desert for forty days. "Now, take off those glasses and look me in the eye for a minute."

She pulled them off, squinting in the glaring sun. "Ow."

"I'm gonna give you the same lecture I gave your mama all those years ago because I think you need it right about now. No more drinking. You're carryin' a baby, and that's a GIFT. I don't know what choices you're gonna make down the road, that's not my bizniss, but right now it's a responsibility that you have to accept, to give that little one the best, most healthy start you can give it."

Jesse paused. "...her." A small crack in her tough facade.

He smiled. "Well, alright now, there you go. The most healthy start you can give *her*."

Del gave Jesse a grandfatherly pat on the shoulder and they joined Jack and Jennifer back at the car where they said their thank-yous and goodbyes to Del before piling in. Jesse, dark glasses back on, picked up Sean and climbed into the backseat with her guitar. Jennifer rode shotgun once again while Jack took his turn at the wheel on this next leg of their drive. They pulled out, waving to Del.

"Y'all send me a postcard when the trip is over," he called after them. "Let me know how it all went!"

· · · · • · • · ·

A few minutes into the drive, Jesse unhooked Sean's bungee-leash. He curled up next to her, and she awkwardly half lay down, resting her head on her guitar. She was out cold within a minute.

Once Jack had backtracked his way out of the tangle of side streets in Del's neighborhood—many of them missing street signs, and often not corresponding to

"Penelope's" GPS directions—they miraculously reached a major boulevard, and Jennifer read Del's printed instructions to Jack.

"Okay, so his directions say to take I-20 South, then exit onto the 459 North, connect back up with I-20 East to Atlanta..."

"Wait, why not just stay on I-20?" he asked.

"The 459 bypasses downtown Birmingham. Then once we hit Atlanta, it's a straight shot down to Savannah on I-75."

"Okay," he said. "Just let me know when the exits are coming up."

That's when "Penelope," from the depths of their GPS box, said pleasantly, "Take I-20 North toward Birmingham."

"I thought you said take I-20 South," he said to Jennifer.

"Don't listen to her. It's South."

Jennifer had also punched the Savannah address into Waze on her phone, just for back-up. That's when Waze joined in on the action. "Take I-20 South toward Tuscaloosa."

Jack turned off Morgan Road and got on the I-20 South.

"Penelope" said, "Make a U-Turn."

"How the hell am I supposed to make a U-turn on an Interstate freeway?" cried Jack.

"No, I told you not to listen to her," said Jennifer. "Don't make a U-turn. This is the right direction."

"Why are we listening to her at all? Can you shut that damn thing off?"

While Jennifer searched for an on/off button, "Penelope" said, "Recalculating..."

Jennifer glanced up at the road just in time to see the exit for 459 North whiz by. "That was our exit! You were supposed to get on the 459!"

"You were supposed to tell me when the exit was coming up!"

Waze interrupted them this time. "Continue straight for forty-three more miles to Tuscaloosa, then take US-82 East to Montgomery."

"No, that's not right," corrected Jennifer. "Do NOT go to Tuscaloosa. We need to find the next place where we can get off and go back in the other direction to the 459."

Jack found the nearest turn-around option and narrowly managed to miss being run over by a truck transporting two hundred live chickens.

"Recalculating..." said Waze.

"Recalculating..." said "Penelope."

Jesse began snoring in the back seat. The absurdity at this point was too much. Jack and Jennifer broke out laughing.

"For God's sake, turn those things off," he said, exiting into slowing traffic on the 459.

She finally located the off button for the GPS, and as she was about to shut Waze down, she said, "Oh no..."

"What now?" asked Jack.

"I see why Waze was trying to route us through Tuscaloosa. There's a major, multi-vehicle accident on the I-20 East about five miles outside of Birmingham. It happened about fifteen minutes ago and they're already expecting an hour and a half delay."

"Okay. What now, Magellan?"

"We need to get off soon. Before the 20." She studied the map on her phone. "So... let's exit onto the 280. Then we can take that to the 80... to the 96... to the 16..."

"Are we going by way of Sheboygan, Wisconsin?"

"Trust me," said Jennifer, "it'll be faster even though it's longer."

Jesse covered her ears in the backseat. "Oh, my God, do you guys have to talk so loud?"

"HAVE to?" said Jack loudly over his shoulder. "NO. It just makes us feel POWERFUL." He turned to Jennifer. "How about a little road music?" He began to sing.

> *"A hundred bottles of beer on the wall,*
> *A hundred bottles of beer..."*

Jennifer grinned at Jesse in the back seat and joined in with Jack.

> *"Take one down, pass it around..."*

"You guys are *not funny*!"

"Don't be silly," said Jack. "We're hilarious."

They stopped singing nonetheless. Jesse unhooked her seatbelt and sprawled out in a more comfortable sleeping position, forcing Sean to relocate to the other end of the backseat. They continued the drive in silence.

··········

They were three-and-a-half hours into their scenic, road-less-traveled drive on the 280 (if you can call Insane Pete's Fireworks, Lulubelle's World of Dance, two

Piggly Wiggly's, three Winn Dixies, and a hundred and forty-seven Waffle Houses scenic). Jesse was still sound asleep in the back seat. Sean, gnawing on Jesse's guitar case, had discovered an expensive new chew toy.

Jennifer turned to Jack. "I don't know about you, but I could use a bathroom break when we get to the next town."

"Okay," he replied. "The sign we just passed said we're coming up on Plains in a few minutes."

"Do you want a break from driving?" she asked him.

"No, I'm good, thanks."

A few minutes later as they approached the town, Jack turned off of the 280, slowed down along historic Main Street, and parked in front of a giant, grinning peanut. For someone with a nut allergy, this place would be a hellish nightmare, because you couldn't spit in the town without hitting something that had a peanut on it or in it.

"Oh, my gosh," it suddenly dawned on Jennifer. "*Plains, Georgia!* This is where Jimmy Carter lives!"

"What gave it away? The giant banner on the building in front of us that says WELCOME TO PLAINS, GA, THE HOME OF JIMMY CARTER, OUR 39th PRESIDENT?"

There was a brief pause as she looked up at the banner in front of them that she had somehow missed. Then she said, "Yes, as a matter of fact, that did give it away." She glanced into the backseat and said, "Hey, Jess, we're stopping for a pee break if you need one." No answer. "Jesse?"

Jesse still didn't respond. She just rolled over and draped her arm over her eyes, so Jack and Jennifer got out and left Jesse there. And her little dog too.

Walking up to the giant, grinning peanut, Jennifer said, "That's hilarious." She handed her phone to Jack and said, "Would you get a picture of me with this?"

"You don't get out much, do you?" teased Jack.

Post-photo session, they entered a shop called Plains Peanuts in search of a restroom. When they left the shop, they had two empty bladders and two "World-Famous" peanut-flavored ice cream cones which they proceeded to eat on a bench next to the giant, grinning Peanut Man.

Four licks in, Jennifer said, "Can I ask you something?"

"Do I have a choice?"

She smiled. "No. So if another nightmare happens and you take off down the road again, is there something, in particular, we should do? Because you said it's not the first time that it's happened."

"Don't try to wake me unless you absolutely have to for safety reasons, because I won't know where I am, and I probably won't know it's you. If you have to wake me, better to make a loud noise from a distance to startle me awake. That way I won't feel like I'm being physically attacked."

"That's happened before?"

"Only once. Not too long after I got back to the States. Anyway, just try and make sure I don't hurt myself. Or anyone else. And help make sure I get back home, just like you did. Oh, and you might want to hide the car keys."

"Good to know. I'm sorry you have to deal with that," she said softly.

He shrugged it off. "Yeah, well, what're ya gonna do? I have it a lot better than some of the other guys I served with..."

They worked on their ice cream cones in silence. Jennifer again tested the waters, delicately broaching the subject of his service in the war. "You already would've been in your twenties after 9/11, so what made you want to enlist?"

Jack paused, then responded, "I had graduated from college that spring, and I was feeling a little lost. Directionless. My best friend had gotten an internship with a company in New York City that was in the Twin Towers. He was killed that day. I had my new direction."

"I'm so sorry."

Jack stood up suddenly, set the car keys next to Jennifer, walked away, and threw the rest of his cone into the garbage. He slid into the front passenger seat and slammed the door. Jennifer watched him go, then grabbed the keys and got into the driver's seat, still working on her ice cream. They drove in awkward silence for a while. Then Jack looked at Jesse in the back seat. She and the puppy were still snoring quietly.

"Okay, my turn for a question. That's a pretty serious scar around Jesse's collarbone and shoulder that she tried to hide with that tattoo. What's that from?"

"Oh. Umm..." She glanced over her shoulder to make sure Jesse was asleep then lowered her voice. "She was in a pretty seri—SHIT!" she yelled suddenly while simultaneously slamming on the breaks.

The tail end of her ice cream cone flew out of her hand and hit the windshield with a loud *splat!* They barely missed the terrified deer that had bolted across the road in front of their car. Jack threw his hands forward and braced himself on the glove compartment as his seatbelt locked. There was a THUD from the backseat. Jesse, not wearing her seatbelt, projectile-rolled and slammed into the back of Jennifer's seat before gravity took over.

"Ow..." they heard her say from the floor behind them.

"Oh, my God, put your seatbelt on! Are you crazy?!" said Jennifer, leaning over the seatback.

Sean jumped up onto the seat above Jesse and stared down at her, wagging his tail. She climbed back up, straightening her sunglasses.

"I have to pee really badly," she said.

"I asked you that when we stopped in Plains a few miles back!" said Jennifer, exasperated.

"*Sorry.* Jeez. I didn't hear you."

"Can it wait until we get to the next town?" Jack asked.

"No, it definitely can't wait. Just pull over and I'll pee on the side of the road."

Jack and Jennifer groaned. A sprinkle of light rain began to dot the windshield. Jennifer turned the wipers on low.

"I'm *sorry*!" Jesse continued. "I have a small bladder! And Del made me drink a gallon of water before we left."

"There's nothing to hide behind out here, Jesse. It's just pasture," said Jennifer, scoping out the immediate terrain.

"I don't care. Just pull off to the side and you guys can stand in front of me and block me from traffic. Not that there is any."

Jennifer pulled off to the shoulder and parked the car. She handed Jesse a wadded-up tissue from her purse.

"Here. This is all I have," she said.

"Eww," said Jesse, holding it gingerly with two fingers. "It's used. That's disgusting."

"Well, would you rather have a little snot on your twat, or underwear that smells like urine?"

"Wow, it's like *Sophie's Choice*," said Jesse as they all piled out of the car, Sean again on the bungee-leash.

"Yeah, that comparison's not offensive at all..." said Jack.

He and Jennifer stood with their backs to Jesse as she unzipped her pants and squatted down, trying not to pee on her clothes. Sean lifted his leg to pee on nothing in particular and barely missed Jennifer's shoe.

"You go, guy!" Jesse whispered to Sean.

The rain began to come down more steadily at that point.

"Oh, God," said Jennifer, trying to shield her hair with her hands, "Pee faster!"

A big rig truck barreled down the road with a clear view of Jesse. He honked at her and yelled out the open passenger-side window, "Yeah, baby!!"

"Thank you, I'll be here all week!" Jesse yelled, with a wave to her appreciative passing audience.

The sky opened up and it began to pour.

"Shit! Hurry up!" yelled Jack, as he and Jennifer bolted back to the shelter of the car, leaving Jesse bare-assed and scrambling to get her pants up as quickly as possible. She ran back to the car with Sean.

By the time they all dove into their Chevy Impala pumpkin-carriage, they were completely drenched. Sean added insult to injury by standing on the backseat and shaking wet-dog-scented water on everyone.

"Well, this sucks," said Jack. "With the exception of a floor-length, blue sequined gown, these are the only clothes I have with me."

"Sorry, guys..." apologized Jesse.

Jennifer attempted to start the car but nothing happened. She tried again with the same outcome. Nothing.

"Can you put on the heat?" Jesse asked.

"No, I can't put on anything," Jennifer said. "The car's dead."

Sunday Afternoon

The soggy trio plus a tow truck driver were packed into his truck cab like sardines. Jack next to the driver, then Jesse with Sean in her lap, then Jennifer at the window. No sound but the steady pattering of rain on the windshield and the metronomic beat of the wipers.

The driver broke the silence. "Where'd y'all say you were headed?"

In flat, unenthusiastic unison they answered, "Savannah."

"Hurricane season over there," the driver informed them.

"Oh, don't even," said Jack.

The driver wisely didn't pursue it.

From the depths of Jennifer's purse, a muffled Bonnie Raitt began to sing her mournful song "I Can't Make You Love Me." It was Jennifer's newly programmed ringtone. She pulled it out of her purse, dismissed the call that said "SEAN," and threw the phone back into her purse as Jesse watched.

"Interesting ringtone there, partial sister."

"Stop calling me that."

"Why didn't you answer his call?"

"Not in the mood," Jennifer said darkly.

"Trouble in paradise?" Jesse teased.

Jennifer shook her head, irritated by the comment, and looked out her window without responding.

They drove in silence for a few minutes until Jennifer turned to Jesse and, with annoyance in her voice, said, "You know, we haven't talked about what happened last night. You shouldn't be drinking while you're pregnant, Jesse."

"Oh, okay, here we go with the judgment again. I *knew* you were going to go there. Don't start in with the lectures, Jen."

"Well, it was really irresponsible of you."

Jesse said, "Oh my God, you never fucking change."

"Yeah, well, apparently neither do you," Jennifer shot back.

They ignored each other for the remainder of the drive. The tow truck pulled off the sleepy, two-lane highway in Milan, Georgia, and into an old filling station/auto repair shop, Ernie's Auto Repair. The brief downpour of rain had stopped by this point, and they all piled out of the tow truck. The tow truck driver spoke to a mechanic near a car that was elevated on the hydraulic lift, then came back to update them.

"Smitty said he should be able to get to it in the next hour or so. Just that one car to finish first."

"I need food," said Jesse. "I'm so hungry."

"Me too," agreed Jennifer, "but I need to change into some dry clothes first. I'm freezing."

"I need some *new* clothes," said Jack. "I don't suppose they'd have a Men's Department across the street at The Dollar Store."

Jennifer took a few steps down the road in order to look down a side street running perpendicular to Route 280.

"How about some new *old* clothes?" she called out to them. "It looks like there's a resale shop down there next to Shecky's House of Chicken and Waffles."

"Whatever. Not really in a position to be choosy at this point," said Jack.

They crossed the road, headed down the side street, and peered in the windows of Audrey and Maudry's Resale Shop. Items from places like Casual Corner, Woolworth's, Montgomery Ward, and JC Penney from the '80s and '90s populated the window displays.

"This should be interesting," said Jesse as she pushed the front door open to the sound of tinkling bells.

The inside of Audrey and Maudry's was kitsch heaven. In addition to clothes and shoes, there was an ungodly amount of porcelain knick-knacks. There were also old dolls (some of them with all their limbs still attached); ancient VCR tapes of *Porky's*, *The Dukes of Hazzard*, *Joe Dirt*, and *God's Not Dead 2*; a velvet painting of Jesus wearing a Georgia Bulldogs football jersey; a box containing an inner thigh device called "Super Kegel"; an assortment of boxed games for girls like "American Dream Date" and "The Sassy Experience Game"; a push lawn mower; and an old Sean Cassidy and Parker Stevenson *Hardy Boys* poster from the '70s.

Audrey and Maudry, identical twins in their late sixties, sat in chairs near the cash register. Audrey, wearing clothing and jewelry covered in brightly colored

Chihuahuas, was knitting. Maudry was decked out in her year-round Christmas attire and was decorating a satin Christmas ball with beads and ribbons and pins from the little table next to her.

"Hello! Welcome! Come on in!" they said in sing-song unison.

Audrey's Chinese Crested Chihuahua, a raggedy little thing with some kind of skin disease and milky eyes, growled at Sean.

"Oh, don't mind Carlos," said Audrey. "He's totally blind. He doesn't even know what he's barking at."

The comment obviously referenced some inside joke, because the twins looked at each other and cracked up in the same bizarre, shrill laugh. Though whether their inside joke was about Carlos, blindness, or skin disease wasn't immediately clear. It was like the three J's had landed on some sort of retro planet ruled by two alternate versions of Bette Davis in *Whatever Happened to Baby Jane?*

"Oh, my! Y'all are soaked to the bone, you poor things!" said Maudry. "Let me get you some hot tea."

Jesse leaned over to Jennifer and whispered, "Do people in the South know that Christmas is not in October?"

Jennifer elbowed her to be quiet as Maudry poured some hot peppermint tea from a large carafe into Styrofoam cups and handed them out.

"Would you mind if we changed right away into the clothes we find here?" asked Jennifer. "We're in a bit of a bind."

"Of course, darlin', whatever you need," answered Audrey. "There's a bathroom in the back corner that you can use to change in."

She and Maudry went back to their craftwork as the siblings browsed. Jack held up an enormous orange and pink floral print muumuu.

"Look, Jesse, some maternity wear for you!" She tossed him a withering look. "What? You'll have the latest fashion from Milan."

"It's pronounced MY-lin," said the twins in sing-song unison, without looking up from their work.

· · · • • • • · · ·

The afternoon sun was out in full force again when the three J's exited the shop twenty minutes later rocking their new resale duds, looking like a pack of seven-year-olds whose parents had let them dress themselves. Jack sported some plaid, madras shorts; a Redneck t-shirt that said "Guns, Girls, and Grits"; a Budweiser cap (an homage to Harville); and brown camo-print water shoes. Jennifer wore tapered Capri mom-jeans from the eighties with pink lace trim and embroidered flowers on the pockets, a fuzzy sweater covered in psychedelic cat appliqués, and red sequin-covered ballet flats because *there's no place like home...* Jesse was wearing that enormous floral muumuu along with a big, floppy, red and green sun hat that said "Christmas All Year Round." And Sean walked beside her in a spider dog-Halloween-costume. He was on an actual dog leash!

They headed next door for food, carrying their wet clothes in plastic bags that Audrey and Maudry had recycled from Cleghorn's Country Pantry & Appliance Repair.

"Chicken and waffles it is!" said Jennifer as she led the way in. "And Ms. Tiny Bladder can pee again. I'll call Enterprise about a replacement car."

Shecky's House of Chicken and Waffles was a very small diner with three empty booths, one booth where a trucker was eating solo, and a short counter where two additional customers were seated, buried in their cell phones. The walls were covered with license plates from every state, and colorful, corny bumper stickers that said things like *I Still Miss My "Ex" But My Aim Is Improving*, and *I Bet Jesus Would've Used HIS Turn Signals*, and *Keep Honking, I'm Reloading*. A five-cent gumball machine with a large, chipped Bozo the Clown head on top of it was perched at the end of the aging Formica counter. The gum inside of it looked as old and faded as Bozo.

A heavyset, middle-aged waitress wearing a name tag that said "Harriet" was behind the counter. She had a disturbing shade of flaming red hair that happened to be on special last week for fifty-nine cents at The Dollar Store. She called over to them as they entered. "Y'all sit anywhere you'd like! Menus are on the table."

Harriet was a lifelong resident of Milan and had watched both the population and economy of the town steadily decline over the years. She had worked for ten years at the peanut butter processing plant in town until an E. coli "mishap" had landed upper management in the federal pen. She had then tried her hand at a local Christian hand-embroidery service, but customers complained when her dyslexia caused her to sew "Dog is Doog" and "Save Jesus" on their shirts. Fortunately, the prior Shecky's waitress had been fired around that time. It was her third "just one tiny little instance" of check forgery, so Harriet landed the job, and due to her affable personality, she was a natural.

The three J's slid into one of the Naugahyde booths and perused their menus. The solo trucker was in the next booth down, his back to them.

"Order me some chicken and waffles with collard greens if I'm on the phone when she comes over," Jennifer instructed them. She pulled out her phone and called 411. "Hi. I need Enterprise Rent-A-Car, please.... A general number.... Thank you."

Harriet approached the table with a bowl of water for Sean and a pot of coffee for the humans. "Would y'all like coffee, iced tea, or something else to drink?"

Jennifer plugged her free ear with her finger. "Hi. I need to order a replacement car. The one we're in has broken down."

"Three coffees," answered Jesse. "And I'll also have scrambled eggs... and... alligator sausage."

"We rented it in Tallahassee, Florida," Jennifer continued, "but we're in Milan, Georgia right now."

"It's pronounced MY-lin," interjected Harriet while filling their coffee cups.

"Jennifer McMahon... Yes."

Harriet looked back at Jesse. "You want fried green tomatoes or sweet potato hash browns with that, darlin'?"

"Sweet potato hash browns, please."

"...Right now it's at Ernie's Auto Repair on Route 280," continued Jennifer.

"And for you, hon?" Harriet asked Jack.

"I'll have the red beans and rice with andouille sausage," he answered.

"What do you mean not until tomorrow or Tuesday?!" exclaimed Jennifer. "We're on a very tight deadline. We have to get to Savannah today!"

"And the angry woman on the phone," Jack continued, "is going to have chicken and waffles with a side of collard greens."

"...No, I'll call you back." Jennifer hung up with a sigh.

Harriet headed off to the kitchen to put in the orders, and Jack and Jesse turned their focus toward Jennifer.

"Well," she said, "we're totally screwed. The nearest Enterprises are in Dublin, Tifton, and Vidalia. However, the problem is that between some big Hillbilly Hog BBQ Throwdown this weekend, and the big Georgia Bulldogs vs. Auburn football game, there are no available replacement cars until tomorrow at the earliest. And maybe not until Tuesday."

"All dressed up and no place to go," lamented Redneck Jack.

"So what do we do?" Jesse asked.

The trucker in the next booth turned around and rested his hairy forearm on the back of his booth seat. His mullet spilled out from underneath his devastatingly stylish John Deere trucker cap. He was of completely ambiguous ethnic descent. If there was such a thing as a medium-skintone-with-freckles, part Black, part Asian, part Irish man with reddish hair, two different-colored eyes, and a southern accent... that would be him. A veritable human unicorn.

As an infant, he had been abandoned in an empty Granny Smith apple shipping crate behind a Piggly Wiggly in Tunica, Mississippi. He was discovered by a couple of migrant farmworkers who had just finished harvesting sweet potatoes in Vardaman and were in town looking for work in the Tunica peanut harvest. The childless couple saw this baby-in-an-apple-crate as a gift from God, the literal "fruit" of their labor, so to speak. They took the first letters of their names, Sosimo and Ysabel, and that's how Sy got his redneck name. The subsequent migrant lifestyle was where he developed his habit of constantly being on the move as an adult.

"Hey there," he said. "The name's Sy. Didn't mean to eavesdrop, but I couldn't help hearing that you're trying to get to Savannah."

"Trying being the keyword," said Jennifer.

"Well, folks, it's your lucky day. That happens to be where I'm headed, and there's room in my pickup truck. Double row of seats in the cab. I'll make a deal with you. As soon as yer done eatin', you buy me a case of Bud Light and a handle of Fireball, you cover the gas costs, and I'll drive you there."

The three of them looked at one another and shrugged.

"Might as well," said Jesse. "What have we got to lose?"

"Do you want me to answer that?" asked Jack.

"Not really," she said.

••••••••••

Back at Ernie's, Jesse and Jennifer stood next to the pile of their rapidly accumulating crap near the lift where their car was balanced in mid-air. Sean ran around in circles at Jesse's feet attempting to bite the spider legs that stuck out from the sides of his costume. Bonnie Raitt started in again with her depressing dirge announcing Sean. Jennifer took the phone out of her purse, dismissed the call again, and threw it back in while Jesse watched.

"Seriously, Jen, what's going on with you guys?"

She hesitated, still somewhat angry about the exchange in the tow truck, but then made the decision to surrender and open up about it. Dealing with it all alone had been eating her up inside, so she figured she might as well share it with her sister.

"I'm pretty sure he's cheating on me," Jen said softly.

"What? *Sean?* Mr. Boy Scout? No way. What makes you even think that?"

"He shuts his computer quickly every time I walk into his office. He's hiding something, Jesse. I know him too well. AND he told me to stay out here as long as I need to. AND he's been out late every night since I've been gone."

"But—"

"AND he's recently started wearing cologne. *Cologne*, Jesse!"

"Oh, shit."

"I confronted him about it, but he says it's all in my head. I honestly don't know what to do at this point," she said, her voice starting to break.

"I had no idea, Jen."

"It's why I didn't want to come on this trip."

"I'm so sorry. That fucker!"

Jack walked over to them, interrupting their conversation.

"Okay, they said they can keep it here until Enterprise picks it up tomorrow or Tuesday. And Enterprise authorized the repair cost, so we're good to go," he said.

Sy pulled his pickup truck into the small parking area adjacent to the auto repair shop. The truck bed was filled with a plethora of wonderful junk—antique furniture, a giant plastic Triceratops, 1950s lamps, a big neon beer sign, and more—all tied down with bungee cords.

Jesse looked at the load apprehensively. "Oh, yeah, plenty of room in there," she said.

"Your stuff will all fit in the back seat with Jack," Sy assured her.

"Why do *I* have to sit in the back?"

Sy grinned. "I'm not passing up the chance to ride with two pretty girls next to me. It's lonely on the road!" He turned to Jesse. "You climb on in first next to me, Joan Jett."

After a quick side glance at Jennifer, she said, "Hold on one second. I've gotta make a quick call first."

Jesse pulled out her phone and moved off to the side for privacy. When Jack opened the back seat of the cab to load their things, he was greeted by an enormous Bloodhound named Ronald Reagan that was sitting underneath Sy's gun rack.

"Okaaaay... This should be interesting," he muttered under his breath.

Jesse was on the phone speaking in hushed tones. "Hey, Tiny Tim, it's Jesse... Oh, shit, I totally spaced about the tattoo. I'm so sorry. I had a family emergency come up and had to leave town... At the moment, Georgia... Long story. I'll tell you all about it when I get back. But right now I need to ask you for a HUGE favor. I just found out my brother-in-law is cheating on my sister... No, they don't have a dog-walker. Listen, can you possibly pay him a visit tonight? Maybe take Spike and Mongo with you... No-no-no, do NOT actually hurt him! Seriously, Tiny, don't. I just need you all to tell him you're friends of mine, that I know he's been cheating on her, and then scare the shit out of him. Tell him you're going to be keeping a close eye on him for me from now on to make sure he does the right thing... Thanks, Tiny. You're the best. I owe you big time. I'll text you their address."

She walked back over to the group, finishing her text, then climbed into the front seat with Sean, followed by Jennifer. Sy took a big swig of Fireball, wiped his mouth on his sleeve, and screwed the cap back on. The front seat was cramped with three of them across, especially factoring in Sean's eight extra spider legs poking out in every direction.

"Why don't you put that pup in the back seat with Jack and Ronald Reagan?"

Ronald Reagan was sitting very close to Jack, staring, breathing, and drooling on him. Jack gingerly pushed Ronald's face away and said, "Sure, why not? There are a few extra inches of breathing room here..."

Jesse passed Spider-Sean back to Jack.

"Oh, and the liquor was forty-five dollars," Sy said to Jennifer.

She handed him some cash out of the Savannah envelope.

"Okey-dokey. Here we go!" he announced as he pulled back onto Route 280. "So where in Savannah are y'all headed?"

Jennifer pulled out the paperwork and read from it. "We are going to... The Worldwide Trading Emporium on Montgomery Street to meet with a woman named Charlene."

Sy guffawed. "Are you *shitting* me?? That's exactly where I'm headed! What kind of crazy odds are those??"

"I have no words..." said Jesse.

"Been selling the little treasures I find to Charlene for years now," he explained. After a minute of driving in silence, Sy asked, "Would y'all mind if I put the radio on?" Without waiting for an answer, he turned it on to a scratchy AM station playing Rush Limbaugh. "I love this guy! He always tells it like it is. No Fake News with him."

Jesse and Jennifer exchanged a horrified look. Jesse turned to Sy and smiled sweetly at him.

"How about some music instead, Sy? I just love listening to music on a long drive."

Sy grinned at her. "Anything for you, pretty lady."

He pulled a cassette tape out of an old, scuffed-up plastic case and popped it into the dashboard cassette player. It was a tape of old TV theme songs from the fifties through the eighties. The theme song from *The Partridge Family* filled the truck.

"Interesting choice, my man," said Jack from the dog boarding facility in the back seat.

"It keeps me pumped while I drive. Good memories," said Sy before launching into the song, completely offkey.

"Travelin' along, there's a song that we're singin',
come on get happy.
A whole lotta lovin' is what we'll be bringin',
we'll make you happy..."

Jennifer looked at Jesse and silently mouthed, "It's better than Rush Limbaugh."

Jesse mouthed back, "And Country music."

Sy stopped singing and put his arm around Jesse and squeezed her right shoulder. "So tell me, beautiful, you got a boyfriend?"

Before she could answer, Jack leaned forward between them and rested his chin and Sean's head on Sy's arm to interrupt. With the perkiness of a baby shower organizer, he said, "So, Jesse, you never did tell us if you've picked out names for the baby yet!"

Sy recoiled his arm quickly, like pregnancy could be contagious. "You're knocked up?"

"She *is!* She's got a little bun in the oven," explained Jack. "We're all so excited for her!"

"Well, bless your heart," said a disappointed Sy.

"...*Names?*" Jack persisted.

"Well," said Jesse, "to stay with the 'J' theme our beloved Dead-Mom started, if it's a girl I'm thinking either Jezebel, or Jurassic, or Jujube."

Sy looked at her warily.

"But if it's a boy," she continued, "I'm thinking Jesús. Or Wedge after Mom's favorite character on *As the World Turns*."

"With a silent 'J' at the beginning of Wedge?" asked Jennifer.

"Of course!" exclaimed Jesse.

"Nice," said Jack, as he and Sean slid back next to a long strand of Ronald Reagan's saliva.

Sy didn't know quite how to react. He opened the bottle of Fireball and took another big swig as the theme song from the 1950's show *I Married Joan* played in the background.

"I married Joan.
What a girl, what a whirl, what a life.
Ohhhh, I married Joan.
What a mind, love is blind, what a wife, ba da da da."

"You know," suggested Sy, "you could go with something like Joan…"

"Giddy and gay, all day she keeps my heart laughin'.
Never know where her brain has flown.
To each his own.
Can't deny that's why I married Joan."

· · · · · • • • · · ·

Twenty-two-point-four miles, one Bud Light, and a third of a bottle of Fireball later, they had just passed through Alamo and were approaching Glenwood. Jennifer was trying to concentrate on *anything* other than Sy's unfortunate singing. She was focused intently on the map on her phone. It was only 113.8 more miles to Savannah, though that wasn't much comfort to her considering that the relatively short drive from Milan had been the longest. Twenty-two-point-four-miles. Ever. Sy's driving had become more "freeform" in direct correlation to his impressive alcohol consumption, and his off-key singing was boring a hole through the temporal lobes in Jennifer's brain. Especially after he insisted on replaying the theme from *Bonanza* seven times in a row (for luck).

Jack rifled through a first aid kit that he found on the floor behind the driver's seat. You know, in case Sy rolled the truck and they needed a Band-Aid or two. Jesse dozed peacefully between Jennifer and Sy. She had fallen asleep almost immediately after leaving Milan.

The theme song from *The Courtship of Eddie's Father* ended and was followed by *Gilligan's Island*. Jennifer stared at Jesse resentfully, thinking, *God, I hate her sometimes. How can she sleep through this? Just like always, she sleeps and I'm wide-awake dealing with everything unpleasant. SO typical! Stop it, she's pregnant. Jesus, I'm a horrible person. No wonder Sean is cheating on me. No, wait, no, I'm not. They're the problem! I'm—*

Then the song switched and Sy attempted some ill-timed harmony.

> *"Come and knock on our door...*
> *We've been waiting for you...*
> *Where the kisses are hers and hers and his,*
> *Three's Company too."*

"OH MY GOD, JUST SHOOT ME ALREADY!" yelled Jennifer reflexively.

Sy stopped singing and looked over, Jack glanced up from his triage prep, and Jesse awoke with a start.

"What is it? What's happening?" she asked breathlessly.

Jennifer, embarrassed, replied, "It's nothing. I'm sorry, go back to sleep."

Jack leaned over the seat and said to Sy, "C'mon, friend, why don't you let me drive for a while?" It was the third time he had offered since Milan.

"You got some kind of problem with my driving?"

"No, no, I just, uh, I get a little car sick sitting in the back seat," he lied. "It helps me if I'm at the wheel."

"*I've* got a problem with your driving!" Jennifer exploded again. Her impulse control was completely shot. "You're weaving down the road like a drunken snake! I don't think you've stayed inside the yellow lines *at all* since we left Milan! AND you're driving seventeen miles over the speed limit!"

The truck was silent for a moment until Sy said, "Damn, you're uptight, woman."

"Tell me about it," Jesse mumbled.

"Shut up!" Jennifer snapped at Jesse.

"Good God," said Jack, "does *everything* with you two end up in an argument??"

"Yes!" the two female J's replied in unison.

Jennifer seethed. Jesse yawned. Ronald Reagan drooled on Jack. Before anyone had time to respond and further exacerbate the situation, Sy caught a glimpse of a rusted yellow and white Dodge pickup truck out of the corner of his eye. It was rapidly passing them across double yellow lines. The man and woman inside were canoodling dangerously in the front seat.

"That *bitch!* I *knew* it!" Sy yelled.

Four hundred yards ahead of them in no time, the pickup truck turned off Route 280 and onto 2nd Street in Glenwood, heading due south. Sy sped up, turned right, and followed them, burning considerable rubber as he went. His passengers all toppled left when he turned, chaotically shouting over one another.

"What are you doing? Slow down!"

"Where are you going? This isn't the way to Savannah!"

"I'm serious, Sy, stop the car and let me drive!"

"Are you kidnapping us?"

"I swear to God, Sy, I've got my finger on the 911 emergency button. I'm about to push it!"

"*Woof!*"

By the time they were speeding past the Glenwood Church of the Holy Mother on their left, the yellow and white pickup truck was disappearing from sight.

"Okay, they're gone now, we lost them, so slow down. You wanna tell us what all of this was about?" Jack asked.

"They're not gone," Sy answered, his foot still on the accelerator. "That was my lying, two-timing, soon-to-be-ex-wife and my ex-best-friend. I know exactly where they're going!"

"You're *married?*" asked Jesse incredulously.

Just before Preacher Ledbetter Road, Sy hung another rubber-burning, two-wheeled turn to the right onto a bumpy, dirt service road that followed Larry Creek. If it weren't for their seatbelts, they'd have hit the roof of the truck cab when they hit the bumps at that speed. It was fortunate for the dogs, who were launched into the air like popcorn, that Jack's reflexes were as quick as they were.

"Oh, my God, I think I'm gonna be sick," Jesse groaned.

"Don't you dare!" Jennifer yelled. "Put your head between your knees and breathe!"

Once Jack had maneuvered the dogs safely onto the floor at his feet, he reached around Sy's neck and put him into a rear naked choke, and said, "You've got a pregnant woman in here, Sy."

"I can't breathe—I can't breathe—" he gasped.

"Snap out of it and slow down," Jack continued rapidly, "or I'm going to choke you until you pass out. Jesse, be ready to grab the wheel if he does, so we don't go into the creek."

"No, seriously, I think I'm gonna be sick," Jesse repeated.

"Oh my God oh my God oh my God," whimpered Jennifer. "We're all gonna die... I should've taken Sean's calls..."

Sy put the brakes on and Jack released his hold. Sy then pulled into a dirt clearing next to a trailer where Shailene and Jimmy were unloading bags of groceries from Jimmy's pickup. Sy barely pulled the truck to a stop before flinging his door open, jumping out, and stumbling aggressively toward the grocery-toting lovebirds.

"I *knew* you were two-timing me!"

"Oh my God, what're you *following me*, you psycho?" yelled Shailene.

"You told me I was too jealous. That I was imagining things. But I was RIGHT!!"

"C'mon, Sy," said Jimmy, "you two aren't to—"

"And YOU," yelled Sy, cutting Jimmy off. "YOU were supposed to be my best friend!"

He lunged at Jimmy, knocking the bag of Minit Market groceries out of his arms and scattering them across the dirt.

"Now look what you've done!" yelled Jimmy. "You owe me $1.69 for those eggs, you fucker!"

"Yeah? Well, you owe me a WIFE! And a heart that's not broken!"

"He should write for soap operas," said Jesse from the safety of the pickup where the three J's were watching the melodrama unfold.

Sy lunged at Jimmy again, grabbed his shirt, and they toppled to the ground, rolling around and swinging wildly at each other in a cloud of dirt. Like two cartoon characters.

Shailene dropped her bag of groceries and ran over, screaming, "Get offa him, Sy!"

She grabbed Sy's leg to pull him away from Jimmy, but only managed to pull off one of his shoes.

"This is ridiculous," said Jen. "We need to do something before someone gets hurt."

"On my way," said Jack.

He jumped out of the truck and rushed over to separate the men, Jesse and Jennifer not far behind. The three of them in their re-sale duds looked like clowns emerging from a car.

Once the mullet twins were on their feet again, with Jack in between them, Sy turned on Shailene and yelled, "And you owe me the money I paid for your haircutting classes. I even let you practice on me!"

Jesse mumbled to Jennifer, "That was his first mistake..."

But Shailene heard her. "And who are *these* hoes?"

"Excuse me?" said Glenview-Jennifer, taking offense. After all, she was wearing very modest, lace-trimmed mom-jeans and a cat applique sweater...

Shailene swung back around to face Sy. "I think maybe *you* been the one two-timin' on *me!*"

Jesse couldn't help herself (of course). "That's right. I'm pregnant with Sy's baby."

"Stop it! Don't make things worse!" implored Jennifer.

Jack interrupted, "Let's all just take a deep breath here and calm down."

He bent down to help collect Jimmy's groceries from the ground; and Jesse bent down to investigate a box of "red-flavored," powdered-sugar-coated dessert cakes called "Hearty Har-Hars" from Shailene's scattered groceries.

Shailene disappeared into the trailer and Sy ran toward his pickup truck. She immediately re-emerged from the trailer with a pair of Purple Dragon haircutting scissors raised over her head. She was headed straight for Jesse who was sampling one of the irresistible, red-flavored treats.

"GIT'CHER HANDS OFF MY HAR-HARS, YOU HO!"

As she ran straight past Jen, sights set squarely on Sy's baby mama, Jen reached out and shoved her, sending Shailene flying. She hit the ground and began to crawl toward her scissors, but Jennifer reached them first. In the midst of the Har-Har-Scissors-Drama, no one noticed that Sy had retrieved his shotgun from his pickup truck. It wasn't until the first shot rang out that everyone froze in place. He had shot out one of the brand-new tires on Jimmy's truck.

"Oh, shit," said Jesse.

"Okay, Sy? Look over here at me," said Jack, extremely calmly. "Put the gun down and step away from it. I don't want you making things any worse for yourself than they already are. We'll figure this out."

But Sy didn't seem to hear him. *Cock*. BANG! He shot another tire. That's when Jack lunged for the gun and disarmed Sy, causing him to fall to the ground.

"Stand up, Sy. Jesse and Jen, get in the truck. Now!"

Jennifer ran to the truck. Jesse bent down first and grabbed the box of Har-Hars before catching up with Jen.

"HEY! GIMME BACK MY HAR-HARS!" screamed Shailene.

"Shut up, Shailene. We'll get more Har-Hars ferchrissakes," said Jimmy.

"Don't you tell me to shut up! *You* shut up!"

Over her shoulder, Jesse said with a big grin, "Yeah, okay, thanks for the Har-Hars!" She waved at Shailene, then added, "And don't run with scissors!"

Jennifer shoved Jesse into the front seat, dove in after her, and locked the door.

Jack said to the lovebirds, "You two get inside the trailer. You can get your groceries once we're gone. Sy, I told you to stand up! And get in the truck. The back seat. You are officially relieved of your driving duties."

Sy stood up, walked to the truck, and reluctantly climbed in next to the dogs. Jack made sure there was no ammo in the gun before placing it on the floor at his feet.

"Holy shit, what just happened?" said Jesse quietly.

That's the last any of them spoke for a while, as the theme from *The Twilight Zone* played, and Jack backtracked his way to Route 280. Sy wiped his runny nose on his shirt and then promptly fell asleep, emotionally drained. They all were.

· · · · • • • • · · ·

Sy's truck, with Jack at the wheel and Sy still passed out in the back with the dogs, pulled into the No Parking zone in front of the Worldwide Trading Emporium on Montgomery Street in Savannah. They'd made it. Jack shut off the engine and reached into the back seat.

"Look alive, Sy. We're here," he said with a firm nudge.

The three J's piled out slowly. They were dazed from hours of mind-numbing TV theme songs, too many Har-Hars, and a narrowly averted kidnapping by a shotgun-wielding, alcoholic redneck. You know, your usual pleasant Sunday drive in the Deep South. Sy stumbled out after them. Jack scooped up Spider-Sean and handed him to Jesse.

"Here you go," he said. Three of Sean's spider legs had been chewed open and white stuffing was hanging from them. "Why don't y'all go inside and find Charlene. I'll help Sy unload some of the heavier things."

Jennifer handed Sy another small wad of cash and said, "This is for the gas."

Sy took the money and attempted to move in for a still-tipsy kiss. She juked to the left and pointed at him like she was playing.

"Oh! You be good now, you... crazy man," she said, quickly moving away and following Jesse inside as the guys went to unload the truck.

The Worldwide Trading Emporium was magical in the way that your grandmother's attic was magical to you when you were a kid. It was filled with cool old treasures, and whimsical junk that inspired flights of mental fantasy... There was a typewriter from the thirties, a TV/stereo console from the fifties, old collectible lunchboxes, a giant lamp with Hungarian folk dancers at the base, a pair of life-sized golden antelopes, Parisian cabinets from the 1800s, a life-sized cardboard David Hasselhoff, antique costume jewelry, and a fifteen-foot fiberglass hippopotamus... Now the items filling Sy's truck-bed made sense. They moved through the aisles slowly, taking it all in as they made their way to a large mahogany desk in the middle of the store where they found seventy-year-old Charlene busy with bookkeeping.

As far back as she could remember, Charlene had referred to herself as a "collector of strays." As a child, it began with stray animals. Because she was the youngest of seven children, the parental supervision was a bit more, shall we say, *lax* by that point. So her family didn't always notice the new additions until they were firmly ensconced in their new digs, namely Charlene's basement bedroom.

By the time she was older and moved into her own place, she had expanded her family's size over the years by a total of seven feral cats, a three-legged pig she found wandering behind the elementary school, a blind guinea pig that was probably brain-damaged from running into walls, and four dogs. They didn't count the fifth dog because, as it turned out, it was actually a baby coyote who didn't take kindly to young Charlene's attempt to dress it in rain boots. He bit her, took off out the back door into a thunderstorm, and is probably, to this day, wandering the outskirts of Savannah proper wearing three booties made of Saran Wrap and duct tape.

Her strays eventually morphed from animals to humans, most notably her ex-husband Tom. She had met him while waiting in line at *The Corn Dog, Cheese Fries, and Krispy Kreme Donut Burger Stand* on the opening night of the Coastal Empire Fair. He proceeded to tell her his sad-sack story about losing his apartment after his roommate skipped out with the rent money. The next thing she knew, she had offered him her couch. Fast forward two years, and it was Tom skipping out this time, abandoning his wife Charlene in search of the next woman's couch. *Oh, well, easy come easy go*, she thought. *Once a Tomcat, always a Tomcat.*

She turned her focus to collecting strays of the inanimate variety—antique furniture and discarded pop culture items for her family's store. Charlene looked up from her work and her eyes lit up, recognizing them right away.

"I'd know you girls anywhere. Welcome!" She hugged them both. "Isn't your brother with you?"

Before they could answer, Jack walked up extending his hand. "He is! I'm Jack."

"Oh, you put that hand away and give me a proper hug, you!"

"As soon as I finish getting my hug," he said putting his arms around her, "Sy wants you to come out and take a look at what he brought you. He's having a beer in the meantime."

"Shocker," mumbled Jesse.

"Okay, let me go out and deal with him real quick if y'all don't mind. There's a bathroom in the back past the pinball machine if you need it. And here's a plate of snacks if you're hungry. Plenty of chairs to relax in. I'll be right back."

Jesse started heading to the bathroom when Jack stopped her.

"I'll watch Sean for you while you're in there if you want," he offered.

He'd been growing quite attached to Sean over the past few days. Jack walked off holding Sean, kissing him, and thinking he was talking quietly.

"Mwah! I love you. Yes, I do. Yes, I do. Mwah!"

But Jesse heard him and smiled.

Jack and Jennifer sat down in the skewed arrangement of mismatched, mid-century living room chairs, and they helped themselves to the butterscotch oatmeal cookies, Rice Krispy treats, and peanut butter with Bac-O-Bits on toast that Charlene had left for them. When Charlene came back inside, she joined them in the chairs.

"Oh, it's so good to meet you!" She smiled sympathetically at the weary travelers. "Y'all look positively beat."

"Oh, you have no idea... It's been a long roller coaster of a week," admitted Jennifer.

Charlene held out the tray of food to Jesse as she rejoined them. "Would you like some PB&B-o-B on toast?"

"I have no idea what you just said, but... don't mind if I do!" said Jesse taking the entire tray, setting it in her lap, and chowing down.

"Are we staying here?" Jennifer asked. "Did you bring our stuff inside, Jack?"

He gave her a thumbs-up.

"No, not here," said Charlene. "You'll be staying at a sweet little bed and breakfast nearby on Pulaski Square. It's owned by an old friend of your mother's and mine named Westley. I'll lock up for a few minutes and drive you there, but I have a little info for you before we head over and get you settled. A quick story about why you came here to this store first."

· · · · • • • · · ·

<u>1979</u>

Thirty-two-year-old Charlene unlocked the padlock on the front door of The Worldwide Trading Emporium and glanced over at nineteen-year-old Angie, seated on the ground with her back against the storefront next door. Angie was wailing on her harmonica. A few early morning passersby seemed oblivious to the young woman sitting on the sidewalk playing her heart out. Charlene strolled over and put a dollar into her tip cup. Angie nodded her thanks as she continued to play. Charlene went into the store and then almost immediately came back out and walked back over to Angie who stopped playing this time.

"I haven't seen you around here before," said Charlene.

"Yeah, I just got into town yesterday," said Angie.

"Where're you stayin', honey? You got family in town?"

"No. This is just how far my ride could take me," said Angie. "I don't have a place to stay yet."

Charlene didn't immediately respond, so Angie went back to her song, Slim Harpo's "I'm a King Bee." Charlene stood there watching her, concerned.

"Have you eaten, hon?" she asked.

Angie shook her head no. Charlene frowned, contemplating what to do.

"You know," she continued, "I could use some help in the store today. Why don't you come on inside with me? We can get you something to eat, and you can make a little money today helping me out. More'n it looks like you're making out here," she added, motioning to Angie's virtually empty tip cup. "Would you be interested?"

"Yes, thank you!" said Angie, scrambling to her feet at the prospect of some food. She quickly put her harmonica away, grabbed her cup, pocketed the dollar bill, and followed Charlene inside.

"What's your name, honey?"

"Angie."

"I'm Charlene, but you can call me Char."

•••••••••

"She worked for me that day, and I let her stay here that night because I didn't want her sleeping on a park bench somewhere."

"You let a homeless nineteen-year-old that you just met stay here overnight with all of your things?" asked Jennifer. "You weren't afraid she might rob you?"

Charlene smiled. "I had a good feeling about her. I'm usually not wrong about people. My ex-husband notwithstanding."

Jack turned to his sisters. "It's called Southern Hospitality. Y'all probably don't know much about that up yonder in Yankee country," teased Jack.

"Yeah," said Jesse. "That's the sense we got about you right away when we first met you. Mr. Southern Hospitality."

Jack laughed.

"Well, she didn't rob me," Charlene continued. "And she stayed on here the next day, and then the next, and then the next. She was very good with the customers—everyone liked her. She was smart and very funny. But she also carried a deep sadness in her that she wouldn't talk about. I tried to get her to, but..." Charlene shrugged and shook her head. "I didn't even know she had children until about five years ago when she found out she had cancer. I encouraged her to reach out to you, but she said she was sure you wouldn't want anything to do with her."

"Well, that's pretty accurate," Jack conceded.

"Honestly, if I had known sooner, I probably would've reached out to you myself. There's always a way to right the wrongs in your past. Unless you wait until it's too late, that is."

"Aaaand flash-forward to right now. 'Too late,'" said Jesse, her bitterness creeping back in.

"So how long did she work here?" asked Jennifer.

"For the next thirty years, even after she got married, until she found out she had cancer and left the store. I felt like I lost my best friend when she stopped working here."

"Did you lose touch with her when she left?" asked Jennifer.

"Oh, goodness, no. We still talked most days, at least touching base by phone. But you know how it is when you're used to someone being part of your daily life for so long."

"No," said Jesse. "I don't know how that is."

Charlene smiled gently at her. "Why don't we get you to Westley's place so you can get settled and get some rest."

SUNDAY EVENING

The Crepe Myrtle Bed & Breakfast was a beautiful townhouse, hundreds of years old. The last of the pink and lavender summer blooms on the large crepe myrtle trees out front had recently given way to splashy autumn foliage. Jennifer, Jack, and Jesse stood on the front porch at the top of a flight of steps as the doorbell played an instrumental version of "Georgia" by Ray Charles.

Westley, a handsome, elegantly dressed Black man in his sixties, opened the ornate wooden front door. Charlene tooted her horn from the curb where she was idling, exchanged a wave with Westley, and headed back to the store.

"Come in! Come in! Welcome! I'm Westley Barnes," he greeted them warmly.

They entered, set down their belongings, and introduced themselves.

Westley glanced at Sean and said, "I didn't know you'd be bringing a little friend. I'll put you in the Live Oak room. No rugs to pee on in that one!"

"Don't worry," said Jack, "Jesse's housebroken."

"Barely..." added Jennifer.

Westley winked at Jesse. "It's the door at the end of the hallway there, on your left. You'll be in the Magnolia Room, Jennifer; and, Jack, you'll be in the Palmetto Room. Those are both upstairs. I'll show you to your rooms, and then we can all meet back down here in the parlor and I'll tell you over some sweet tea what the agenda for the evening is."

"It's not bed?" asked Jesse with an exhausted sigh.

"Eventually," Westley assured her.

・・・●・●・●・・・

The parlor was impeccably decorated in warm hues of red, gold, and brown. Jesse wandered around the room looking at the old photos and framed historic maps of Savannah that were on display. She sipped from a tall glass of sweet tea with mint leaves and munched on one of the Brown Sugar & Corn Meal Cookies with Peach Jam and Chopped Pecans that Westley had prepared for them that morning.

Westley, Jack, and Jennifer descended the creaking staircase and joined Jesse in the parlor. Westley handed the two of them glasses of iced tea, held out the plate of cookies for them, and the three siblings sat down.

"I know you must be exhausted, but I'm hoping the tea and cookies will give you enough of a caffeine and sugar boost to keep you going for another two hours."

He continued talking as he headed to the kitchen to retrieve their dinner, while Jesse picked Sean up and put him on her lap.

"I'm taking y'all on a little adventure," he called out from the other room.

Jennifer mouthed with fake excitement, "An adventure!"

Sean climbed out of Jesse's lap and over onto Jack's.

"Oh, fine. I see how it is," she said to Sean.

Westley re-entered with five boxes of food that said Zunzi's on the side. "Best sandwiches in Savannah! We're going on a traveling picnic. There's a young couple, just got married, staying here tonight too, so they're going to join us. I hope you don't mind."

Duke and Ivy Parker had met at the Monster Truck Destruction Tour in Lubbock, Texas a mere two weeks ago. Christian Rock radio station KZOL was having their annual Monster Truck ticket giveaway to the first two callers who could answer these two questions correctly:

1) What former WrestleMania star has driven a Monster Truck in a movie and has also founded a church? (answer: Dwayne "The Rock" Johnson); and,

2) According to Wikipedia, what Christian Grindcore band has said that their band name was inspired by Revelations 3:15-16? (answer: Vomitorial Corpulence)

Complete strangers, Duke and Ivy had been the first two correct callers, at number fourteen and number thirty-one, respectively. When they both showed up at the Monster Truck event wearing the same vintage edition Bigfoot Monster Truck t-shirt, they were convinced that it was The Lord that had guided them to each other in Section 104 Row 25 Seats 16 and 17. They knew it was literally "a match made in Heaven," and so they eloped.

Right on cue, Ivy and Duke, an excruciatingly gung-ho couple in their early twenties dressed in color-coordinated NASCAR gear, entered, holding hands.

"Oh," said Westley, "here they are now. Your ears must've been burning, kids."

The seated group stood up and Westley introduced them all.

"Westley just told us you're newlyweds," said Jennifer. "Congratulations."

"Thank yooooouu!" said Ivy in a high-pitched squeal that sent all the dogs in the neighborhood to DEFCON 3.

She turned to Duke and they did the little signature kiss they had created while on their second date at the local Wienerschnitzel after Duke's shift there had ended. (They were taking advantage of the special 2-for-1 employee discount on the Blazin' Bacon and Mayo Pork Schnitzel Footlongs). They cradled each other's face, kissed three times quickly with sound effects "Mwah!Mwah!Mwah!" and then he pinched and shook her nose, making them both giggle.

Duke said, "I'm taking the ol' ball and chain on a—"

"Oh, you stop that, you silly!" Ivy swatted him and they both giggled again.

"Oh, let's *all* stop it!" said Jesse in her most uber-bubbly voice.

"Stop it," Jennifer silently mouthed to Jesse. Then she asked, "Where are you taking her, Duke?"

"On a NASCAR / Monster Truck / WrestleMania / Ghost Tours honeymoon!"

Ivy squealed again and clapped her hands.

"God Bless 'Merica." Jack grinned.

"God Bless America!" they echoed, without a trace of irony. Which, of course, sent them into an encore of their ridiculous signature kiss.

"No more caffeine for you, little lady!" said Jennifer, only half teasing.

Westley said to Jesse, "You'll need to leave the puppy here," he said. "You can just close him in your room. We won't be gone too long."

Jesse picked Sean up from Jack's lap where he was sound asleep and carried him to her room as everyone else stood up and headed out the front door. It was getting dark by this point. Westley gathered the group around a renovated hearse parked across the street.

"Wooo! This is AWESOME!" yelled Duke, pumping his fists into the air.

Westley was passing out the Zunzi's sandwich boxes when Jesse ran up. "What the hell? Is this yours?" she asked.

"No, it's not mine. Though I worked for this company for about ten years before I opened the bed and breakfast. The owner's still a friend of mine, and he let me borrow it tonight." He winked at them. "Special occasion."

Westley pulled out a small step ladder, set it up directly behind the hearse, and helped everyone climb into the back. The rear of the hearse where the coffins were originally transported had been renovated into an open-air, raised platform with a hardtop black roof raised up on support poles over the seats. Westley climbed into the driver's seat, pulled the retooled hearse away from the curb, and they were off! With the siblings still in their resale duds, the perky peppy Parkers in their matching NASCAR suits, and Ivy continuing to squeal and clap, it

THE KEY TO CIRCUS-MOM HIGHWAY 207

looked like the inmates at the asylum were going on a field trip.

They all dug into their food boxes, trading sandwiches, as Westley turned on a mike in the front seat to start the ghost tour spiel. He drove them around Savannah, stopping at the well-known "haunted" spots, regaling them over the mike with tales of war, yellow fever epidemics, accidental deaths, murders, insanity, and other fun honeymoon stories.

The rather uncomfortable, hard, plastic seats in the back had been mounted onto heavy-duty metal springs so that every time the hearse would stop and start, it punctuated the stories with a *boing!* and intensified the experience by inducing mild nausea. Always a great addition while you're eating South African Sausage on French Bread with Gravy, Red Onions, and Mustard.

"I don't even know what's happening anymore," said a weary Jennifer.

"It's like a week-long episode of *The Twilight Zone*," said Jesse.

"Right?" agreed Jack. "Where's Sy's TV theme song tape when you need it?"

•••••••••

Meanwhile, back in Illinois...

Sean (the human) walked into the foyer with a small carry-on suitcase and his computer bag. He was talking on his Bluetooth headset again. "She's in Savannah now... No, there's no way she knows... Because she *definitely* would've said something." He set his bags down next to the front door. "Are you all packed? Because I'll be swinging by to pick you up in just a few minutes... Okay, good. I'll see you soon... I love you too."

He ended the call and opened the hallway coat closet to grab a jacket for his secret rendezvous. He slipped it on and was picking up his bags when the doorbell rang. He couldn't imagine who it would be. He opened the door, suitcase in hand, and found himself staring at three immense, tatted-up bikers.

"Can I... can I help you?" asked Sean, a little weak in the knees. He immediately regretted not looking through the peephole before opening the door.

Tiny Tim, Spike, and Mongo looked down at the weekend bag in his hand.

"Going somewhere?..." asked Tiny Tim ominously.

"What do you want?" Sean was trying to figure out an escape route if needed, and wondering if his neighbors would hear him if he yelled.

"We have a message for you from Jesse, you little shit."

• • • • • • • • •

The hearse finally pulled up to the closed gate at the Bonaventure Cemetery and Westley shut off the engine. He got out of the hearse, walked around back, and pulled out the stepladder for his passengers to disembark.

"This is our last stop," he said. "We're actually going to get out and walk."

"Looks closed," said Ivy as Westley helped her climb down.

A pale, lanky, Ichabod Crane-ish cemetery worker stepped out from behind the wall at the gate. He had a flashlight shining under his chin for effect, and a shovel in the other hand. Ivy screamed (of course) and grabbed Duke's arm. Jack slowly leaned in between them from behind.

"Shhhh. We don't want to wake the dead..." he whispered.

He withdrew his head and Duke pulled Ivy in close.

"Come in... if you dare!" the cemetery worker warbled.

Jesse rolled her eyes. *At least it's the right October holiday,* she thought. Ichabod unlocked the gate and pushed it open, allowing the rag-tag group of asylum mates to enter.

"You have thirty minutes," he whispered to Westley who entered last, "then I have to get you out of here. I don't want to get fired."

"Thanks, Jimbo," said Westley, slipping him some cash.

Westley took them on a very abbreviated walk through the beautiful old cemetery as he narrated.

"This is Gaston's Tomb... graveyard for the elite citizens of Savannah... John Muir's book *A Thousand Mile Walk*... Gracie, a six-year-old girl who... singer/songwriter Johnny Mercer who was also the founder of Capitol Records..."

He eventually brought them to a stop in front of an ornate, weather-worn tomb.

"We need to head back now, I don't want to get my friend Jim in trouble, but I wanted to show you this one last grave."

"This must be hers!" Jennifer whispered to Jesse with anticipation.

"This is the grave of Thomas Caldare and his parents, Missy and Guyton."

The sisters exchanged a confused look.

"Wait. We're not seeing our mom's grave?" Jesse said to Westley.

"No, she's not buried here." He continued on with his story. "Guyton and Missy were from two of the oldest families in Savannah. In fact, Missy's relatives can be traced all the way back to General James Oglethorpe. He was one of the founders of Savannah who arrived on the galley ship *Anne* in 1733. I wanted to show you this..." He turned to the three siblings. "Because Tommy was a very dear friend of your mother's."

"Ohhhh," said Ivy.

Westley magically produced a single red rose from an inside pocket of his jacket and laid it gently in front of the tomb.

"And of mine. Soon he'll be important to you too."

He walked away softly down the path, back toward the entrance of the cemetery. The others followed in silence, accompanied by the song of the crickets, the call and response of two Great Horned owls, and the scraping of the oak tree branches in the breeze. It was a beautiful tableau of the cemetery at night with the silhouettes of giant oaks and dogwoods dripping with Spanish Moss set against the moon-drenched sky.

・・・●●●●●・・・

Back at the Crepe Myrtle Bed & Breakfast, Jesse, Jennifer, and Jack stood in a huddle in the foyer, conferring.

"Guys," said Jesse, "I'm sorry but I HAVE to go to sleep. I don't know what's wrong with me."

"First trimester of pregnancy, that's what," said Jennifer. "I remember practically falling asleep every time I sat down."

"Well, I'm beat too," Jack agreed. "Though I'm pretty sure I'm not pregnant. At least the last time I checked."

"Famous last words, *Jackie, Oh!*" said Jesse with a yawn.

"But I do think we ought to press on and hear the rest of the story tonight," he added. "Our time is basically up with this week-long deadline, and we don't know how much is left for us to do."

Westley entered the room and interrupted their discussion.

"So what's the verdict?" he asked. "Do you want to hear the rest tonight, or in the morning?"

In unison, Jesse and Jennifer said, "Morning," while Jack said, "Tonight."

Westley chuckled. "Looks like you're outvoted, Jack. Tomorrow it is." Jack sighed. "Breakfast is anytime between eight and ten. In the meantime, just knock on my door tonight if you need anything else."

"Okay, thanks," said Jack.

"Sweet dreams," said Westley as he turned to go up to his room.

Jennifer followed him up the stairs. Jack climbed a few stairs then paused and went back down. He caught up to Jesse in the hallway outside her room, about to take Sean for a quick trip outside.

"Hey, I was just wondering... Do you think Sean could sleep with me tonight?" asked Jack.

Jesse grinned. "Aww, look at you all warm and fuzzy."

He gave her a playful shove. "I am not," he said in the most ultra-deep, masculine voice he could muster.

Jesse said, "Yeah, he can sleep with you."

· · · · · · · · ·

Jesse was awakened in the middle of the night by the sound of a dog frantically barking. She quickly glanced at the clock on the bedside nightstand and saw that it was 3:31 a.m. She dragged herself out of bed, threw on her floral muumuu, and went out into the hallway to see what the ruckus was about. Sean was frantically pacing and barking at the front door.

"Oh, my God, I don't think I've ever heard you bark like this before. What's the matter, baby?"

She went over to him with the intent of picking him up, but he dodged her hands when she bent down and reached out. He continued barking at the door. Jennifer came down the top few stairs from the second floor.

"What's going on? Is everything okay?" she asked.

"Yeah, I think maybe he just needs to go outside to pee. Go back to bed, I've got it under control. Sorry he woke you."

Jennifer headed back up to her room.

Jesse looked at Sean and said, "Okay, okay, baby, hush! We're going outside!"

Worried he was going to wake the entire house, she didn't bother going back for his leash. She opened the door, a bit surprised it wasn't locked. She could've sworn she remembered Westley locking it when they got home. She was planning on a quick trip down the front steps to the grassy area at the curb, but as soon as she opened the door, Sean took off down the steps and ran across the street. Jesse took off after him in the light, pattering raindrops that were just beginning to fall.

"Sean! No! Come here!"

But he didn't listen. He ran into the center of Pulaski Square, Jesse running after him in her bare feet, calling his name.

"Goddamn it, Sean! Come!"

He stopped, turned around, and barked at her. Just as she had almost caught up to him, he turned again and ran to the far corner before he came to a stop, barking madly at a tree.

"What the hell has gotten into you??"

When she caught up to him again, she saw that on the other side of the enormous Live Oak was Jack, standing with his back against the tree. He was awake now, looking confused, not quite sure where he was. Sean's barking—a "loud noise from a distance"—had woken him up. He slid down the tree into a sitting position leaning against the trunk, knees bent, his elbows resting on his knees, his hands clasped.

"Oh, my God. Jack. Are you okay?"

"Yeah.... What happened this time?"

"Honestly, I have no idea," she answered, sitting down next to him. "I didn't even know you were gone. This little one woke me up, barking like a madman at the front door, otherwise, you'd still be out here wandering around in the dark by yourself."

"Oh, thank you, little buddy."

Sean nuzzled Jack's leg.

"You sure you're okay?" she asked again.

"Yeah, I guess," he said, staring at the ground in front of his feet.

"We should probably head back then... You need to run any errands while we're out?" she said, trying to lighten the moment. She could see in his expressionless face the toll that his nighttime wandering was taking on him.

He smiled wanly. "Nah, I think I'm good."

But they made no move to stand up.

"I don't know what to do about this anymore," he continued. "It's exhausting."

He leaned forward and rested his forehead on his clasped hands. She watched him for a moment, wishing she knew how to help him. She put her arm around his hunched shoulders and leaned her head against him. They sat there together, in the silent camaraderie of two people who understood being chased by demons from the past. The umbrella of the giant tree sheltered them from the rain that fell softly on the surrounding streets in the glow of the antique street lamps.

DAY SEVEN

*"When the day becomes the night
and the sky becomes the sea,
when the clock strikes heavy
and there's no time for tea;
and in our darkest hour,
before my final rhyme,
she will come back home to Wonderland
and turn back the hands of time."*
– The Cheshire Cat,
Alice's Adventures in Wonderland

Monday Morning

The bright morning sunlight streamed through the stained-glass windows of the Crepe Myrtle dining room, bathing everything in rich, kaleidoscopic color. Jennifer, back in her original outfit, sat at the table by herself working on the last of her hot griddle cakes. Westley cleared the plates left by Ivy and Duke who had already finished and checked out. They were off to Macon, Georgia to watch men with shaved chests and Lycra spandex pants fling each other through the air and sweat on each other in the manliest of ways. God Bless America!

"Should we wake them? It's getting late. It's after ten o'clock," asked Westley.

"No, let's—"

Jack entered the dining room, also back in his own set of clothes.

"Well, speak of the devil," said Jennifer.

"And the devil appears!" said Jesse, entering on cue, looking bright-eyed and bushy-tailed (relatively speaking).

"Good morning! I hope you both slept well," said Westley.

Jack and Jesse shared an understanding look with one another.

"Have a seat," Westley instructed them as he carried the remainder of the Parkers' empty plates to the kitchen. "I'll bring you two your breakfast."

"Look!" Jesse grinned, indicating her clean clothes. "The Laundry Fairy came last night."

"For me too. I feel so pretty!" said Jack, twirling.

Jesse laughed, sat next to Jennifer, and leaned over to give her an unexpected peck on the cheek. Jack seated himself at the long table across from them.

"I'm assuming this was you?" Jesse asked Jennifer.

Jennifer shrugged it off. "Habit."

They thanked her as Westley re-entered with two plates piled high with fluffy omelets, corned beef hash, grits with homemade peach jam, and griddle cakes.

"Wow!" exclaimed Jesse at the sight of the approaching feast.

"Now that's what I call breakfast," said Jack.

"More griddle cakes, Jennifer?" asked Westley.

"No, I'm good, thanks. It was delicious. I wouldn't turn down a little more of that chicory coffee though."

He grabbed a heated carafe from a side table and set it down in front of her. "Plenty in here. Help yourselves." He sat down at the head of the table between Jack and Jennifer. "I'm usually not one for business over a meal," he continued, "but we do have somewhere important to go today, and there's a little more to the story about Thomas Caldare that we didn't get to last night.

"Tommy met your mom because he spent a lot of time at The Worldwide Trading Emporium. He loved to shop there. He liked to furnish his house with an eclectic mix of antiques and quirky pop culture items. Partly, I think it was in rebellion against his family. They had more money than God; and they were fine with expensive, traditional, Savannah antiques, but they hated what they called his 'ridiculous, used junk' purchases. So he did it to get under their skin."

"Why was that?" asked Jack.

"Well... They were a very prominent, ultra-conservative family, very active in their church, and Tommy was gay. That was absolutely NOT acceptable to his parents. He tried to come out to them once when he was in his early thirties, but they refused to acknowledge it. They told him that if he ever pursued that lifestyle, or even spoke of it again, he would be disowned and cut out of the family estate. And, to be honest, he liked having money. He was very accustomed to that lifestyle."

"That's ridiculous. Wasn't this in the seventies? Weren't people more accepting by that time?" asked Jesse.

"Not down here they weren't. At least not the older generation."

"So how exactly does our mom fit into all of this?" asked Jennifer.

"There was a lot of pressure on him, being an only child, to find a nice girl and get married. Even though Tommy was about twenty-five years older than Angie, they had become very dear friends. She had some trust issues with men, as I'm sure you understand now, but Tommy was exceptionally kind and non-threatening, so he felt safe to her. She appreciated his presence in her life. She knew that he was gay, and it angered her the way his family had treated him and that he wasn't able to be with the man he was in love with, so she proposed a plan. Your mom offered to marry him, just for appearances, so his family would be satisfied and get off his back, and then he could be together with his lover."

"Wait, hold on. He was in his early fifties and was still getting pressure from his parents to marry?" asked Jennifer. "You'd think they would've come to terms with him being a confirmed bachelor by then."

"You'd think," Westley replied. "But his parents actually got worse the older he and they got. They were constantly badgering him about it, telling him they wanted to see him married before they died. The only thing Angie asked for in return was that in Tommy's will he would leave her some money."

"Let me guess. So he added her to the will, then she murdered him and buried him in Bonaventure Cemetery," Jesse posited with a smirk.

Westley smiled patiently at her. "No. She asked for the money so that she would have something to leave her children someday. She said she wanted to be able to do something good for them at the end of her life since she wasn't there for them at the start."

The three J's sat there, taking all of that in.

·········

<u>1986</u>

Twenty-six-year-old Angie stood facing fifty-one-year-old Tommy in front of the priest at Christ Church Episcopal, "The Mother Church of Georgia."

Jesus was towering over them from the giant stained-glass Ascension Window behind the pulpit. It was the oldest house of worship in Savannah, established in 1733. The original site had been set aside for the colony's first church by General James Oglethorpe, Missy's great-great-great-great-something-or-other.

The church was filled with lavish bouquets of flowers. Cascading waterfalls of white lilies, white freesia, blush camellias, and peach roses adorned the end of every pew, lining the aisle. Elaborate arrangements of white lilies, white and blush ranunculus, freesia, peach roses, and stephanotis were stationed on either side of the pulpit.

A large crowd was assembled for the ceremony, just as you would expect for one of the most prominent families in town. The crowd was so large, in fact, that the spillover from the groom's side of the church filled the bride's side as well, much to Angie's relief since she had been rather short on family names for the guest list. As in zero. The pews on the ground level as well as the pews in both balconies were filled to capacity.

Angie's Maid of Honor, Westley, and her one other bridesmaid, Charlene, stood behind her dressed in, what else, Georgia peach. Tommy's closest friends since childhood, Lyman Theus Jr. and Brantly Upshaw, stood behind him. Missy and Guyton Caldare watched happily (and with more than a small measure of relief) from the front pew. They were blissfully unaware of Angie's three teenaged pregnancies out of wedlock, two the result of rape, three abandoned children, and her short stint as a traveling circus performer. *But hey,* Angie had rationalized, *who doesn't have a skeleton or two in their closet?*

The Caldares' initial concern about Angie's troubling lack of family pedigree, and her disturbingly unorthodox choice for her Maid of Honor, were forgiven due to the fact that Angie was small enough to fit in the heirloom wedding dress that had been passed down in Missy's family for generations. They were also thrilled that she was finally making an honest man out of their son who had been "momentarily confused" in his thirties.

Before the exchanging of the rings, Angie stole a quick glance at the gargantuan stained-glass Jesus behind the minister. Never much of a church-goer, she nonetheless had a momentary pang of guilt about lying in church. She hoped that the floor didn't open up and swallow them into a pit of eternal flame, or whatever it was that was supposed to happen.

But just then, she heard the voice of the minister say the words, "Let us love one another for love is of God," and she was immediately renewed in the knowledge that helping Tommy and Westley in this way was the good and right thing to do, "for love is of God."

"Thomas, you have taken Angela to be your wife. Do you promise to love her, comfort her, honor and keep her, in sickness and in health; and, forsaking all others, to be faithful to her as long as you both shall live?"

"I do."

Missy and Guyton were beaming.

"Angela, you have taken Thomas to be your husband. Do you promise to love him, comfort him, honor and keep him, in sickness and in health; and, forsaking all others, to be faithful to him as long as you both shall live?"

"I do."

All eyes were on the positively radiant bride at the moment, so no one noticed Westley's lips move imperceptibly as he gazed lovingly at Tommy over Angie's shoulder, also whispering, "I do."

··········

"So she married him. She played the part socially, went to all the events as his lovely young wife, and made him an acceptable man in his parents' eyes and in the community's eyes... and he could be with his lover at home."

"How did that work exactly?" asked Jack. "With the other guy, I mean."

"He lived in a wing of their house," answered Westley.

"Really?" asked Jennifer. "That didn't look a little suspicious to his parents?"

"The man he loved was also Black, even a bigger taboo back then. But, even in the eighties, when the wedding took place, it wasn't uncommon around here to have a full-time maid or butler that was 'colored' who had a room in a different part of the house. So that's what they did."

"It was you," said Jesse.

"It was me."

"I'm so sorry that you had to live like that, in secret," said Jennifer.

"It is what it is. At least we were able to be together. And that's all thanks to your mom. It was a pretty selfless thing that she did for us."

"Well," interjected Jesse with disdain, "it's not like she didn't get something out of it. She got rich. That's not entirely selfless."

Westley turned to her. "She didn't have to worry about keeping a roof over her head," he said sternly, "or worry about where her next meal was coming from, that's true. That's an extremely stressful thing for a young woman to always be worrying about. Yes?"

The comment hit a little too close to home.

"Yes," she answered softly.

"It took a huge weight off of her. But she never took advantage of that. She was a loyal friend, she lived modestly, and when Tommy died seven years ago and left money to both of us, the majority of hers went into an account for the three of you, and that's where it's stayed. Though some of it did go to medical bills when the cancer hit.

"He left me the house and she and I stayed there for a while, but it was too painful for us to be there without him, so I sold it. That's when I bought this bed and breakfast and Angie moved out to the old Caldare family summer home on Isle of Hope. He had left that to her. That's actually where I'm taking you today. Her final home."

"Is there anyone living there?" asked Jack.

"Yes, there is, but we have permission to visit today. So… If you'd like to see it, I'm ready to go as soon as you're finished eating. You'll be going to the airport from there, so take your bags with you."

"It's the end of our journey?" asked Jack.

"Finally!" said Jennifer.

"Well," Westley smiled, "it's never *really* the end of the journey. But the end of your trip this week? Yes, I suppose it is. Let me know when y'all are ready."

"We're not taking the hearse, are we?" asked Jennifer apprehensively.

"Not unless you're *dying* to!" joked Westley.

Westley and Jennifer laughed at his bad joke as he cleared her empty plates off the table. Jesse was pensive.

"Why the long face, Droopy Dog?" said Jack. "We're almost there. *We did it.*"

"I don't know," she said softly, staring down at the table in front of her. "I'm just gonna miss this. It's the first time in a long while that I haven't felt so alone."

Jennifer put her arm around Jesse's shoulder and pulled her in. Jack reached across the table and took Jesse's hand.

"You're not alone," said Jennifer.

Monday Afternoon

Westley was at the wheel of his Mercedes, barreling down the freeway. Jack rode shotgun, and Jennifer and Jesse rode in the back with Sean. Jesse gazed out the window and tracked a road sign saying "Isle of Hope" as they flew by at sixty-five miles per hour. Westley exited the freeway and navigated the back streets, turning down West Bluff Drive which was lined with pretty little Victorian homes across from riverfront docks.

"The Isle of Hope community was established in the 1800s as a retreat for Savannah's prominent families," he told them. "It was a refuge from the summer heat and the periodic outbreaks of malaria."

The car was silent. The three J's watched passively out the windows, each lost in his/her own thoughts. Westley continued driving to their final stop, the home that marked the end of the woman they would never have the chance to know outside of photo albums, yellowed junior high and high school articles, circus programs, and a velour drawstring bag full of rocks.

Westley turned down a private road lined with Spanish Moss-covered trees. He turned the car off the road and drove between two decorative brick walls that flanked the driveway entrance, proceeding slowly toward a beautiful, enormous, old, white house. It was surrounded by a good-sized wooded yard with waterfront at the far end of the property through the trees. The car came to a stop.

"Now before we go inside, I just want to say to the three of you that you might have some emotion come up in there, and that's okay. Feel what you're going to feel, but also keep an open mind."

"About what?" asked Jesse.

Before he could answer, Charlene opened the front door and waved to them.

"There's Charlene," said Westley. "Let's go on in."

They got out of the car and walked toward the house, Jesse carrying Sean. Poppy and Harville unexpectedly appeared in the front doorway as they approached, and greeted them all with hugs.

"What's going on?" asked Jack.

"You weren't expecting to have to see us again so soon, I imagine!" joked Harville.

"Eulalie sent you some more of her medicinal tea, Jesse. She wasn't able to make the drive with us."

"That was a helluva long drive just to bring me tea, but... thank you!"

"C'mon in," said Harville, ushering them into the foyer.

"Let's head into the living room, and you can make yourselves at home," said Westley.

The living room was bright and comfortable, with a large wall of windows looking out onto a big screened-in porch. Seated on couches and chairs in front of a freestanding fireplace were Sean (the human), Connor, Maggie, and Sydney who, as it turned out, was female and who had a prosthetic leg.

"What the hell?" said Jesse. "Is this some kind of intervention?"

A very surprised Jennifer hugged her family members. "What's going on?" she asked.

Jack took Sydney in his arms and kissed her. No one was there specifically for Jesse.

"Jack, this is my husband Sean, and my kids Connor and Maggie. Guys, this is my *brother* Jack!"

"And this is my fiancée Sydney. Syd, these are my sisters Jennifer and Jesse."

Jennifer was shocked. "This is Sydney?"

"We thought you were gay," added Jesse.

"Why did you think I was gay?"

"Uh, I dunno. Blue sequined evening gown, women's high heels, and a partner named Sydney?" answered Jesse.

"Okay, for the record, wearing women's clothes doesn't make you gay. But, no, I'm not. That's just something I have fun doing."

"It started as a goof, comedically lip-synching to women's songs," explained Sydney. "Something to entertain the guys when we were deployed and had time to kill. He had a knack for it."

"You served together?" asked Jennifer.

"That's where we met," said Sydney, with a loving look at Jack.

Jesse noticed another woman who had been sitting quietly during all of the family introductions. Jesse pointed at her with a look of hazy recognition. "You look vaguely familiar."

"We've never officially met. I was around a lot while you were growing up, but I was careful to keep my distance. I'm Patricia Sinclaire. I'm your mom's friend Patsy."

"Wow," said Jennifer, staring. "It feels like meeting a character from a book I just finished."

"Why don't we all have a seat," encouraged Charlene.

Jesse set the puppy down. They all took their seats, and the three Js looked around at all the familiar faces, utterly confused.

"Okay, sooo... this is a little weird," said Jennifer. "I mean, nice, but..."

"We thought it might be good to have some extra support on this stop," said Harville.

Jack furrowed his brow and said, "Y'all are starting to freak me out."

Westley turned to all of the supporting family members and said, "Why don't we head out to the porch for a few minutes, and I'll fill you in with more of the details that you've missed this week. There's a lot to catch you up on."

Sean (the human), Connor, Maggie, and Sydney headed out with Westley and settled into lounge chairs on the porch. They tried to focus on what he was telling them, but couldn't help glancing inside occasionally to see how the show in the living room was playing out.

"There's no money, is there?" asked Jesse. They didn't respond. "Oh my God, I'm *right*, aren't I? I quit my job to come here, and this was all just a wild goose chase. Goddamn it!"

"There's plenty of money for you," said a female voice from the doorway of the hall leading to the back bedrooms.

Jennifer, Jack, and Jesse turned to see who was speaking. They found themselves staring into the face of a woman who looked like a slightly older version of Jesse. It was their mother, fifty-six-year-old Angie Hartley, and she was very much alive. They stood up slowly, absolutely stunned.

"Ohhh, no, you did not," said Jack.

"I know you have questions," said Angie.

"What is going on??" asked Jennifer, looking to Harville, Poppy, Charlene, and Patsy for an answer.

"What. The. Fuck?" said Jesse, furious. "How about *that* for the first question?"

Angie remained calm. "How about just 'hello' to start? Then we can go from there."

She walked over to greet her kids. She hugged Jennifer and Jack, who only partially responded to her. Not overwhelmingly enthusiastic, mostly just stunned.

"And Jesse..." Angie continued.

She moved toward Jesse, but Jesse was having none of it. She held up a hand and took a step backward, away from Angie's attempted embrace.

"No. Don't you dare hug me. What, are we just supposed to call you 'Mom' and fall into your arms, and cry and hug, and everything's suddenly water under the bridge because oh yay, you're suddenly alive?"

"Of course not," Angie said gently. "And you can call me anything you want to."

"I don't think I'd open that door with her if I were you," Jack said to Angie.

Jennifer tried to get a handle on all of this. "Okay, let's just—let's just—just—"

"Let's just sit down and see what she has to say," Jack suggested, stone-faced.

Jesse turned on him. "*You* didn't even want to come on this trip! *You* didn't want to have anything to do with her! So when exactly did you 'drink the Kool-Aid'?"

"Uh, when you forced it down my throat at gunpoint in Louisiana."

"You did *what?*" asked Charlene.

Jennifer waved it off. "It's okay. It was plastic."

Just then, a man a couple of years younger than the three J's crossed through the entrance hallway on his way from the kitchen to the bedrooms. He was carrying a toolbox. He kept his head down, trying to be as inconspicuous as possible, but Jesse spotted him.

"And who the hell is *that?*" she asked.

"I'm sorry. Don't mind me," he apologized with a little wave, quickly disappearing down the hallway.

"Is that another brother we haven't heard about yet??" Jesse continued.

"No, Jesse," said Patsy. "That's my son Lex."

"Calm down," Jennifer said to Jesse.

"Don't tell me to calm down. *You* calm down!"

"Good one," said Jack.

"Oh, that's really mature, Jesse," said Jennifer.

"Okay, let's all try to stay focused here," suggested Charlene.

"Everybody needs to cool yer britches and take a deep breath," added Harville in his commanding tone.

Jennifer composed herself and said to Jesse, "Look. I didn't want to come on this trip. Jack didn't want to come. *You* wanted us to come, and now we're here. So you need to park your butt down on that couch so we can listen to what she has to say."

The trio sat back down on the couch together, Jesse in the middle, fuming.

"So you faked a big, sad, death-by-cancer story to trick us out here." Jesse turned to the rest of the group. "And it worked thanks to all of you being in on this big, fat lie. Well," she said to Angie, "we're here. NOW what?"

Angie took a deep breath before launching in.

"Yes, I faked my death, but the cancer part of the story was real. I did have colon cancer, which is currently in remission. I'm very sorry about the way I did all of this, I know it's a shock, but I didn't know any other way to get you here."

"True dat," said Jack under his breath.

"I was hoping," she continued, "that by hearing the whole story, directly from the people who were involved, it might be a helpful introduction."

"I don't understand why you didn't try to make contact all these years," said Jennifer.

"I did try to, once you were a little older," she explained. "I wrote so many letters over the years. To you girls through Carolyn and Jim, and to you, Jack, through your adoptive family. I never got a single response from any of you."

"No. I'm calling bullshit on that. I didn't get any fucking letters," Jesse said to Jennifer. "Did you get any letters?"

"No."

"I did," said Jack.

They all faced him, waiting for him to elaborate.

"Well, my parents did, but I didn't read them. I wasn't interested. My mom said she'd keep them in case I ever changed my mind, so I'm sure they're in a box somewhere."

"Fair enough. I understand," Angie nodded. "So let me ask you, if I had tried to contact you to ask you to come and meet me, would you have come?"

He looked at her for a moment without responding, then shook his head and said, "No. I wouldn't have come."

"Exactly. I didn't think so. And with no response from you girls over the years, I assumed you wouldn't either. So... I came up with this elaborate alternative. I figured if I wasn't in the picture, if you knew you weren't going to have to deal with me personally, the odds were better that you'd come."

Jennifer conferred with Jesse, quietly saying, "Maybe they saved them. We never finished going through all of their things after they died. Maybe they're in one of the boxes in storage somewhere."

But Jesse wasn't about to let Angie off the hook so easily. "Yeah, and what about THAT? Jesus. Your sister and brother-in-law die in an accident, and your daughters are left without parents, and even THEN you can't pick up the fucking phone?"

"I didn't tell her about Carolyn and Jim right away," said Patsy who had been quiet up until this point.

"I don't understand. Why not?" asked Jennifer.

Angie started to explain. "That's right when—"

"This is *bullshit!*" yelled Jesse.

She stood up and rushed out a side door in the direction of the water at the edge of the property. The family members on the porch were attempting to inconspicuously watch the developments in the living room that were now spilling out into the yard.

"Excuse me," said Angie as she stood up and followed Jesse quickly.

"Should we go out there?" Jack asked Jennifer.

"And by 'we' you mean me?" she said.

"No, I mean we."

"Fergodsakes," interjected Harville impatiently, "quit yammering about it and go!"

Jack and Jennifer took off out the side door.

"Uh-oh. That's not looking like a happy reunion," said Sydney to the other porch dwellers who were now standing up, trying to peer through the trees in the distance to watch the drama unfold.

"Well," Sean responded with a smile, "the story was about due for a good high-speed chase, don't you think?"

Jesse and Angie were mid-conversation at the end of Angie's sun-bleached wooden dock by the time Jack and Jennifer hurried over. Jesse was effectively cornered. She couldn't go any farther unless she decided to swim for it (which she briefly considered until she wondered if there were alligators).

"Patsy didn't tell me about Carolyn and Jim and the accident right away because I was in a very difficult period with the chemo when it all happened. By the time I found out about it, I didn't think I should contact you because I didn't know at that point if I was going to beat the cancer. Making all of you lose another parent seemed like a cruel thing to me at that point."

"Do you have any idea what I was going through? Not just losing my parents but feeling like I'm the one who killed them?"

· · · · · • • • · ·

2012

Jesse pulled her car up to the curb where Jim and Carolyn waited. They opened the doors, climbed in, and fastened their seat belts.

"Thank you so much for coming to this today," said Jesse. "It means so much to me that you'll be there."

"Oh, honey," said Carolyn, "don't be silly. We wouldn't miss it for the world!"

Jesse pulled away from the curb and then came to a stop at the four-way stop sign on the corner.

"I can't believe I'm finally going to get to hear these songs you always seem to be working on. I don't even care that I have to pay for it!" joked Jim.

"You only have to buy a cup of coffee and a pastry, and I'm treating, so you don't even have to pay for *that*." Jesse laughed, accelerating through the intersection.

A car speeding toward the intersection on their right didn't even slow down as it approached. The speeding car barreled through the intersection just as Jesse pulled out. The driver was looking down at his new cell phone, oblivious to the four-way stop sign. He broadsided her car at more than twice the residential speed limit. There wasn't even time for Jesse to react. Her car was totaled.

Carolyn and Jim, sitting on the right side of the car, were killed instantly upon impact. Jesse was alive but was bleeding profusely from an enormous, jagged cut around her fractured collarbone and shoulder where the crumpled metal from the passenger door and roof had ripped into her flesh.

A neighbor, screaming for help, ran toward the demolished car dialing 911 on his cell phone.

· · · · · • • · · · ·

"Do you know what it was like feeling like every time anyone looked at me that they were blaming me for it? I needed someone on my side then!"

"*Nobody* ever blamed you for it, Jesse. It wasn't your fault. It was the other driver," said Jennifer, trying unsuccessfully to comfort her.

"You don't know, Jennifer. You didn't feel the looks people gave me. Like they wondered why I was the one who lived and not them. And I can't ever get away from it. Every goddamn time I look in the mirror and see this hideous scar."

Jack meets Jennifer's gaze with a look of comprehension and she nods.

"Hey," he said gently, taking a step toward Jesse. "I know what survivor's guilt feels like... I was in a supply convoy in Afghanistan when we were ambushed."

・・・・・●●●●・・

2003

A convoy of trucks and Humvees was traversing the arid landscape in the Khyber Pass, on their way to resupply food and military armament to NATO forces. This area connecting Pakistan to Afghanistan was considered relatively safe due to the Pakistani government paying the Pashtun clans living in this region to provide security.

The convoy march column was broken up into smaller groups of two- to four-vehicle march units. Jack was in the second vehicle of the lead march unit, behind the commander's vehicle. He was riding with three others from his platoon. As they enjoyed the mercifully cooler November temperature outside, they laughed and talked. At the moment, they were giving Sam Drabinsky unrelenting shit for writing letters to his mother every week without fail since they were deployed.

"Hey, it's not *my* fault that *your* mothers don't want to hear from *you*." He laughed.

"What Drabinsky isn't saying is that he's afraid his mom won't let him move back in with her when he gets home if he skips a week," said Jack.

"Yeah, well, I'm not living with her for *me,* I'm living there to help *her* out," he countered unconvincingly.

"Oh, do you pay rent there?" Jack continued, already knowing the answer.

Drabinsky took a deep breath. "So, what I offer her in exchange for the room is—"

As soon as he started justifying, the rest of them exploded with laughter.

"Okay, so that's a 'no, I pay zero rent,'" said Jack, answering his own question.

"You help her out by eating her food and making long-distance calls on her tab? Just to make her feel needed?" added Chris Kellum. "What a good son."

"Hey, I'd 'help my mom out' too if she had a swimming pool and a free guest house in the backyard," said Sydney Winters, laughing. "Come to think of it, maybe *I'll* start helping out Drabinsky's mom if I get out before he does!"

"Let's all start writing to his mommy. We'll see whose letters she likes best," said Jack. "You got any extra butterfly or kitten stationery we can borrow, Drabinsky?"

"You guys are hilarious, but writing letters will first require that you learn to read and write, and I'm guessing none of you graduated from the second grade," Drabinsky shot back.

"Does your mom like music?" asked Jack. "I'll tell her I can do a mean Beyoncé impression."

"Sorry, loser, but my mom is strictly a Sinatra gal."

"Which Sinatra? Nancy? Because *I've* got some boots that are made for walkin'." Sydney laughed, lifting up her feet and propping her army boots next to Drabinsky's head.

Drabinsky shoved Sydney's feet down with an exaggerated grimace. "Daaammnn, girl! You'd better wash your feet first because I can smell them through your shoe leather. They smell like ass! My mom'll smell them through the front door before she even opens it. She won't let you in."

"Uh, I believe those are *Jack's* feet you're smelling, thank you very much," Sydney joked.

"Don't worry, as soon as we get to our hotel today, I'll soak them in a nice hot bubble bath," Jack continued, as they bounced down the winding road, entering Middle of Nowhere, Afghanistan. "My feet'll smell like rose petals by the time I move into your old bedroom, Drabinsky."

The group laughed at the thought of their convoy ending up at a hotel. Suddenly, the sound of an automatic rifle cut through the air of the mountain pass like a jackhammer. Rifle fire in combination with mortar shells hit the back of the commander's vehicle in front of them and somewhere close behind them. They had been ambushed by a small group of insurgents who had been lying in wait behind an outcropping of boulders on the steep incline above them.

The voices of troop members' rapidly shouting orders could be heard from the vehicles in front and to the rear of them. But before they could grab their weapons to mount a defense, another mortar shell exploded on the road directly in front of them, severely damaging the front of their vehicle. When Jack, bleeding from a few non-life-threatening injuries, was able to get his bearings, he saw his two buddies in the front of the vehicle slumped over.

"Oh, my God! Kellem! Drabinsky! Can you hear me?" He could barely hear himself due to the severe ringing in his ears. He flung open the door on the opposite side of the vehicle from the mountain incline and stumbled out into the road. "Men down! Men down! We need a medic!" he shouted toward the vehicles at the end of the convoy, but his voice was swallowed by the sound of troops returning fire at the rock outcropping above. His buddies hadn't survived the blast. Everything seemed to be moving in slow motion when he heard a cry and saw Sydney's body shift slightly in the back seat.

"Winters!" he screamed. "Come on! Get out here and take cover!"

"My leg..." Sydney whimpered. "Help. I can't move... It's my leg."

That's when Jack saw the extent of the damage. Sydney was bleeding profusely. He dropped his weapon and dove back inside, looking for anything he could find to help stave off the blood loss. Medics from the rear of the convoy had been incrementally moving forward with emergency first aid equipment since the first shell had exploded. They were ducking for cover behind each consecutive vehicle as other troops covered them and maneuvered to get a better shot at their attackers.

"Goddamn it, Syd," Jack sobbed as the medics reached his vehicle. "Don't you die on me! Do you hear me? Don't you die!"

・・・・●・●・・・

"That's how Sydney lost her leg. I was in therapy for years dealing with the survivor's guilt. 'Why me? Why was I spared?'"

"And what did your shrink tell you?" asked Jesse.

"That there's no easy answer to that other than the answer you *choose*. *You* decide the meaning, and then you *live* it. Because perception is always a choice."

He holds her gaze as she lets his words sink in.

"I can't change the past, Jesse," said Angie. "I wish to God I could. I wish I had been in a better place emotionally when I was young so that I could've been there for all of you. But wishing isn't going to change the past. All I can do is focus on right now."

"And why reach out to us now?" asked Jennifer. "I don't understand."

"When I went to my five-year follow-up appointment recently and I was still cancer-free, I felt hopeful again for the first time in very a long while. Like I was in a place where I *could* contact you. I suddenly, miraculously, had more time. I felt like I had been given a second chance," she explained. "Just like the two of you, Jack and Jesse. I decided that *I wasn't going to waste it.*"

She let that statement land.

"There aren't enough words to convey to you how sorry I am about the past. Truly I am. But what I can offer you is that I'm here for you *now*. Whatever you need, for as long as I have left. If you're interested." No one immediately responded, so she turned to Jack and Jennifer and said, "Would you two mind if I spoke to Jesse alone for a few minutes? I'll catch up more with each of you back at the house. I promise."

They nodded and turned to walk away. Jack put his arm around Jennifer's shoulders as they continued toward the house. She glanced back over her shoulder at Angie and Jesse who were now seated on the weather-worn benches at the end of the dock, facing one another. Jesse was saying something, but they were out of earshot by this point.

"How could you do it? I don't understand. How could you just leave like you did?"

Angie paused to formulate her answer. "I know that nothing I say is going to be a good enough answer for you because it *is* hard to understand from the outside. I just couldn't handle my life back then. I was so young, and so many difficult things happened in such a short time span. I really thought I was doing the best thing for you and Jennifer because I knew that Carolyn and Jim would be great parents."

"But you just left. Just up and left with no explanation to anyone."

Angie paused again, and then asked, "I'm not trying to change the subject, but can I ask you something?" Jesse shrugged, and Angie continued, "You were in college studying art, you were in your senior year, and from what I heard you were doing really well there. And then you quit. With only one semester to go before you graduated, you dropped out and went to Europe. You left suddenly, with no explanation to anyone. Why did you leave so abruptly?"

"What's the point of this? I don't want to talk about this with you! It has nothing to do with anything!" said Jesse, extremely agitated.

Angie continued to gently press her on this. "Why did you leave, Jesse? What happened?"

"Look, just because you're my 'birth mother,'" Jesse said with sarcastic air quotes, "doesn't make you my shrink!"

She stood up abruptly to head back to the house. But she didn't leave. She walked to the edge of the dock instead, thrust her hands into her back pockets, and stared out over the water. Angie watched her, sensing that something from the past was bubbling up inside of Jesse. She rose from the bench and joined Jesse at the edge of the dock. She didn't say anything, but pulled out a small, flat, round stone from her pocket, and side-armed it, skipping it across the water six times. Like a *boss*.

Without looking at Angie, Jesse said, "I can't believe you still do that. It's so stupid."

Angie smiled to herself, and then reached into her pocket again and pulled out a handful of the small stones, extending half of them to Jesse like an olive branch. Jesse stared at the "stupid" stones, wanting to take them, but not wanting to give Angie the satisfaction. Angie held out her hand until Jesse finally reached over, took the wishing stones, and skipped one across the water. They continued until Jesse stopped, still staring into the distance. Angie waited.

"I haven't ever told anyone about this," she finally said, almost to herself.

She hesitated again, so Angie tried to coax her along, very gently saying, "Well, if ever you had a captive audience with absolutely zero right to judge anything you might say, that would be me."

No response.

"You know, I can tell you one thing from personal experience. The difficult things we keep locked up inside, because of guilt, or shame, or fear of judgment, don't do anything but eat away at us from the inside out.

Jesse was shaking at this point, but still no answer.

"It's okay," said Angie. "Maybe I'm not the person you want to tell. I understand. But I'd encourage you to tell *someone*. Do that for yourself, so you don't continue to carry it—"

Jesse cut her off, quickly blurting out, "One of my professors sexually assaulted me. My faculty mentor in the art department, actually." She started sobbing to the point of having difficulty breathing, as her eighteen-year-old secret came spilling out. "It didn't get as far as what happened to you, but when I tried to stop it, he started saying how *I* had been the one coming on to *him,* and that the department wouldn't look very kindly on it if he were to tell them. Which was *bullshit!* I never came on to him. I just wanted his guidance in school. I trusted him. So when he made that threat to report me for what *he* had done… I don't know. I just snapped. I was so angry! I punched him in the face as hard as I could. I'd be shocked if he didn't have a black eye the next morning, or a broken nose, but I didn't stick around to find out, or to be the one in trouble with the school. I ran out of his office but didn't know where to go. So, I withdrew all the money from my campus account, bought a plane ticket, and got as far away as I could. Barcelona was the next international flight leaving that I didn't need a visa for when I got to the airport."

She paused briefly to catch her breath, then continued, "I didn't tell my family where I was until a couple of weeks later, once I had a job. I had been wandering down Las Ramblas, crying, and this woman having a cigarette break in front of her tattoo shop saw me and brought me inside. I didn't tell her why I was really crying, just that I was in town alone, and needed a job. She hired me to answer phones, and do general office stuff. Eventually, I started apprenticing with her. But I was vague with my family. I told them I was there for school, a 'studying abroad' kind of thing."

That's where Jesse stopped, and her breathing slowed. Angie watched as Jesse took a very deep breath. As she exhaled, it was like a hundred pounds of dead weight fell off of her. It wasn't until then that Angie finally spoke.

"I'm *so very sorry* you had to go through that, Jessica."

The use of Jesse's full name caught her off guard and made her shoulders twitch. No one had called her Jessica in over five years, not since she had lost her parents. She turned to face Angie, but this time without the virtually impenetrable, defensive wall around her.

"So, what brought you back home?" Angie asked softly.

"My boss there got very ill and went to go live with her daughter. She was pretty old," said Jesse with a shrug. "I left Barcelona and traveled around Europe for a few weeks after that, mostly visiting art museums, but I was too sad to stay."

"So, you do understand," said Angie, "at least a little bit, why someone might choose to leave suddenly."

"I don't *want* to understand. I'm so mad at you right now," said Jesse as she turned and headed back over to sit on the bench. "This was different. You had *kids*."

Angie walked over and sat down next to Jesse, and tried a different tack. "What was high school like for you, Jesse?"

"I don't know. It was good, I guess. I had a fun time."

"You always looked very happy in the pictures Patsy sent me."

"That's really creepy you had her spying on us, by the way."

Angie smiled. "Yeah, maybe. But I was so grateful for it. It was my only connection with you and Jennifer. She was my lifeline." She paused, then went back to the subject of high school. "Anyway, so I want you to imagine yourself at age seventeen, where you were, how you spent your days, what kinds of things you thought about. Now... picture yourself at that age as a single mom with a toddler, and pregnant again for a second time after being raped. Your old friends ostracizing you and whispering names about you, not even bothering to do it behind your back. It was overwhelming at age seventeen. I just didn't have the emotional maturity to know how to deal with it. And then, in the middle of all of *that,* at age seventeen, imagine your mom, your only living parent, suddenly dying. My mom had been my rock during that time. She was the hand I had been clinging to, that was keeping my head above water, keeping me from drowning. And then she was suddenly gone."

They're both quiet. Silent tears rolled down Jesse's face as the picture Angie had just painted sunk in.

"I'm not saying you have to forgive me, Jesse," Angie continued. "I'm just asking that you try to understand why I might have made those choices when I was only seventeen."

Neither one of them spoke. Their attention was diverted into the sky, their heads following the path of a flock of migrating birds as they changed formation and then course-corrected over the water. Just like the two of them were doing. They could hear the faint sound of laughter back at the house, as the guests set up the yard for dinner.

Jesse asked Angie, "Were you telling the truth about the letters? Did you really send letters to us?"

"I did. I waited until you were a little older, sixteen and eighteen, when you were both around the age I was when I left. I guess I can't blame Carolyn and Jim for not giving them to you. I'm sure they were still angry, and probably didn't trust that I wouldn't hurt you all over again, and at a time when you were old enough to really be affected by it if it happened again. But... I do wish they would've given me a chance."

"What did they say? The letters, I mean."

"Well, I tried my best to explain what I just told you. I described what my life was like now, and I said I'd love to come back and meet you and try to re-establish a relationship with you, if and when you were ready. I wrote every few months for a couple of years. After a while, I stopped writing, because I never heard back. I didn't know if they weren't giving you the letters, or if they did and you just weren't interested. For one hot second, I even considered just showing up on your doorstep, but I was too full of shame and guilt to follow through. I guess I felt like I had given up the right to force myself back into your lives if you didn't want me there. Or if Jim and Carolyn didn't want me there. I was afraid to try. I didn't feel very good about myself back then... I know they were wonderful parents to the two of you. You know, from all of Patsy's 'creepy' reports and photos."

That last sentence made Jesse smile. "Yeah. They really were."

"I know it had to be devastating to lose them."

"It was. Though it wasn't just the 'what' but the 'how.' I was at the wheel when that car broadsided us. I was a foot away from them when they died. I know Jennifer said that everyone knew it wasn't my fault, but talk about the looks people gave me... and their judgment."

"Well, if anyone understands that, it's me. But the difference is, as painful as it was for you, you stayed. You were stronger than I was. That was a big part of my fear about coming back, facing the judgment from people about what I had done. But in *my* case, the choice I made *was* my fault." She paused and shifted to face Jesse better. "At least you had Jennifer through that difficult time. She was there for you, wasn't she?"

"Yeah, I guess. She bailed me out of so many difficult situations as I fell into this downward spiral. And this isn't her fault, but ultimately, her help made me feel even more 'less than' in comparison to her. She's *always* had her shit together. Our whole lives. It was really fucking annoying having such a 'perfect' older sister growing up."

Angie laughed. "I know the feeling. I had one of those too. It's why I knew she'd be a better mom than me. I didn't have much self-esteem back then. It took a lot of years to turn that around. Honestly, it was the cancer scare that did it. At first, I felt like it was punishment for everything I had done in my past; but ultimately, it's what made me realize I could make different choices from here on. And that's when I became *this...*" She pointed to Jesse's phoenix rising from the ashes tattoo.

Jesse contemplated the tattoo. "I haven't quite gotten there yet."

Angie put her hand gently on Jesse's shoulder, and said, "Choose it. Choose it *today*. Because that's all we really have. The past is gone, and the future doesn't exist. We have today. So, Jessica, choose to be the phoenix rising from the ashes, starting right now."

Jesse held her gaze for a long moment, then said, "I'm still mad at you."

"It's okay. You're entitled... Hey, speaking of those tattoos, Del called after you all left his place. He told me about a certain song you wrote. I'd love to hear it sometime."

Jesse shrugged in a noncommittal way. "Maybe later."

"It seems like we share a lot of things in common, Jesse. Some of them aren't such great experiences, but a pretty wonderful thing that we also share is music. Maybe that's where we can start, you and I. We can meet each other through our music."

Jesse considered that, and with a small nod said, "Okay."

"And I have one other idea..." continued Angie.

Monday Evening

Two hours after Jennifer and Jack had left Angie and Jesse on the weathered dock, strings of soft white globe lights strung between the trees illuminated the colorful table set up in Angie's ample backyard as dusk settled in. Tall citronella torches burned on the periphery, casting dancing shadows along the ground. Everyone was pitching in, carrying large serving dishes piled with food to the table as they chatted and laughed.

Westley set a bowl down and said to Jennifer and Jack, "Can one of you two go get Angie and Jesse and let them know that dinner's ready?"

They turned toward the dock, but Jennifer elbowed Jack and pointed to their mom and sister heading back in the distance. The tension between Angie and Jesse seemed to have lifted as they entered the softly illuminated backyard area talking quietly. Everything about Jesse seemed softer than Jennifer had seen in her for years.

Angie surveyed her guests with great pleasure as she walked over and sat at the head of the table, Jesse to her

THE KEY TO CIRCUS-MOM HIGHWAY   249

right, then Jack and Sydney, Jennifer to her left followed by Sean and then Lex. Patsy, Maggie, Westley, Charlene, Poppy, Harville, and Connor filled in the remaining seats around the large table, in a configuration based on the conversations they were in the middle of. As people passed bowls and plates of food around and served themselves, Angie listened to the random snippets of conversation.

"You're a private investigator?" asked Maggie, fascinated. "How did you get into that?"

"Well, the funny thing is," said Patsy, "I spent so many years spying on your mom and Jesse when they were growing up, so I could send Angie pictures, I got really good at it. I got a degree in police science and then worked for a local P.I. for a couple of years so I could get my license. Oh, and speaking of pictures taken! Make your mom show you the hilarious picture I took of her first-grade musical when she played the role of a door. She was excellent, by the way!" That cracked Maggie up.

In the next seat over, Harville was teasing Connor. "Well, that's clearly because your pecker's too small, son!"

"Oh my God, who says that?" Connor laughed.

Poppy said, "Come and spend a week with us, Connor, and you'll get an education on lots of sayings you've never heard. *Lots* of sayings!"

Angie watched them all, her heart overflowing with gratitude.

Jennifer, sitting across from Jesse, caught her sister's eye and mouthed, "Are you okay?"

Jesse gave her a little smile and nodded.

Angie turned to focus on Jennifer and said, "I have *lots* of grandkid pictures to catch up on, Jennifer. After Patsy moved to Ohio eight years ago, her days of spying on my kids and grandkids ended and she wasn't able to send me any more photos."

"Well, you're in luck. I happen to have hundreds of family pics on my phone here!"

"No," corrected Jesse, "she has *thousands* on her phone. She's a photo hoarder. We're gonna see her on a reality show one of these days with people from Verizon showing up at her front door to do a cell phone intervention."

Jennifer pulled out her phone and excitedly began showing Angie photos, while simultaneously continuing to serve and pass food. So she missed the entirety of the conversation that Jesse and Sean (the human) were having with each other across the table and right next to her.

"So. Jesse. I met some friends of yours yesterday. Delightful gentlemen."

Jesse grinned. "So I heard! Tiny Tim and Mongo really enjoyed meeting you. Spike thought you were kind of a jerk, but he's so hard to please."

"Just so you know..." He lowered his voice. "That thing you told them about me? You're completely wrong, it's not what you think."

"Oh, yeah?" she whispered. "What is it then? Tiny Tim's message just said 'He doesn't seem like the type.' He didn't elaborate past that. So enlighten me."

Sean continued in hushed tones, glancing furtively at Jennifer who was joyfully regaling Angie with eight years of photos and nineteen years of stories. She was completely focused on connecting with her mom, but he still shielded his mouth as an extra precaution.

"I joined another Civil War club, and I didn't tell her because I know I wouldn't hear the end of it. We've been meeting at night and on weekends."

"You can't *possibly* be serious. That's all that's been going on? You're lying."

"That's it. You have my word."

Jesse looked over at Jennifer and then shielded her mouth as well. "Uh huh. And the cologne?"

"Oh, my God, what is it with you women and cologne?"

She raised her eyebrows and stared at him, waiting for a more convincing answer.

"It hides the smell of gunpowder, okay?" he whispered.

"Oh my God, this is the dumbest thing I've ever heard. Either you tell her or I will because she has wasted *so much energy* worrying about you cheating on her, you sorry-ass fake soldier."

"Fine," he said.

Jesse rolled her eyes and shifted her focus away from him to keep herself from reaching across the table and slapping him upside the head. She noticed that Lex, seated next to Sean, had been watching her.

"What?" she asked him.

"Nothing. I was just appreciating your tats. They're nice. I've been thinking of getting one myself."

"Oh, yeah? Well, I don't have my equipment with me, but if you have a ballpoint pen and a nail, we could take care of that tonight," she joked.

"Ah, prison yard style. Nice." He laughed.

"If that's what you're into," said Jesse. "We aim to please."

She turned her attention to Jack and Sydney.

"So, Sydney, Jack told us what happened to your leg. I hope you don't mind. That must've been incredibly difficult for you to adjust to. I can't even imagine."

Jesse continued passing the endless train of bowls of food.

"Yes, it definitely was. Partly because I had trouble for years with the original prosthetic leg, but we couldn't get the VA to approve an upgrade. So, for a long time, I just tried to focus on the gratitude I had for being alive at all. Then about a year and a half ago, we were notified that it had been fully funded through a private hospital in New Orleans. It was so unexpected—we thought it had been buried in red tape permanently—and it changed everything for me."

Sydney and Jesse continued talking about it as a sudden realization hit Jack. *Private hospital.* He looked over at Angie who had been listening to them after Jennifer's attention had turned to her husband.

He mouthed silently, "Was that you?"

She nodded.

"You changed our lives. Thank you," he mouthed again, very moved by her generous act.

"It was my great pleasure," she mouthed.

The endless stream of bowls and platters of food had finally been dished out at that point.

"Before we start to eat..." said Angie over the chatter, as a couple of the men sheepishly stopped chewing and slowly lowered their forks onto the table. "I wanted to take a moment to give thanks. For the food we're about to eat. For the dear friends who have been there for me all these years, and who worked *very* hard to help make this night and this improbable reunion possible... To second chances."

Jesse smiled.

"And to family!" Angie continued. "However you come to find them."

"To family!" they all responded in unison, glasses raised.

The laughter and conversation (and chewing) resumed. And so it continued... the night, the dinner, and the reunion of family old and new. With one small shift in the fabric of space and time—well, and a lot of planning and coordination by some dear old friends—a new, more hopeful reality was being birthed for them all.

・・・・●●●●・・・

It was late at night, long after their raucous family dinner had come to an end. Most of the guests had retired for the night, but Jennifer, Jesse, and Jack were still out on the screened-in porch. They were stretched out on the reclining lounge chairs. It was quiet except for the sound of the crickets that seemed to have followed them across the country, chirping their version of the "Hallelujah" chorus, the faint clattering of dishes being put away in the kitchen by one last straggler, and Jesse snoring.

"That was a *really* nice evening," said Jennifer, almost to herself.

"It was," agreed Jack.

"I wasn't expecting that," she added.

"*That's* the understatement of the year," said Jack. Then he continued, "Hey, did you catch the way Lex was flirting with Jesse?"

"No. Really?"

"I can hear you guys," said Jesse with her eyes still closed.

"You can?" asked Jack. "Because I can barely hear myself over your deafening sleep apnea."

"Very funny," she said. "I don't snore."

"Oh, I'm sorry, I must've confused you with the jet engine they're testing in Angie's back bedroom."

Jesse laughed, her eyes still closed.

"I have to say," said Jennifer, "he's pretty cute, Jesse."

"And he's thirty-four. A younger man," teased Jack. "It's like you'd be robbing the cradle. How exciting for you!"

"A cradle is probably not the best analogy at the moment," Jesse interjected, "all things considered."

"Yeah, you're probably right," he said.

There was a long pause before Jennifer commented, "So, Sydney seems pretty great."

"She is," he agreed. "She really is."

"When did you two get engaged?"

He thought for a moment. "Uh, 2008 I think it was."

Jesse's eyes sprung open and she turned to him. "You've been engaged for *ten years*? Jesus," she laughed, "commitment phobia much?"

"Why so long, Jack? Are you having doubts?" asked Jennifer.

"I don't have any doubts about *her*," he said. "I don't know. A part of me has felt broken ever since I came home. And right when I think it's getting better, it gets worse again. I guess I'm just afraid of saddling her with that for the rest of her life."

"Honey," Jennifer said, "you've been together for, what, about fifteen years now? Sixteen? Engaged for ten of that, and she hasn't left you yet. I'd say she's already saddled and halfway around the track at this point... Please don't tell her I just compared her to a horse."

"Is that part of the survivor's guilt you talked about earlier?" asked Jesse.

"I don't know. Probably. I had a lot of difficulties connecting with people back home for a while. Sydney helped some with that because we had both gone through a lot of the same things. It made me feel like I wasn't completely alone because she understood better than anyone. We also met with family members of our buddies who were killed. Delivering the last letter that Drabinsky had written to his mom, but that hadn't been mailed yet before he died, was one of the hardest things I've ever done. It was difficult, but it also helped us, to be able to share stories about our buddies with their families.

"Sometimes, though, when the nightmares come back, and the sleepwalking gets more frequent—it seems to go in cycles—I can feel myself pull away from Sydney a little because I don't want to make things harder for her than it's already been."

No one spoke for a moment.

"Maybe you should talk to someone again," offered Jesse. "And look into some kind of support group, if you're not in one already. You know, so you can actually move forward with your life. You deserve that."

Jack looked at her. "Yeah... ditto," he said pointedly.

Jesse studied him for a moment and then leaned back in her chair. "Touché," she said.

Jennifer sighed. "Maybe we should *all* talk to someone. I think I need to move forward too."

"Jen, the only person you need to talk to is your damn husband," said Jesse. "Promise me you'll do it in the morning. I'm serious. Jack and I can even hold him down if you need us to."

Jennifer laughed. "You gonna use your ninja neck punch on him and pin him in the dirt, Jack?"

"Hey, whatever it takes," he said.

"Oh, yeeaah. Speaking of that..." Jesse said to Jack. "I had a little question for you, Jackie Chan."

"Uh oh," he said.

"So here you are with all of your fancy military training and your lightning-fast reflexes. You disarmed me in the car on the way to Thibodaux before I knew what was happening, you subdued a horndog redneck in Alabama before he had time to react, you saved us from an accidental kidnapping, but you didn't do *anything* when I had that plastic gun to your back in the middle of a crowded street. You even said you knew I wouldn't shoot you. And yet you didn't make a move."

"My arms were full!" he protested.

"Your life is in danger, but you don't want to mess up your *wig?*" Jesse laughed. *"*Bullshit."

"She's right!" said Jennifer.

"You *totally* wanted to come on this trip with us," continued Jesse. "You just didn't want to admit it, you big liar."

"I'm sorry, was there a question somewhere in that?" asked Jack.

"Yeah, what do you have to say for yourself, ol' brother ol' pal?" answered Jesse.

Jack leaned back, closed his eyes, and crossed his arms.

"I plead the Fifth."

Jesse said to Jennifer, "He obviously found us irresistible."

Jack laughed and admitted, "There might have been a *little* curiosity."

"Aha!" said Jesse. "I rest my case."

"But I'm not technically admitting anything," he added.

Jennifer shook her head and said, "Too late."

The door to the porch slowly opened a few inches and Lex stuck his head out.

"Sorry to interrupt," he said. "I just wanted to see if any of you needed anything from the kitchen before I turn out the lights and head to bed."

They all said no, they were good. Lex rested his eyes on Jesse.

"Okay, well, goodnight then," he said.

Jack and Jennifer said goodnight.

Lex smiled at Jesse. "See you in the morning."

"Goodnight," she said sheepishly, feeling Jack and Jennifer's eyes burning holes into her.

Lex closed the door and headed to his room. Jesse turned around and saw the other two grinning at her.

"Shut up," she said.

They all leaned back in their chairs, smiling to themselves, lost in thoughts of friends, family, and the existential meaning of life. Their gratitude permeated the thick, sweet southern night air.

DAY EIGHT

"When a great adventure is offered, you don't refuse it."
-Amelia Earhart

TUESDAY MORNING

Early the following morning, the house was bustling with energy. Sean (the human) entered the foyer with Connor. They deposited their small suitcases by the front door and then headed to the kitchen for some coffee. Maggie had melted into the living room couch across from a roaring fire that was piercing the crisp, autumn morning air. She was texting Northwestern friends on her cell phone at a furious pace. *You guys will NEVER believe what I've been doing the last couple of days! Also, I think I'm changing majors!* Some of the others milled about the common area carrying Angie's handmade ceramic mugs, nursing their coffee, and continuing unfinished conversations from the previous night. Jennifer and Connor were on the screened-in porch with Poppy and Harville, finishing plates piled high with breakfast food and scheduling Connor's trip to Thibodeaux. The happy, overlapping conversations were music to Angie's ears. The success of this long-overdue family reunion had surpassed even her wildest dreams.

Jesse had spent the last hour watching the sunrise from Angie's dock, marveling at how effortlessly the flocks of migrating birds changed direction and pivoted into new formations. She thought about how much easier things would be if she could do that in her own life without all of the crippling doubt, self-recrimination, and second-guessing. No bitching and moaning, just *Hey, it's time to change direction.* Because that's what a phoenix rising from the ashes would do, and a phoenix is what she had chosen to be. Starting today. No more excuses.

She was now walking back to the house, mid-conversation with Lex who had finished his morning jog just as she was standing up to head back and join the others. Behind them was a romcom-worthy backdrop—a pink, orange, and blue morning sky infusing the world with a hopeful glow.

"Well," said Lex, "I'd been living in Cincinnati for a while and was feeling very burnt out at my job, and I—"

"What was the job?" asked Jesse.

"Middle school vice principal," he replied. "And I had just gone through a rough divorce aft—"

"After she found out you were into eighth-grade boys?" Jesse joked.

Lex laughed. "No, but thank you for your insightful character assessment. It was after she decided to leave me for her business partner," he continued. "Sharon."

"Ouch," Jesse winced.

"So," continued Lex, "when my mom called and told me Angie was struggling down here during her chemo treatments and needed someone full-time to help her out, it just seemed like a good time to make a move in a new direction. She couldn't take care of things around the house, and I desperately needed a change of scenery. I've been here ever since. I kind of like this place."

Angie and Patsy were standing inside, peering out the window at Jesse and Lex walking and talking in the yard, thoroughly enjoying each other's company.

Patsy turned to Angie. "Well, that's an interesting development," she marveled.

Angie nodded. "Isn't it though?"

They shared a conspiratorial smile and then drifted off to join the others. Patsy joined Maggie on the couch to continue their P.I. conversation from the previous night, and Angie headed to the kitchen.

Back in the yard, Jesse continued her friendly interrogation. "So what exactly do you do here now that she's better?"

"Yardwork, handyman stuff, whatever needs to be done," he said.

"'Whatever needs to be done.' I see. So should I give you a big tattoo across your chest that says BOY TOY?"

Lex laughed his easy, comfortable laugh. "Nothing against your mom, she's great, but I'm not really into women that are my mom's age. Call me crazy."

"So you're not into eighth-grade boys, and you're not into your mom's peer group. What exactly *are* you into?"

Lex cocked his head and smiled at her. "You asking 'for a friend?'..."

Jennifer and Angie walked out of the kitchen together, looking at vacation brochures.

"Here are your plane tickets, hotel info, and a few other surprises in there I think you'll all enjoy," said Angie.

"This is so generous of you!" exclaimed Jennifer. "We haven't been on a vacation as a family in *so long!*"

"And," continued Angie, "your father's information is in there too, Jennifer. Daniel McCallister. I tracked him down and it turns out he's back in Illinois doing real estate law out of Winnetka, so he's not too far from you. I called him and told him you might be getting in touch sometime soon."

Lex opened the door for Jesse who stepped inside and headed over toward Angie and Jennifer. Lex joined his mom and Maggie on the couch.

When she saw that Jennifer was thrown by that sudden father information, Angie assured her, "Just so you know, he was *thrilled* about that possibility! But no pressure at all. Whenever you're ready, and only if you decide you want to."

"No pressure about what?" asked Jesse, inserting herself into their conversation.

"Getting in touch with Riverdance-Dad," said Jennifer.

Jack and Sydney joined the other departing guests in the foyer with their belongings as Sean (the human) and Connor headed outside with their bags.

"What? Everybody's leaving already? This is ending too soon," said Jesse.

"Syd and I have to get back to work, Jesse," said Jack. "There are busloads of tourists being deprived of their *Jackie, Oh!* fix."

"Not to mention I had no idea how this was all going to play out," said Angie. "I wasn't sure you'd even want to stay for the night once you got here."

"Nothing's ending. It's just a brief pause," Jennifer assured her. "We'll all be back next month for Thanksgiving, right?"

"Yep," confirmed Jack.

THE KEY TO CIRCUS-MOM HIGHWAY 263

Jesse looked confused. "Wait. What?"

Jennifer said to Angie, "You didn't tell her?"

"Well," Jack said to Jesse, "after spending the last week with you, I totally understand why she didn't invite you."

Jesse laughed. "Asshole."

"Where's your bag, Jess? You can ride to the airport with us," said Jennifer.

"Um... well, here's the thing..." Jesse began. She looked to Angie for help.

"Jesse's going to spend some time here with me," Angie explained.

"Well, that's unexpected," said Jack.

"I don't have a job back in Chicago as of last Tuesday, or a place to live anymore, for that matter," Jesse explained.

"And she's going to need some help with the baby when the time comes," Angie continued.

Jennifer, shocked to hear that Jesse was going to continue with the pregnancy, said, "Yeah?"

Jesse shrugged.

Jennifer looked at Angie then back to Jesse and nodded. "That's nice. I like the symmetry of that.... *Oh my God, I'm going to be an auntie! I thought this would never happen!*" she said with an Ivy-Parker-worthy squeal.

Jennifer grabbed Jesse in a rib-crushing hug. Once Jesse was released from the soon-to-be-auntie death grip, she grabbed Jack and Jennifer's hands.

"Come over here for a second," she said, pulling them off to the side, while Angie headed over to her other departing guests in the background.

"I don't want our adventure to end," said Jesse.

"I know, me too," agreed Jennifer. "Thank you for guilt-tripping me into coming."

Jesse laughed. "I will happily guilt-trip you anytime you need it."

"It seems like it's been a lot longer than a week, doesn't it? In a *good* way, I mean," continued Jennifer.

"It does," agreed Jack. "I want you guys to know that I've really appreciated the time with you. You're not nearly as horrible as you first seemed."

"Well, I wouldn't jump the gun on that." Jennifer laughed.

"Man, who knew what a crazy fucking week this would end up being," Jesse mused.

"Well, not to beat a dead horse," said Jack, "but you kidnapped me at gunpoint wearing a Mardi Gras boob shirt, so I had a vague idea."

The three of them laughed at that memory as Sean (the human) came back through the front door.

"Jen, honey, c'mon. We've gotta hit the road if we're gonna make our flight."

"Okay, I'm coming."

The three J's shared a wordless moment, enjoying their new and completely unexpected bond formed over the last roller coaster of a week.

"Oh, come here, you lunatics," said Jack. "Group hug." Mid-embrace, he added, "Just please don't name your daughter Jujube."

Sean (the puppy) ran up into the middle of them and broke the moment. Jack scooped him up.

"Aw, I'm gonna miss you most of all, little buddy." He kissed Sean's furry little Beanie Baby head and handed him off to Jesse.

"Walk me out to the car, Jess," said Jennifer, putting her arm around Jesse's shoulders.

They headed out of the house to the cars in the driveway. Jack picked up Sydney's belongings and joined Sydney, Angie, and Westley at Westley's Mercedes.

As Jesse walked with Jennifer toward the McMahon family rental car, Jesse said quietly, "Has Sean talked with you yet about... things?"

"No. I expect we'll be hashing that out when we get back home. I'm going to try really hard not to let it overshadow our family vacation. Who knows, these next few days might be really good for us."

"Goddamn it, I'm gonna punch that man in the fucking head." Jesse sighed. "Listen, Jen, you don't have to worry about him cheating on you. That's all I'm gonna say for now."

"How do you know that?" Jennifer asked.

"Insider information... Ask him about the Civil War," Jesse said cryptically.

"Oh, God, do I have to?" Jennifer groaned.

"Trust me."

"Okay, I will. I love you, Jesse."

"High-five, partial sister!" Jesse said, holding up her puppy-free hand.

"Shut up and hug me," Jennifer said, pulling her sister and Sean (the puppy) into one last sisterly embrace.

"Man, a girl can't get a high-five to save her life these days... I love you too, sis," Jesse added, not really wanting to let go.

But they eventually did. And as Jennifer headed over to say goodbye to Angie and Jack before getting in the car, Jesse approached Sean (the human). She pointed to her eyes with two fingers and then pointed them at him, signaling "I'm watching you." She hugged him goodbye, maybe just a little *too* hard, for emphasis.

"You're even crazier than I thought, you know that?" he said.

"That's right, don't you forget it. Also, you officially have twelve hours and counting to tell her before I do it. Tick fucking tock. And just so you know, Sean, I'm gonna laugh my ass off when you accidentally shoot your nuts off in service to The Union."

The McMahon family piled into the rental car and drove off, leaving Jesse to say her goodbyes to Westley and Sydney.

"I hope you might reconsider reading those old letters I wrote to you," Angie said to Jack. "I'd really love for you to read them sometime."

"I will. I'll get them from my parents as soon as I get home. I promise."

"Good."

Angie put her hand on her heart, trying not to cry, and she hugged him.

"And, Sydney," Angie continued, "it was lovely meeting you. I look forward to getting to know you better over Thanksgiving when we have more time to talk."

"You too, Angie. And thank you again... for everything."

They finished their goodbyes, and Jack and Westley loaded Sydney's bag next to Jack's sequined gown and wig in the trunk. When Jack turned around, Jesse was standing directly behind him holding Sean (the puppy) out to him.

"Here," she said. "I want you to have him."

"What do you mean?" he asked.

"I mean I want you to keep him. You seem to sleep much better at night when he's with you. And when you don't, he keeps an eye on you. Plus, I think he likes you better anyway. Damn dog... what does he know?"

Jack laughed.

"Anyway," she continued, "I'll have enough on my plate with a new baby without having a puppy in the mix too. Think of it as something to remember me by as he pees on your rugs."

Jack happily took the puppy from her, Sean's tail wagging a mile a minute. Jesse pulled a folded letter out of her back pocket and offered it to him.

"Here, I made the human Sean write up a new doctor's note for you this morning, so you can bring him on the plane with you as an emotional support dog. It won't even be a lie for you!"

In his best Ren Hoak voice, Jack said, "You are one of the good ones, Stimpy."

Jesse smiled, kissed him on the cheek, and then punched him in the arm to send him off.

As Westley's car pulled away, Jesse waved, and Angie called out, "See you next month!"

Jack leaned out of his window and yelled, "To be continued!"

Jesse and Angie stood together in silence, watching until the car disappeared around a bend in the tree-lined driveway. As they turned to head back inside, Jesse bent down, picked up a small, flat stone, and quickly shoved it into her pocket.

Angie looked sideways at Jesse, a twinkle in her eye. "I saw that," she whispered.

Jesse smiled sheepishly.

Poppy, Charlene, and Patsy stood waiting for them in the doorway, all of the new "aunties-to-be," as Jesse and Angie walked side-by-side back toward their home, into the next chapter of the adventure, and into their shared *second chance*.

THE END

"In the universe, there are things that are known
and things that are unknown,
and in between, there are doors."
-William Blake

ABOUT THE AUTHOR

Allyson Rice is a writer, mixed media artist, and producer currently splitting her time between Los Angeles and Rehoboth Beach, Delaware. She's a graduate of Northwestern University with a Bachelor of Science in Communication. After spending many years as an actress on stage and on television, she left the business to found the company *The Total Human* and spent the next decade running yoga/meditation retreats, women's retreats, and creativity retreats around the country. After that, she pivoted to focus on her own creative work. In addition to her writing and art, she's also a photographer.

Some random bits of Allyson trivia: 1) She's been skydiving, paragliding, bungee jumping, zip-lining through a rainforest, and scuba diving with stingrays; 2) she has an extensive PEZ dispenser collection; 3) she played Connor Walsh on *As the World Turns* for seven years; 4) she's been in the Oval Office at the White House after hours; 5) she's related to the Hatfields of the infamous Hatfield/McCoy feud; and 6) her comedic rap music video to her rapper son, "Fine, I'll Write My Own Damn Song," won numerous awards in the film festival circuit (https://youtu.be/7Xe3nuVDkC4).

Also available from Allyson Rice is her line of women's coloring books (*The Color of Joy*, *Dancing with Life*, and *Wonderland*), and *The Creative Prosperity PlayDeck*, an inspirational card deck about unlocking and utilizing your creative energy in the world. They're available on www.Allyson-Wonderland.com. She's currently at work on her next novel, *Normal is Overrated*, and her fourth women's coloring book.

Follow her on Instagram: @AllysonRiceAuthor, @OfficialAllysonRice, and @AllysonRiceArt.

And on Twitter: @CircusMomHwy and @TheColorOfJoy.

If you enjoyed *The Key to Circus-Mom Highway*, please leave a review. It helps other readers discover the book. Thank you!

CARROLL COUNTY
FEB 2023
PUBLIC LIBRARY

 CPSIA information can be obtained
at www.ICGtesting.com
Printed in the USA
LVHW101152141222
735154LV00003B/43